Kaitlin tightened her grip on the broom.

"Have you changed your mind? Do you want to back out?"

"No, I'm not backing out. I'm fixing up the place. I'm keeping my end of the bargain."

"Can't you at least be pleasant in the process?"

Tripp rolled his eyes. "It's not enough for you that I'm doing it? I have to *like* it, too?"

Kaitlin swung the broom at him, swatting him squarely on the chest. "Yes! Yes, you have to like it!"

Tripp fell back a step, stunned.

She advanced on him, clenching the broom in her fist. "Yes, you have to like it, Tripp Callihan! This is *my* life you're a part of now, and I won't have you griping, moaning and complaining about everything. Life's hard enough without your own partner dragging you down! Do you understand me?"

He understood, all right. Better than Kaitlin Jeffers would ever imagine....

Dear Reader,

Welcome to Harlequin Historicals—stories that will capture your heart with unforgettable characters and the timeless fantasy of falling in love!

Rising talent Judith Stacy is back this month with *The Dreammaker,* set in 1880s Nevada. Known for her light, feel-good stories, Judith has again written a tale about family and finding oneself—and love—along the way. Here, two very different people, a single father and an aspiring actress, are swindled by the same man and become business partners to recoup their losses and realize their dreams. Ironically, love—the dream of a lifetime—is right in front of them!

Award-winning author Gayle Wilson returns with a mesmerizing Regency-style romance, *Lady Sarah's Son,* about sweethearts, torn apart by tragedy, who reunite in a marriage of convenience and can no longer deny their enduring love.... In *The Hidden Heart,* a terrific medieval tale by Sharon Schulze, a beautiful noblewoman must guard her heart from the only man she has ever loved— the Earl of Wynfield, who has returned to her keep on a dangerous secret mission. And don't miss *Cooper's Wife* by rising talent Jillian Hart, a heartwarming Western about single parents—a sheriff and a troubled widow—who marry to protect their kids, and find true love.

Enjoy! And come back again next month for four more choices of the best in historical romance.

Sincerely,

Tracy Farrell, Senior Editor

P.S. We'd love to hear what you think about Harlequin Historicals! Drop us a line at:

> Harlequin Historicals
> 300 E. 42nd Street, 6th Floor
> New York, NY 10017

Also by Sue Grafton

The Dreammaker

Judith Stacy

HARLEQUIN®

TORONTO • NEW YORK • LONDON
AMSTERDAM • PARIS • SYDNEY • HAMBURG
STOCKHOLM • ATHENS • TOKYO • MILAN • MADRID
PRAGUE • WARSAW • BUDAPEST • AUCKLAND

ISBN 0-373-29086-1

THE DREAMMAKER

Visit us at www.romance.net

Printed in U.S.A.

Books by Judith Stacy

Harlequin Historicals

Outlaw Love #360
The Marriage Mishap #382
The Heart of a Hero #444
The Dreammaker #486

JUDITH STACY

began writing as a personal challenge and found it a perfect outlet for all those thoughts and ideas bouncing around in her head. She chose romance because of the emotional involvement with the characters, and historicals for her love of bygone days.

Judith has been married to her high school sweetheart for over two decades and has two daughters. When not writing, she haunts museums, historical homes and antique stores, gathering ideas for new adventures set in the past.

To Judy and Stacy, who keep me grounded

To David, who gives me wings

Chapter One

Nevada, 1884

Every conception should be this delightful.

Kaitlin Jeffers turned sideways, studying her round belly in the big oval mirror. She stretched out her arms and rested her palms on the bulge. Goodness, she could hardly reach all the way around.

A wide grin parted her lips. Perfect. Absolutely perfect.

Kaitlin faced the mirror making sure the folds of her black dress hung straight. She looked down to be certain the hem touched the tops of her kid shoes, and laughed aloud. All she could see was her big stomach.

Looking up, she saw her reflection in the mirror and forced the smile from her face. She'd have to remember not to make that mistake again. Maybe she should have rehearsed more.

A metal key scraped in the door behind her, and in the mirror she saw Isabelle Langley walk into their hotel room. Tall and thin, her friend was even more a contrast to her now.

Kaitlin turned sideways and dropped her hands onto her belly. "Come to admire your brother's handiwork?"

Isabelle's eyes widened and she fell back against the closed door. "Saints alive, Kaitlin, I can't believe you!"

Kaitlin's smile broadened and she wiggled back and forth. "Looks good, huh?"

"It looks horrible!" Isabelle sheltered her eyes, then drew in a breath and looked at her again. "I can't believe my brother let you talk him into this."

She patted her round belly affectionately. "He does good work, wouldn't you say?"

"You're disgusting." Isabelle tossed her armload of packages onto the brass bed. "I found a bonnet like you asked for in a millinery shop down the street—it's the ugliest one in this whole town. Of course, there's not much here to choose from."

"And just as well." Kaitlin turned back to the mirror and tucked a stray lock of brown hair behind her ear. "The smaller the town, the better. We need to be in and out of this place quickly."

Isabelle unpinned her hat. "Please, Kaitlin, think this over. It's not too late to change your mind."

Kaitlin sighed impatiently. "You promised you wouldn't nag if I let you come along."

"You don't know what might happen. You don't know these people. What if they toss you in jail?"

Kaitlin planted her hands on her hips. "Who in their right mind would throw a woman in my condition in jail?"

"You don't have a condition!"

She bounced her fists off her belly. "Yes, I do."

"I'm going to kill my brother." Isabelle shook her head slowly. "He'd better stick to harness making from now on."

"Leave him out of this. He only did what I asked. And did it very well, I might add." Kaitlin leaned her shoulder closer to her friend. "You can't see the straps, can you?"

Isabelle glared at her, then walked over. "No."

"How about in the back?" Kaitlin turned around.

"No."

She looked over her shoulder. "Are you sure?"

"I'm sure."

"Good." Kaitlin turned and lifted the bulk of her belly higher. She frowned. "This might be uncomfortable, if I were really pregnant."

Isabelle moaned and covered her face with her hands. "Kaitlin, please don't do this. You can't go around pretending to be pregnant. Somebody will find out."

"No one will find out. We've never been to this town before—neither of us. No one recognized us on the stage this morning, or when we checked-in. We'll be out of here on the afternoon stage. What can go wrong?"

"A thousand things!"

Kaitlin drew in a determined breath. "That crook Harvey Stutz stole every dime I had in this world. Tricked me out of it, and waltzed away with a big smile on his face. I'm getting it back—no matter what I have to do."

"But Kaitlin—"

"You know what I'd been saving that money for."

Isabelle's shoulders sagged. "Yes, I know."

"Harvey Stutz stole my dream."

She nodded sorrowfully. "I know."

"He pretended he liked me, pretended he cared about me, until I told him about all the money I'd saved. Then he broke into my room and took every cent." Kaitlin squared her shoulders. "Well, he's dead now, and if it means pretending to be his pregnant widow to get back what belongs to me, then so be it."

"I guess you're right."

"Of course I'm right. Now, help me get ready."

Isabelle pried open the hat box she'd tossed on the feather mattress and took out the black, straw bonnet. "Try this on."

Kaitlin winced. "It's ugly, all right."

She turned to the mirror and pinned the hat in place, then lowered the thin black veil over her face. The hat was a trifle too big, and that made her look small and vulnerable; her stomach bulging beneath the black dress completed the effect.

"How do I look?" She turned to Isabelle.

"Awful."

"Good." Kaitlin drew in a deep breath. "Well, I'm going now. The sheriff is expecting me."

"Do you have everything?"

Kaitlin held up her left hand displaying her mother's gold wedding band, then patted her stomach. "Ring and baby. That's all I need."

"Are you sure you remember your story?"

"Of course. My dear husband Harvey—the rat—

and I were married some time ago. I knew little about him, except that he traveled a great deal. When I read his obituary in the newspaper I was devastated, of course. So, here I am to collect his belongings. What could be simpler than that?''

''What if the sheriff doesn't believe you?''

Kaitlin wagged her finger at Isabelle. ''Are you doubting my acting abilities?''

''But what if there really is a Mrs. Harvey Stutz?''

''He's been dead over a month now. Any legitimate wife would have already come forward—if there's a woman out there stupid enough to have actually married a crook like him.'' Kaitlin nodded confidently. ''And, if one should show up, I'll just be devastated that Harvey married me too, and run crying from the sheriff's office.''

''Well, I guess you've thought of everything.''

''Don't worry.'' Kaitlin patted her belly. ''Junior and I will be back within the hour, then we'll be on our way home.''

Isabelle wrung her hands. ''Just be careful.''

Kaitlin left the hotel room ready to give the performance of a lifetime. She'd learned about performing, mostly from her mother. But then Harvey Stutz had come along and taught her what it could really mean, what it could lead to. Harvey, who used his own acting talents to con unsuspecting young women out of their money. Even now, it galled Kaitlin that she'd been so gullible.

In the hallway she made certain no other hotel guests were about, then hurried down the stairs to the lobby. The young man behind the desk was busy with a couple and their three fidgeting children and didn't even look her way as she crept out the front door.

The noon sun brightened everything, even from behind her black veil. Horses, wagons and carriages crowded the dirt street, pedestrians moved slowly along the boardwalk.

Odd, but everyone seemed to get out of her way, stepping aside, giving her plenty of room to pass. Men she didn't know tipped their hats. Kaitlin thought her black mourning dress was the reason, then realized every man she passed gazed at her belly first before looking at her veiled face. Decidedly uncomfortable, Kaitlin hurried to the sheriff's office down the block and went inside.

The place smelled of coffee and gun oil. Across the small office sat a desk cluttered with papers. Rifles hung in racks on the walls flanked by Wanted posters. A dark corridor allowed Kaitlin a glimpse of iron bars. She shuddered, Isabelle's dire warnings coming back to her.

"Help you, ma'am?"

The deep voice from the opposite side of the room startled her. She jumped as she saw two men standing at the potbellied stove in the corner, and touched her hand to her bulging stomach.

"Take it easy now, ma'am."

A man—his gaze glued to her belly—hurried over. Gray hair showed below the brim of his hat and a badge hung on his vest. He cupped her elbow.

"Just come have a seat, ma'am. Don't get yourself all upset. Doc's out of town and we don't want no surprises."

The sheriff led her to the chair in front of his desk.

"Get some water over here for the lady, will you Callihan?"

Kaitlin plopped into the chair, her huge belly bulging out in front of her. She shifted awkwardly. Mercy, this thing was uncomfortable.

"You want to put your feet up? My missus, she always wanted to put her feet up," the sheriff said.

Kaitlin nearly gasped aloud. Good grief, if she raised her feet she'd surely tumble backward out of the chair.

"No, thank you, Sheriff."

"You just take it easy. Callihan, get that water over here, will you? Ma'am, you want me to get Mrs. Neff from next door? She's birthed a bunch of young'uns herself. I'll go get her. She's right next door."

Kaitlin nearly panicked. That was the last thing she needed. "I'm fine, Sheriff, really. Thank you."

"Here, just drink some water. Callihan, give her the water."

The other man stepped to her side. She sensed him before she actually saw him, a forceful, masculine presence. Slowly she lifted her gaze. Long legs, lean hips, a broad chest covered in black. A strong jaw, lips set in a thin line, a straight nose. Eyes, blue as the ocean. A black hat pulled low on his forehead.

Kaitlin's mouth sagged open as her heart pounded its way into her throat. Breath left her in a sickly wheeze.

"Here."

He shoved the tin cup at her. Kaitlin gulped and reached for it. Their fingers brushed. For an instant they both hung there, their gazes locked. Then he turned quickly and walked to the opposite side of the desk.

Kaitlin lifted the veil off her face wishing she could dump the water down her bodice to cool the strange heat that enveloped her. Instead, she sipped slowly.

"You feeling better, ma'am?" the sheriff asked.

She cleared her throat and set the cup aside. "Yes, Sheriff, thank you."

"Good." He dragged his sleeve across his forehead. "I guess you must be Mrs. Stutz?"

"Who?"

The sheriff frowned. "Harvey Stutz's widow."

"Oh, yes. Yes, I am." Kaitlin glanced at the man in the corner and shifted in her chair. She lowered her eyes demurely. "Yes, dear Harvey was my husband."

The sheriff touched his finger to the brim of his hat. "Real sorry about your loss, Mrs. Stutz. Real sorry."

"Thank you. You're very kind."

"Well, let's get on with this." He bustled around his desk. "I'm Sheriff Newell and this here is Mr. Callihan. Tripp Callihan."

Kaitlin dared lift her gaze to the man in the corner. He was already watching her and spared her no more than a brief nod.

Who was this man? Kaitlin looked away, but felt the heat of his gaze burning into her face. Was he a deputy? He had no badge pinned to his chest. Surely not a criminal, walking freely in the sheriff's office, but Mr. Tripp Callihan had a dangerous look about him, just the same.

Kaitlin forced her gaze away from him. "I understand, Sheriff, that you have my husband's belongings."

Sheriff Newell cleared his throat and glanced at Tripp. "Well, yeah, I do. But there's a little problem, Mrs. Stutz. You see, Mr. Callihan read my notice in the paper and came to town just like you. He's put in a claim on your husband's things, too."

Kaitlin's back stiffened. So that's why he was here. She hadn't counted on this. And she didn't know if that meant Tripp Callihan was Harvey Stutz's partner in crime, or another one of his victims.

She touched her hand to her forehead. "I—I don't understand."

"It seems Mr. Callihan here had some… dealings…with your husband."

The realization of Callihan's purpose in the sheriff's office caused Kaitlin's spine to tingle. Harvey Stutz had conned him, too. Callihan was a victim, the same as she.

From the corner of her eye, Kaitlin glanced at Tripp Callihan. What had Harvey Stutz taken from him? Money? A dream? A dream like the one he stole from her when he'd taken her life savings?

Kaitlin drew in a determined breath. Whatever Harvey Stutz had taken, Tripp Callihan had a better opportunity of getting it back than she did. Right here, right now was Kaitlin's only chance.

She gasped and clutched her belly. "Oh, dear."

The sheriff's eyes widened. "What's wrong?"

"It's nothing serious…probably." Kaitlin drew in a ragged breath. "Now, you were saying?"

Sheriff Newell shifted uncomfortably. "Tell me, ma'am, do you know what your husband did for a living…exactly?"

"Certainly." Kaitlin blinked up at him. "Harvey was a salesman."

The sheriff and Tripp exchanged a troubled look.

Kaitlin smiled innocently. "We weren't married very long, but my Harvey was always off working as hard as he could, providing for me and our child." She caressed her belly. "Why do you ask, sheriff?"

"No reason, ma'am. No reason."

Kaitlin gazed at Tripp. "Is that how you knew my husband, Mr. Callihan? Were you two business partners?"

He hung his thumbs in his gun belt. "Not exactly."

"Well, the fact is, Mrs. Stutz, that it's up to me to decide on who gets what. With both you and Mr. Callihan here filing a claim, well, I—"

"Ohhh.…" Kaitlin pushed herself out of the chair, bracing her hand at the small of her back.

Sheriff Newell jumped. "Maybe I ought to go get Mrs. Neff."

"No, no. I don't want to be a bother." Kaitlin smiled bravely. "It will help if I stand a while…maybe."

"You want some more water?"

"I'm just a little tired, that's all. It was a long journey here, and not very comfortable on the stage. So much time alone to…think." Kaitlin pulled a lace handkerchief from the pocket of her dress and pressed it to the corner of her eye. "The memories, you know. So many memories. I've no other family. Did I tell you that?''

Sheriff Newell shook his head. ''No ma'am, you didn't.''

Kaitlin sniffed and patted her belly. ''It's just me and Little Harvey here. I'm trying to preserve all I can for him, so he'll know his pa in some small way.''

''That's good of you, ma'am.''

She sniffed again and dabbed at her eyes. ''Could we get on with this, please, Sheriff?''

''Yes, ma'am.'' Sheriff Newell opened his desk drawer and withdrew a small sack. ''This here's everything your husband had on him when he died. And since you're his only rightful kin, Mrs. Stutz, I guess it all belongs to you.''

Kaitlin nearly kicked up her heels, but forced herself to lower her eyes. ''You're so kind.''

''Hold on a minute.'' Tripp advanced on the sheriff. ''I've got a claim on Stutz's belongings, too.''

''For heaven's sake, Callihan, can't you see she's his wife? And with a young'un on the way, too? What kind of a man are you, trying to take away from a widow and orphan?''

He flung his hand at Kaitlin. ''What proof has she got?''

Sheriff Newell sucked his gum. ''Well, you've got a good point there. How about it, Mrs. Stutz? You got a marriage license or something?''

Kaitlin pressed the handkerchief to her lips to hold in the curses burning her tongue. Darn that Tripp Callihan, he was ruining everything.

She clutched the handkerchief to her chest. ''It

was lost in the fire. Didn't you know? No, of course you had no way of knowing. Our home—our little love nest, Harvey called it—burned to the ground right after he died.''

''Well, mercy ma'am, you've had your share of hardship, that's for sure.''

Tripp snorted his disbelief. ''Sheriff, you're not going to fall for—''

''Hush up, Callihan. I'm the law in this town, and I say this here little lady deserves Harvey Stutz's belongings. Besides, you've got no proof of your claim, either.'' Sheriff Newell straightened his shoulders. ''Believe me, if I thought for one second that she was lying, she'd be seeing the inside of my jail cells quick as a wink. Same goes for you, Callihan.''

Kaitlin gulped and pressed the handkerchief to her lips.

Sheriff Newell grunted. ''Hell, maybe I ought to just give everything to the church.''

Tripp clamped his jaw shut and walked back to the corner.

''Now, let's get this over with. I'm getting hungry for my supper. I don't know what all the fuss is about, anyway. Harvey Stutz didn't leave enough for anybody to be fighting over.'' The sheriff pulled an envelope from the sack and handed it across the desk to Kaitlin. ''There's some money.''

Kaitlin's heart lurched. ''Cash?''

''Not much, but something to tide you over for a while.''

''Oh...''

''And a deed to some property over in Porter.''

Kaitlin eyed the envelope. "Property? What sort of property?"

The sheriff shook his head. "Don't know. Didn't look."

"That's all?"

"Well, yeah. Except for this." He pulled a gold locket from the sack. "Looks like a family piece. I guess that's what you're looking for, huh? You don't want those family things to get away."

From the corner of her eye she saw Tripp tense as she took the locket from the sheriff. She ignored him. "It's been passed down for generations. I want Little Harvey to have it when he gets grown."

The sheriff dusted his hands together. "Well, that's about it."

Kaitlin felt Tripp's hot gaze on her as she dropped the envelope and locket into the sack.

"Thank you for everything, Sheriff Newell. Goodbye." Kaitlin headed for the door. Such a performance. Her mother would have been proud.

"Not so fast." Sheriff Newell blocked her path. "There's one more matter we need to get cleared up before you leave here."

"A memorial service?"

"Yes, a memorial service." Kaitlin pulled her wrapper closed over her chemise and pantalettes, and yanked the sash tight. Afternoon sunlight filtered through the eyelet curtains on the window, brightening the hotel room. "For my dear departed. The Sheriff thinks it's what I want. It's set for tomorrow morning."

"Tomorrow!" Isabelle waved her arms wildly.

"But we're supposed to leave tonight! Tonight, Kaitlin, tonight! Miss Purtle will fire me if I'm not at work in her shop first thing tomorrow morning. She'll fire me!"

"Don't worry." Kaitlin pulled the pins from her hair and shook her head, sending her thick tresses curling down her back. "You'll leave this afternoon on the stage, just as we planned, and tomorrow after the service, I'll leave too."

"No, Kaitlin." Isabelle shook her head frantically. "It's dangerous. Somebody will figure out what you're up to."

Kaitlin dropped her hairpins on the washstand. "What else can I do? Tell the sheriff I don't want a service for dear ol' Harvey?"

"Let's just sneak away. He probably wouldn't recognize you, even if he saw you get on the stage."

"And what if he does?" Kaitlin asked. She wouldn't take the chance that the sheriff might give Stutz's belongings to that Mr. Callihan, or turn it over to the church.

"Kaitlin, please, come with me—"

"No. It's all settled. When you leave the hotel, pay for another night and asked them to send up a tray for me. I'll stay here in the room until tomorrow and catch the midday stage after the service. What can go wrong?"

"A thousand things!"

Kaitlin picked up Isabelle's carpetbag from the bed. "You'd better go before you miss the stage."

Isabelle hesitated, then took the carpetbag. "All right. But you be careful."

She opened the door. "I will. See you tomorrow."

Kaitlin waved goodbye, then closed the door and turned the big metal key in the lock. She fell back against the wall, heaving a heavy sigh.

Darn that Harvey Stutz. Judging from what was in the sack the sheriff had given her, Harvey had spent nearly all of her money. Gambled it away, probably. But that deed to the property over in Porter might be promising, and the locket. If she sold them both, maybe she could get back the rest of her money.

Kaitlin's spirits soared. Yes, she could get back her money—and her dream—after all.

A knock sounded at the door. Thank goodness the kitchen sent up her meal quickly. She was starved.

"Just leave the tray, please," she called.

The knock sounded again, harder this time.

"You can leave the tray outside. Thank you."

The pounding continued.

Kaitlin rolled her eyes. Good grief, was the kitchen help deaf?

Standing behind the door, she turned the key and opened it a crack. "I said, just leave—"

Tripp Callihan glared down at her.

"You're a fraud and a liar, lady. And I can prove it."

Chapter Two

Kaitlin threw her weight against the door, but Tripp was too fast and too strong. He pushed it open, sending her flying backward across the bed.

"Who do you think you are!" Kaitlin sprang to her knees in the center of the soft, feather mattress, anger flushing her cheeks. "Get out of here!"

He slammed the door shut and strode in the center of the room, his legs braced wide apart. "I'm not going anywhere, lady, until I get what I came here for."

She pushed her tangled hair over her shoulder. "I've got nothing that belongs to you!"

"You're a liar. You're a—"

He stopped, his gaze homing in on her belly.

Kaitlin followed his line of vision to her wrapper gaping open, the sash hanging loose at her sides exposing her flat stomach. She gasped and crossed her hands over her middle.

His eyes narrow. "What happened to your baby?"

Kaitlin scrambled off the opposite side of the bed,

her anger gone, ribbons of fear in its place. She gulped. "I—I gave birth."

He advanced on her. "Yeah? Where's the kid?"

Kaitlin backed away waving her hands around the room. "It's here…somewhere."

Tripp rounded the end of the bed. "Hell, you're not even a good liar."

Kaitlin pointed a finger at him. "Keep away from me." She tried to sound harsh, threatening, but her voice was nothing more than a squeak.

She bumped into the corner and looked around frantically. There was no place to run. He towered over her. He came closer, hemming her in.

"I'll scream. I'll scream my head off and have everybody in the hotel up here."

"Go ahead! Scream until you're hoarse! Get the sheriff up here, too. I'm sure he'd love to hear you explain *this*." Tripp grabbed a handful of her wrapper at her belly, and yanked it. Kaitlin fell against him.

Her arms wrapped around him, her nose burrowed into his neck. Her breasts, unbound, snuggled against his chest; her thighs brushed his.

Stunned, they both froze.

Fingers of fire raced through Kaitlin. He was hard and strong, muscles everywhere. He smelled like leather and soap.

Slowly, she lifted her face. His breath was hot on her cheeks, his eyes piercing. Kaitlin's knees weakened. Afraid she'd fall, she shifted. The thick ridge beneath his fly settled intimately against her.

Her senses reeled. Her whole body tingled. Heat rolled off him in waves. She saw the quick intake of his breath, felt his muscles tense. She knew she should pull away, but couldn't.

He pushed her away, gently, and stalked across the room. Kaitlin gulped and closed the sash of her wrapper with trembling hands.

He stood with his back to her for a moment, then turned and stepped behind the rocking chair in the corner. He pulled his hat lower on his forehead.

"Just give me what I came here for, lady, and I'll go."

His voice was softer now, unsteady. Kaitlin didn't trust herself to say anything, so she smoothed down her wrapper, reaching for a modicum of dignity.

Finally, she lifted her chin. "Everything Harvey Stutz had belongs to me, Mr. Callihan."

His eyes narrowed. "So you're in on his con games?"

"No!" Her back stiffened. "I most certainly am not. My name is Kaitlin Jeffers. I have an honest job and I come from a respectable family. I had nothing to do with Harvey Stutz, except to get everything I owned stolen by him. But I have it back now—part of it, at least."

"That's a lie. What you got from the sheriff belongs to me."

"Oh?" She tossed her head.

"Where's that sack the sheriff gave you?"

Tension coiled in Kaitlin's stomach, and she knew she'd be wise to be scared of this man. But he could have hurt her already, and hadn't. She'd felt the power he possessed. His touch was gentle; he was a man used to tempering his anger.

She pulled in a breath. "Those things are none of your business."

He pointed to the bureau. "I'll tear this place apart to find it, if I have to."

She knew he was capable of doing just that. Still, she wouldn't make it easy for him. Kaitlin planted her hands on her hips. "I'm not giving you anything."

"It belongs to me."

"It's mine. And you can't prove any different."

He advanced on her. "Yeah? It belongs to you? Then what's the inscription on the back of the locket?"

"Inscription?" Kaitlin shifted. There was an inscription on the locket? She hadn't even taken time to look it over. "Well..."

"It says, 'To my darling with all my love.'" Tripp held out his palm. "Hand it over, Miss Jeffers."

Obviously, the locket belonged to him. Darn. It would have fetched a good price. As much as she hated to see it go, it was only right.

For a moment she felt a kinship with Mr. Tripp Callihan, both taken advantage of by Harvey Stutz. Briefly she wondered what else the con man had taken from him, but doubted Tripp was the kind of man to divulge that.

Kaitlin opened the top drawer of the bureau and kept her back to him as she dug beneath her clothing. She glanced over her shoulder. "I had nothing to do with stealing this."

He snorted his disbelief.

Kaitlin pulled the gold locket from the sack and

turned it over in her hand. On the back was the inscription, just as Tripp had said.

She shrugged. "I guess it does belong to you."

He snatched it from her hand and dropped it in his shirt pocket. "Now I want what else is mine."

"But—"

Tripp jerked the sack from her hand.

"Hey! Give me that!"

She lunged for it, but he held it out of her reach, easily fending off her grabbing hands. He was so tall, so strong, she had no chance.

"Listen, Mr. Callihan. Let me explain." Kaitlin drew in a deep breath. "Harvey Stutz stole my life savings—every cent of it. I'm just trying to get it back."

"By pretending to be his widow—his pregnant widow?" He shook his head in disgust.

"Well, it worked. Or would have, if it hadn't been for you."

"Stutz stole from me, too."

"Your life savings?"

He looked away. "Something like that."

"You can have your locket. But the sheriff already said everything else belongs to me."

"You want to get the sheriff involved again?" Tripp's eyebrows drew together. "Fine. Let's find out what he has to say when he sees you like this. Maybe you can explain exactly where your *baby* went."

"You're not exactly his favorite person either, Mr. Callihan."

"I'll take my chances."

"And what if Sheriff Newell decides not to give

it to either of us? He threatened to give it to the church once already, remember? Both of us could end up with nothing.''

''Dammit...'' Tripp walked across the room and stared through the window at the street below. ''I didn't wait all this time, and come all this way, to end up with nothing.''

Kaitlin didn't say anything, just studied his profile outlined in the window. He looked grim.

Finally, he turned to her. ''All right. We split everything fifty-fifty. Deal?''

''Fifty-fifty? No, I was thinking more like—''

''You'd rather I let the sheriff settle this?''

She huffed impatiently. There really was nothing she could do. At least this way she'd end up with something.

''All right. We'll sell the business and split it down the middle. Agreed?''

''Agreed.'' Tripp strode across the room and opened the door. ''We'll head over to Porter at first light. Be ready.''

''Wait.'' She braced her hand against the door. ''How do I know you'll be here in the morning? How do I know you won't take off with the money and the deed?''

Tripp held up the sack. ''You'll have to trust me.''

''Trust you? I don't even know you.''

He looked down at her belly. ''At least I didn't start off with a lie.''

Tripp left the room and slammed the door behind him.

Dawn's first rays of light seeped over the horizon as Tripp dropped his satchel beside the front desk in the hotel lobby. A circular red velvet couch stood in the center of the room beneath an ornate chandelier. At the desk along the back wall, a man scrawled his name on the registration book while the clerk searched the cubby holes for a room key.

Tripp paused in the doorway of the hotel dining room, looking over the few customers already seated there. A couple of men wearing cravats and jackets, an old man with a dusty beard, a family with three wiggly children. An odd sense of disappointment crept over Tripp. No sign of Kaitlin Jeffers.

That proved it, he decided. She was a crook, just like Harvey Stutz. Probably hightailed it out of town during the night, fearing he'd go to the sheriff after all.

Tripp wound his way through the white-linen-covered tables, ignoring the murmured conversations around him, and took a seat along the back wall. He hadn't expected any different. Hadn't he learned a long time ago how women act when things got tough?

Tripp tossed his black hat on the chair beside him and scrubbed his hands over his face. He'd hardly slept a wink last night. Worries, then dreams, kept him awake until nearly dawn. The worries he was used to. But the dreams—he hadn't had dreams like that since he was a kid.

He shifted in his chair as a familiar stirring claimed him, then looked around the room for a distraction from his own thoughts.

A woman stepped into the doorway of the dining room. Tripp drew in a sharp breath. God, she was the prettiest thing he'd seen in a month of Sundays, all done up in a green skirt with a matching print overskirt, and a blouse that hugged her breasts and outlined her trim waist. A green hat sat at a saucy angle among her dark curling hair.

Pressure behind his fly increased considerably as he watched her hips sway across the dining room. She took a seat at the corner table facing the wall, her back to the door.

A sweet scent wafted over him. Tripp reeled back in his chair. Good God, it was Kaitlin Jeffers.

What had happened to her? Brown eyes, so dark they reflected the light from the window, darted quickly around the room. Her oval face shone with full lips, soft delicate features, and porcelain skin. Why hadn't he noticed those things last night?

Or maybe he had. Images that had frolicked in his dreams last night came back to him now with the same urgency.

Tripp turned his attention to two old men seating themselves at the table next to him, and listened to their conversation. He sure as hell needed something to occupy his attention. But his gaze drifted back to Kaitlin.

She looked all delicate and soft, tugging off her lace gloves, smoothing down her skirt, tucking a wisp of hair behind her ear. Womanly movements, feminine and artful, without trying to be. Tripp's chest tightened.

She glanced at him, then looked away quickly.

"Miss Jeffers?" The words slipped from his lips before he realized it.

She glanced at him from the corner of her eye, then looked away once more.

He knew damn good and well she'd seen him.

"Miss Jeffers?"

Kaitlin turned to him, her lips pursed, her brows furrowed. "Shh! Not so loud. I'm trying to be inconspicuous."

How in the name of heaven did a woman as pretty as her think she could be inconspicuous in a little town like this?

"Look, Miss Jeffers—"

Her eyes bulged, silencing him, and she waved him over.

Slowly he walked to her little table in the corner, holding his hat in front of him.

Kaitlin huffed impatiently. "For heaven's sake, sit down. You'll have everybody in the room staring at me."

Tripp lowered himself into the chair across from her. "Somebody you're trying to avoid, Miss Jeffers?"

"As you so delicately pointed out last night, Mr. Callihan, it wouldn't do me any good to be seen by Sheriff Newell in my...condition."

"Or lack of it."

"Exactly."

Tripp pulled on his chin. "I figured you'd left town."

"As if you should be so lucky." Kaitlin smiled sweetly at him. "I'm not going anywhere without you, Mr. Callihan, until our business is settled."

The serving girl stopped at their table and filled their cups with hot coffee.

"Give me steak and eggs with lots of potatoes and some biscuits." Tripp gestured across the table. "Same for her."

"Coming right up." The serving girl smiled and left.

Tripp sipped his coffee. "So you're still agreeable with the deal we made last night?"

"No, I'm not agreeable at all. I'd much prefer keeping everything for myself. But since half is the best I can do, I'll settle for that."

"I guess we might as well get down to business." Tripp reached beneath his vest and pulled a small tablet from the pocket of his white shirt. He studied it for a moment. "I figure it'll take us two hours to get to Porter this morning, about a half hour to find the place and look it over, then another hour to get it listed for sale."

Kaitlin peered across the table. "You wrote that down?"

He flipped over to the next page. "Once the place is sold, we'll meet, sign the papers, and divide up the profit. Any questions?"

She rolled her eyes. "I don't know. It's so complicated, I'm not sure I follow you."

"We'll take the deed to the bank and transfer it to both our names—just to be safe."

She tilted her head. "You don't trust me?"

He dropped his forearm on the table. "Look, Miss Jeffers, the sooner we get this over with, the better. I haven't got time to fool around."

"Nor have I, Mr. Callihan." Kaitlin pushed her chin higher. "In fact, thanks to Harvey Stutz, I've had to change my plans considerably."

He glared at her, then drank his coffee. He didn't pursue her comment, didn't really want to know what Harvey Stutz had done to her. Tripp couldn't muster his compassion for another of the man's victims; it just didn't stretch that far.

The serving girl brought them plates of hot food.

Kaitlin wagged her finger at his pad of paper as she ate. "Do you have written down somewhere the kind of property we own?"

"A store." He waved his fork toward her plate. "Eat your potatoes."

She sat up straighter. "A store? Really?"

"Finish your meal. We've got to go."

Tripp turned his attention to his plate, hoping to discourage any more conversation. The sooner he got this over with—and this woman out of his life—the better.

He paid for their meals, then followed Kaitlin's bobbing bustle to the lobby. Tripp pulled his tablet from his shirt pocket, forcing himself to look at the notes he'd made.

"I checked the stage schedule last night. Nothing going to Porter until this afternoon. I'll rent us a buggy down at the livery and pick you up out front in a few minutes."

"I'll meet you out back," Kaitlin said.

Tripp shook his head in disgust. "If you hadn't told a lie in the first place you wouldn't have to hide from the sheriff."

"Thank you so much for that pearl of wisdom, Mr. Callihan." Kaitlin jerked up her carpetbag from beside the front desk and marched toward the back of the hotel.

* * *

The streets of Porter were quiet with a wagon or two lumbering along when Tripp and Kaitlin drove into town. A few men gathered outside the barber shop, cowboys and miners moseyed along, women and children moved down Main Street.

At the far edge of town Tripp halted the team at the blacksmith shop. The big double doors stood open; horses waited patiently in the corral.

Tripp set the brake and jumped to the ground. He strode away from the buggy drawing in deep breaths of hay, horses, and dust. Riding next to Kaitlin Jeffers, breathing in her sweetness for two solid hours had been torture. He wished he'd waited for the stage coach.

"Morning!" A tall, muscular, man around thirty years old walked out of the stable, smiling and pushing his blond hair off his forehead. "Name's Rafe Beaumont. What can I help you with?"

"My horses need tending." Tripp waved toward the team; he'd driven them harder than he should have, thanks to Kaitlin Jeffers's scent.

Rafe stroked one of the horses's thick neck and nodded toward Kaitlin. "You and the wife plan to be in town long?"

Kaitlin came to her feet. "We are not married."

Rafe glanced back and forth between them and his cheeks turned red. "Oh…"

"We're business partners," she said.

"Oh!" Rafe looked relieved. "What sort of business?"

"Maybe you can help us with that." Kaitlin gathered her skirts and turned to climb down from the buggy.

Tripp hurried over. "Hold on. Do you want to fall? You need to be more careful." He caught her waist and lifted her to the ground.

Kaitlin shrugged out of his grasp. "We're looking for a store, Mr. Beaumont."

"Got a few of those in town." Rafe smiled and patted the horse's forehead.

"This one's called Finch Dry Goods. Used to be owned by an Everette Finch." Tripp nodded toward town. "Didn't see it when we drove in."

Rafe's eyes widened. "You two bought Finch's place?"

Tripp and Kaitlin glanced at each other.

"Let's just say it's ours now," Tripp said.

"I can tell you how to find the place, but—"

"Rafe, why don't you take them over there yourself?"

Two men walked out of the stable, grinning broadly. Like Rafe, they were tall, muscular and blond.

One of them slapped him on the back. "Yeah, Rafe, take these nice folks over to the Finch place."

Rafe blushed and ducked his head. "These are my brothers, Ned and Wade."

Greetings were exchanged and proper introductions made.

"So you're the new owner of old man Finch's place?" Wade asked. "Well, all I can say is good luck to you."

Ned chucked Rafe on the shoulder, grinning. "Take them over there. Show them the store."

Rafe shifted uncomfortably. "I got work to do here."

"Ned and I will look after the place." Wade elbowed him in the ribs. "And if you're a little late getting back, we'll understand."

Ned and Wade both broke out laughing, bringing another blush to Rafe's face.

Rafe grumbled under his breath. "All right. Let's go."

The late morning sun warmed the breeze as they walked the short distance to town. The men's boots echoed on the wooden planks of the boardwalk drowning out the scuff of Kaitlin's shoes as she walked between the two of them.

"Have you lived here long, Mr. Beaumont?" Kaitlin asked.

"Just call me Rafe. My family's lived here a while. I took over the livery after our pa passed on." He gestured toward the street. "Yeah, Porter is a nice place, all right. Quiet. Not much going on. Your store's right up here."

Kaitlin's heart thumped in her chest. Visions of her recaptured dream filled her mind.

Rafe flung out his hand. "Well, this is it."

Kaitlin's heart sank into the pit of her stomach.

Dust covered the boardwalk in front of the store. Dirt streaked the display windows beside the door, and several panes were broken. The shade over the windowed door hung askew.

Rafe shrugged apologetically. "I guess it doesn't look like much on the outside."

Her spirits lifted. "It's better on the inside?"

"Well...no," Rafe said. "Still want to look around?"

Kaitlin squared her shoulders. "Yes."

Rafe pushed open the door. Cobwebs clung to the corners. Barren shelves dangled from the walls. A potbellied stove lay on its side. Gray ashes swirled in the slight breeze.

"It's been empty for a while. Kids got in and tore it up," Rafe said. "I guess it's not what you expected."

Kaitlin looked around. "No, not exactly."

Tripp gazed down at her. "I don't know what your dream was, Kaitlin, but you can kiss it goodbye."

Chapter Three

"It just needs a little fixing up."

Kaitlin gazed hopefully at the two men. Rafe offered her a sickly smile. Tripp snorted and turned away.

She walked slowly around the room. "It has possibilities."

"To tell you the truth, old man Finch was never able to do much with the place. Tried to sell it, but never got a nibble," Rafe said. "I heard he finally got rid of the place by betting it in a poker game, then losing on purpose."

Kaitlin's gaze collided with Tripp's across the empty store. So that's how Harvey Stutz had acquired the deed. It was small consolation to think that for once, Stutz had been the one getting conned.

"Of course, with a lot of hard work and a little luck, maybe you two can make a go of it," Rafe said. "You—"

"Rafe?"

A young woman walked through the front door.

Shapely and attractive, her blond hair gathered in a neat bun, she headed straight for Rafe.

"I didn't know you'd be here." She reached for him.

Rafe backed up a step and caught her hands before they circled his waist. "I brought these folks over to look at the store. They're the new owners."

She turned to Kaitlin and Tripp. "New owners? Oh, how wonderful."

Tripp tipped his hat and introduced Kaitlin and himself. "Nice to meet you, ma'am."

"This is Julia, my wife." Rafe caught her hand as it splayed across his chest. "Just a minute now, darling. Julia owns the millinery shop next door. She makes hats."

"You'll have to come over, Kaitlin, and see the shop," Julia said as she eased her bosom against Rafe's side.

Rafe's cheeks turned pink and he stepped away from her. "For a while we thought business would pick up some around here. There was talk of the railroad coming through. They even laid the tracks and started work on the depot. But then the railroad changed its mind, for some reason."

Tripp nodded. "That'll happen. I've got a friend working for the railroad. Never knows where he'll be laying track next."

"Porter is a real friendly town. You'll like it here." Julia gazed up at Rafe. "We sure like it here, don't we?"

"I've got to get on back to work," he said.

"So soon?" She eased up next to him again. "Things are real quiet at the shop, Rafe, and I'm not expecting anybody in until this afternoon. Why don't you—''

''I've got work to do.'' Rafe said, fending off her wandering hands. ''If you need anything, Tripp, let me know.''

''I'll do that,'' Tripp said, as Rafe went out the door.

Julia hurried out after him. ''Rafe? Wait!''

The heat seemed to leave the room with them, causing Kaitlin to shiver. She wandered around the store. This certainly wasn't what she expected, although with Harvey Stutz involved she should have known better.

Why couldn't it have been a nice, clean, prosperous store? Just once, couldn't things have gone well for her? Did everything always have to be so hard? She'd worked diligently and suffered so many setbacks already. Briefly, she wondered if her dream was meant to come true.

Kaitlin drew in her resolve and squared her shoulders, reminding herself that those sorts of thoughts would do her no good. She had to continue on, to keep going.

Kaitlin turned to Tripp, standing at the broken remains of the counter.

''Well, I guess we'd better get to work,'' she said.

''Get to work? Are you loco?'' His eyes widened. ''This place is hopeless.''

''We have to clean it before we offer it for sale. Who would buy it looking like this?''

He waved away her comments with his big hand. ''Forget it. We'll never see a dime from this place. Didn't you hear Rafe say that the last owner couldn't get rid of it? We'd be better off signing it over to the town before they charge us for tearing it down.''

Kaitlin's mouth flew open, but she didn't say anything. She'd had her own doubts a moment ago. Surely Tripp was entitled to the same feelings.

"I understand why you feel that way, Mr. Callihan. Just think it over a while longer."

"I've already done all the thinking I need to do," Tripp said. "Getting rid of this place is the only sensible thing."

He meant it. She saw the determination etched in the hard lines of his face. He really wanted to walk away.

Kaitlin advanced on him. "I have plans, Mr. Callihan, and those plans require money. This is the only chance I have to get back what Harvey Stutz stole from me, and I'm not walking out on it."

He glared down at her. "I've got plans of my own, Miss Jeffers, but I'm not crazy enough to think I'll get anywhere with this place."

"I'm not about to give up my dream."

He studied her for a moment. "Then what do you suggest we do?"

She pushed her chin higher. "We'll fix it up and run it ourselves. It's the only possible solution."

"Look at this place." Tripp waved his arms around the room. "It's got to be scrubbed from top to bottom. The shelves have to be replaced, the counter rebuilt, the walls painted. Part of the floor's rotted—probably because the roof leaks. And that's only what's wrong with this section of the building. God only knows what needs doing in the back room and upstairs."

"I didn't say it would be easy."

He stalked away, then turned back to her. "Besides, I don't know the first thing about a store. Do you?"

She slid her finger across her lips. "Of course."

Tripp eyed her for a long moment, his brow furrowed, his gaze intent. Finally, he shook his head.

"Look, Miss Jeffers, if you want to get your money back, why don't you just get a job somewhere? You can earn back what Stutz took from you."

"And what sort of work would you suggest, Mr. Callihan? What job could a woman get to earn that kind of money?"

Tripp shrugged his wide shoulders. "Restaurants are always needing serving girls. And hotels need somebody to clean."

"I've worked those types of jobs, Mr. Callihan, for pennies a day. Pennies," Kaitlin said. "It took years for me to save up what Harvey Stutz stole in one night. I don't want to wait that long again."

Kaitlin pressed her lips together. "We both know there's only one profession where a woman can earn good money."

Tripp straightened, his expression grim. "Don't talk like that. That's no kind of life for a woman like you."

The intensity of his words stunned her. She'd certainly never considered turning to prostitution, but did envy the whores their money.

Kaitlin shrugged. "You can see that my choices are limited. Running my own business is the only chance I have to earn the money I need. You have to agree with that.''

Tripp stepped away. Obviously, he wasn't ready to concede anything.

"Fine.'' Kaitlin squared her shoulders. "Just sign over the deed to me and I'll run it myself.''

His frown deepened. "You can't fix up this place by yourself. It's too much work. You'll hurt yourself.''

She tilted her head. "Maybe you're afraid I'll succeed?''

Tripp glared down at her. "That wasn't my first thought.''

"Maybe it should be.'' Kaitlin pushed past him and strode to the middle of the room. "Look, all we have to do is run the store long enough to earn back the money Harvey Stutz stole from us. I saw only one store when we passed through town. This place is hungry for variety. And what about those ranches and miners near here, and those small settlements? We'll pull in people from miles around.''

Tripp stared at her, unconvinced.

Kaitlin kept going. "Everybody will come. The novelty of a new store will draw them in. They'll buy. We'll be lucky to keep stock on the shelves, and we'll make a big profit very quickly. Once we've done that, we can list the store for sale and go our separate ways. If it never sells—who cares? We'll have our money.''

Tripp paced back and forth in front of the toppled stove, rubbing his chin. He stopped and looked at her again.

"I'm hungry.''

"Hungry?" Kaitlin threw her hands up. "Haven't you been listening? How can you think of food at a time like—"

Tripp strode out the door without a look back.

Two blocks down the street he slowed enough to glance around. The town of Porter was much like other towns he'd seen. Good people. Churchgoers, businessmen who didn't cheat their customers, families planting roots. As towns went, Porter didn't seem so bad.

Tripp went inside the Red Rose Café on the corner, took a seat at a table near the front window, but didn't look out. He needed to think.

Propping his elbows on the red-checkered table cloth, Tripp dug the heels of his hands into his eyes. No, he didn't want to think. There was nothing to think about.

An older woman with an apron spanning her considerable girth stopped at his table. "We've got chicken or ham today. What will it be?"

"Both."

Lately, all he wanted to do was eat. A craving had come over him and he couldn't control it.

"Sure thing." The woman disappeared into the kitchen.

Tripp scrubbed his palms over his face, refusing to think about the general store down the street he'd just left. He'd made up his mind. The whole idea was crazy. It would never work.

The image of Kaitlin Jeffers flashed into his mind. Headstrong, determined, resourceful…beautiful.

Tripp slumped in the chair. Looks meant nothing. And neither did any of those other qualities. Any

woman could display them. But how many would
act on them when things got tough, when plans
didn't turn out as expected?

A deep ache settled over him, old and familiar. He
allowed those feelings to wash through him. It was
good to be reminded, from time to time. Good not
to forget.

He drew in a deep breath. For all her talk of
dreams and plans, Kaitlin Jeffers would forget the
whole thing at the first sign of trouble. And Tripp
didn't intend to be left behind to pick up the pieces.
Again.

Belly full of chicken, ham, vegetables, corn bread
and two slices of peach pie, Tripp ambled down the
boardwalk. When he reached the store, he cringed;
the place looked worse every time he saw it.

Reaching for the doorknob he stopped. Singing.
He heard singing. Looking up and down the street
Tripp saw nothing, then peered into the store through
the crooked shade over the door. In the middle of
the floor, all alone, Kaitlin waltzed back and forth.
Gracefully she swayed, her sweet voice rising in a
lovely melody.

Tripp pushed open the door and walked inside.
''Did you hit your head or something while I was
gone?''

''Of course not, Mr. Callihan.'' She finished her
dance and smiled up at him. ''Don't you know you
can dance on air when your dreams come true?''

God, she looked pretty. So full of hope and wonder and optimism. Tripp rubbed his hand across his
belly. How could he feel hungry again?

"Let me tell you what I've decided on for the store." Kaitlin gestured toward the back wall. "I'll put candy jars on the back counter, and along the other walls, fabric and linens. The display windows will be for the newest merchandise, of course, and in that corner I'll put—"

"Hold on a minute. You don't really think you can make a go of this place, do you?"

Kaitlin smiled up at him. "Mr. Callihan, that's exactly what I intend to do, with or without your help."

Tripp looked around the dismal store. "You believe you can turn a profit here?"

Kaitlin glided past him. "Too bad you won't be here to share it. Unless, of course, you've changed your mind."

Tripp watched her move about the store, her bustle bobbing as she thoughtfully considered each angle of the room. He cleared his throat.

"So, you know about running a store?" he asked.

She looked back over her shoulder at him. "A display of dishes and pottery would look good right inside the door, don't you think?"

Tripp rubbed his chin. "And where do you plan to get the money to fix this place up and buy inventory?"

"From the cash that Harvey left behind. I've got a little money put away, too, money I've saved since Harvey took everything I had. It's not enough to replace what he stole from me. But total, it's enough to do the repairs to the store and buy the inventory. That's all I need to get started."

Tripp shook his head. "I don't know."

"It's called investing," Kaitlin said. "It's not so unusual. I'll invest in this store, earn back my money, plus make a profit—all the money I need to make my dream come true."

"Do you really think you can do that?"

"Of course," Kaitlin said. "And best part is that this way I can earn the money quickly. A new store will make tons of money when it first opens. There's no other respectable way I can do that. And I'm not willing to wait years again, working for a few dollars a week."

Tripp stepped closer. "You intend to drop everything and move here with the wild notion of running a store?"

"Running a store can hardly be called a wild notion, Mr. Callihan," Kaitlin said. "But I suppose you're too busy to speculate on a blossoming business opportunity like this. You already have a business, I suppose?"

"Well...no."

"You're working someplace special, then?"

"Not exactly." Tripp pushed his hat higher on his forehead. "Don't you have a family, or a job, or something?"

"If I had a family I would have asked them for money long ago and already been living my dream," Kaitlin said. "I do have a job that I'll be more than happy to quit."

She nodded toward the torn curtain in the doorway along the back wall. "There's lots of storage space for stock. We'll need it, once word gets out that we're here."

Tripp glared at her, then shook his head. "This whole idea is loco, just plain loco."

"Suit yourself, Mr. Callihan." She shrugged. "Of course, it would be a shame for you to miss out on this opportunity, when you were so close. Maybe I can find another partner."

"Another partner?" Tripp's shoulders stiffened.

She brushed past him. "Yes, someone who isn't afraid of a little hard work."

"Now hold on a minute. I'm not afraid of hard work. Hard work has nothing to do with this." Tripp rounded on her. "It's you I'm worried about."

"Me!" Kaitlin's eyes widened. "You're worried about me?"

"Hell, yes." Tripp pointed toward the front door. "I'm not partnering with somebody who's going to run out on me at the first sign of trouble."

Irritated to no end, Kaitlin stretched up until her nose was even with his chin. After what he'd seen her do in the past twenty-four hours, he thought she wasn't committed to her goals?

"Maybe you hadn't noticed, Mr. Callihan, but *you're* the one who keeps backing away from this deal—not me!"

Tripp reeled away. Good God, she was right.

Silence hung in the still, cool room. Minutes dragged by while they contemplated each other. Finally, Tripp drew in a deep breath.

"So you intend to see this thing through?" he asked.

Kaitlin nodded confidently. "I'll have my dream, Mr. Callihan, and not you, or Harvey Stutz, or a room full of cobwebs is going to stop me."

She offered her hand. "So how about it? Is it a deal?"

Tripp gazed at her outstretched hand. God knows, he'd be crazy to accept an offer like this. The store was a losing proposition if he'd ever seen one. Hell, he'd be better off walking out the door now while he still could.

But Kaitlin…Kaitlin burned with determination. Kaitlin caused something to flicker inside him. That determination, surely.

Tripp grasped Kaitlin's hand, soft, delicate, fragile. A knot jerked in his stomach.

"It's a deal," Tripp said, and wished to God he'd never touched her.

"A little more to the right. That's it…just a little more. Stop. Perfect."

Kaitlin nodded with satisfaction as Rudy Langley positioned her big oval mirror in the corner of her new bedroom. Not the biggest room in the world, or in the store, but it was perfect for her, situated off the kitchen in the back room of her new business enterprise.

"Thanks, Rudy."

Isabelle's harness-and-pregnancy-making brother nodded and glanced around the room. "I guess that's everything."

"Everything but a dose of good sense." Isabelle pursed her lips as she opened the lid of Kaitlin's trunk.

"Honestly, Isabelle, you worry too much." Kaitlin grabbed a handful of pantalettes from her carpetbag and shoved them into the bureau drawer. "What can go wrong?"

"A thousand things!" Isabelle waved her arms wildly.

Kaitlin turned to Rudy. "Talk to your sister. Make her understand."

He backed away. "I just came to drive the team and unload your things. You two can fight this out on your own." Rudy disappeared out the door.

Kaitlin pushed more of her belongings into the bureau drawer. "Nothing will go wrong."

"Kaitlin, listen to reason." Isabelle followed her across the room. "You don't know this man. What if he's a murderer? What if he was in prison? What if he's one of those men who...takes advantage of women?"

Kaitlin stopped at the armoire. "Mr. Callihan hardly seems the type. But if it will make you feel better, when he gets here I'll ask him if he's ever killed anyone."

Isabelle shook her head frantically. "Please, be serious about this."

"Listen, Isabelle, if Mr. Callihan were a criminal, he certainly wouldn't have showed up in Sheriff Newell's office to claim Harvey Stutz's belongings, now would he?"

"Well, maybe not." Isabelle eyes narrowed. "But how do you know he won't run off with your money like Harvey Stutz did? Hmm? How do you know that?"

Kaitlin shook out the pink skirt she pulled from the trunk and hung it in the armoire. Tripp Callihan could have run off with everything—cash and deed—the night he'd left her in the hotel, but he hadn't.

"He seems like an honest man. He gave me his word, and I believed him."

"His word?" Isabelle rolled her eyes. "And I suppose you shook hands, too?"

A hot rush crackled through Kaitlin at the memory of Tripp's big, strong hand closing over hers. It had sealed their deal in a way she hadn't expected.

Kaitlin turned quickly to the armoire again. "Isabelle, you worry too much."

"Of course I worry too much!" Isabelle wrung her hands together. "Think about what you're doing. A partnership with a man you hardly know—a man you'll be living with here in this store, all alone. Kaitlin, what will the townspeople think of you? Have you considered that?"

Her hands stilled on the blue blouse she pulled from her trunk. Color stung her cheeks, but she forced it down.

"Mr. Callihan and I are business partners. That's all. The townspeople will just have to accept it. And once they've been in the store and seen what's going on, no one will think any differently."

"People talk, Kaitlin."

"Well, let them talk." She closed the trunk. "This is what I must do to get my money back. And if things go as planned, I won't be in town long enough to care what anyone thinks."

"Kaitlin, please, think this over."

Reaching out, Kaitlin took her friend's hands. "Stop worrying, Isabelle. Everything will be fine."

Isabelle's shoulders slumped. "All right. But if

you need anything, you let me know. Rudy and I will come right over. It's only a few hours' drive.''

Kaitlin smiled. Isabelle had been her friend since they were just girls. They'd been through a great deal together. She didn't know how she would have managed the trip to Porter—and a lot of other things—without her help.

Rudy stepped into the doorway of the bedroom. ''We'd better go. Need anything else before we leave, Kaitlin?''

She gazed at the bedroom. Since Isabelle and Rudy had driven her to Porter this morning, they'd spent most of the day cleaning. Now, filled with her brass bed, bureau, mirror and armoire, the room looked a little more like home.

''No, Rudy, you'd better go if you want to get back before dark.'' Kaitlin stretched up and gave him a peck on the cheek. ''Thanks for everything.''

Rudy ducked his head and grinned. ''We'll miss you.''

Kaitlin led the way through the kitchen—which they hadn't touched yet—and out the back door. Across the little dirt alley stood a small barn and corral. Rudy's wagon waited at the edge of the covered boardwalk.

''When is that Mr. Callihan supposed to get here?'' Isabelle gazed down the alley, past the rear of the other businesses that faced Main Street.

''We agreed to meet here today. I'm sure he's on his way.''

Isabelle's eyes narrowed as if she doubted it.

''He'll be here.'' Kaitlin urged her toward the

wagon and stepped back onto the boardwalk. "Goodbye. Thanks again."

"Remember what I said," Isabelle called as she settled into the wagon seat.

Rudy climbed aboard and tipped his hat as he headed the team down the alley. Kaitlin stood on the boardwalk, watching and waving until her friends disappeared from view.

After they were gone, she stood there a while longer. The town seemed suddenly quiet now, the breeze cooler. Clouds drifted over the afternoon sun turning everything a pale gray. Vague sounds from the street wafted through the air; somewhere, a dog barked.

Kaitlin glanced down the alley. Suddenly, she wished Tripp Callihan would get here. Odd, but it wasn't like her to think such thoughts. She'd been alone for so long now, she was used to it.

No, she was just in a hurry to get the store ready, she decided. Kaitlin nodded confidently and brushed her hands together. Yes, that was the reason she was so anxious to see Tripp Callihan.

Kaitlin went inside the store and dumped the last of her clothing out of the carpetbag and onto the bed. As she sorted through them she heard the jangle of harness and the creak of a wagon out back.

Kaitlin hurried through the kitchen and opened the back door. High on the wagon seat sat Tripp, his black Stetson pulled low on his forehead, his shoulders straight, his hands holding the team steady.

"You came," Kaitlin said, stepping outside. "I was beginning to think you'd changed your mind."

He set the brake and tied off the reins, then

jumped to the ground and stretched his long legs. "I gave you my word, didn't I?"

"Yes, you did." Kaitlin waved at the back of his wagon, loaded with furniture and crates. "I can see that now."

Tripp reached into the wagon just behind the seat and a child sat up. The little boy yawned and ground his fists into his eyes, then raised his arms to Tripp. He lifted him from the wagon and set him on the boardwalk.

Kaitlin stared at the dark-haired child dressed in black suspendered pants and a rumpled white shirt. Finally she looked up at Tripp.

He glowered at her from beneath the brim of his hat.

"He's my son."

Chapter Four

She'd expected most anything from Tripp Callihan—a change in the terms of their deal, not showing up at all, actually turning out to be a convicted murder. But a child?

Kaitlin knelt in front of the boy. He was a beautiful child. Black hair, like Tripp's. Deep-blue eyes, the same hue as his father's. The family resemblance hidden in the boy's soft face made Tripp's features harder, sharper.

Kaitlin glanced up at him, towering over them both. He looked big, powerful, masculine. That strong chin and straight nose, those intelligent eyes would be the child's someday. It was only a matter of time.

She smiled at the boy as he rubbed his eyes again. "What's your name?"

He latched on to Tripp's trouser leg and looked up at him.

"This is Miss Kaitlin." Tripp touched his hand to the back of the boy's head. "It's all right to talk to her."

"Charlie." His forehead wrinkled in a little frown. "And you can't call me Charles 'cause Papa gets mad."

Kaitlin grinned and glanced up at Tripp. "We certainly don't want that to happen, now do we?"

"Uh-uh." Charlie shook his head emphatically.

"How old are you?"

"Six."

"My, but you're a big boy for six."

Charlie looked past her to the store. "You got any kids?"

Kaitlin rose and shook her head. "No. Sorry."

"Papa?" He tugged on Tripp's trouser leg. "I'm thirsty."

"Come on, Charlie." Kaitlin reached for his hand. "I'll take you inside and get you a—"

"No." Tripp dropped his hand on the boy's shoulder and looked Kaitlin hard in the eye. "I take care of him."

Kaitlin stepped out of the way. "Sorry…"

She followed them inside the store and found Tripp holding the boy up to the sink while he pumped water; Charlie stuck his mouth under the flow, lapping it with his tongue. Tripp set him down, then cupped his hand under the water and rubbed it over his face.

"Can I go outside, Papa?" Charlie asked.

Tripp pulled a handkerchief from his hip pocket and wiped his face. "Stay by the wagon. Nowhere else."

"I will, Papa."

Kaitlin stepped aside as the boy scooted out the door. She nodded outside.

"Have you got a wife inside that wagon, too?"

Tripp frowned at her. "No."

"Will she be joining us later?"

His frown deepened as he shoved his handkerchief into his hip pocket. "No."

Kaitlin stepped closer. "Will she—"

"It's just Charlie and me." Tripp dragged the sleeve of his pale blue shirt across his face. "We'd better get down to business."

Obviously, he didn't intend to give her more details and, really, it wasn't any of her business. But the deep pain she saw in his blue eyes for a fraction of a second told Kaitlin a great deal of what she needed to know.

"Yes, I guess we should." She motioned out the door. "We'll get your wagon unloaded, then we can—"

"Hold on. We need to talk about a few things first."

"Talk?" Kaitlin waved her hand outside. "There's only a few hours of daylight left and lots to do. We can talk later."

"No, now. There're some things we have to get straight, and I'm not unloading my wagon until we do."

Kaitlin huffed impatiently. "Fine."

Tripp walked to the rickety table leaning against the wall, wiped the dust away with his handkerchief and righted two crates at either end.

"Sit down."

Kaitlin waved her arms around the room. "Couldn't we discuss this while we work?"

He blinked at her, taken aback by her questioning. "No. First things first."

She perched on the edge of the crate, holding on to her patience. "Well, just hurry, will you?"

Instead, Tripp walked across the room and looked out the back door.

"Don't play on that, son, you might fall."

He stood there a moment longer, watching, then strode to the table and sat down across from her, the crate beneath him groaning.

"Now, let's see." Tripp pulled a small tablet from the pocket of his shirt. "First, I want to go over our partnership agreement."

Kaitlin sighed heavily. "We've gone over that already. We split everything fifty-fifty, and sell out when we've made our money back."

Tripp shook his head. "It's not that simple."

"If it were any more simple, a dog with thumbs could run the place."

Tripp glared at her, then flipped to the next page. "I've done some figuring on expenses—repairs, buying the inventory, things like that. We need to decide on a budget."

Kaitlin shrugged. "We'll spend what money we have, and that should be enough to get things going."

"What the hell kind of idea is that?" Tripp reared back.

"What more can I tell you, Mr. Callihan? I'm putting every dime I have in the world into this place. Aren't you?"

"All the more reason for us to make a plan."

She bit down on her lip. "We have a plan."

"We need to decide on the extent of the repairs, how much we can spend on them, what kind of inventory to buy." Tripp tapped his finger on the tablet. "We have a lot of decisions to make."

Kaitlin pressed her lips together, holding in her rising temper. "Are you this methodical about *everything* you do, Mr. Callihan?"

Their gazes collided, and the implication of what *everything* might entail sprang up between them as if it were a living thing. Kaitlin blushed and looked away. Tripp cleared his throat and shifted on the crate.

"Well, uh, maybe this can wait a while," Tripp said.

"Good idea." Kaitlin hopped off the crate and hurried across the room.

"As long as we're straight on this deal."

She whirled around. "You've made your position perfectly clear, Mr. Callihan. And the fact that I want to get to work while you want to discuss things should prove my position. Now, can we please get your wagon unloaded?"

Tripp just looked at her, all puffed up with emotion. His belly began to ache.

"All right, let's get to work." He headed across the room. "Are you hungry?"

"Hungry?" Kaitlin shook her head and hurried out the door. "Good grief."

Tripp opened the tailgate of the wagon and unloaded some of the lighter items onto the boardwalk, crates, cane-back chairs, a trunk, a small table. Charlie scooted over.

"Can I help, Papa?"

Tripp handed him a small box. "Take it inside. And be careful."

"I figured you'd use the room upstairs," Kaitlin said as she picked up a chair. "We'll need all the space downstairs for the stock."

Tripp lifted one of the heavier crates. "Let's have a look."

Inside the kitchen, Charlie waited at the door to Kaitlin's bedroom.

"That room's mine, Charlie," Kaitlin said. "You and your papa will be upstairs."

They placed the items they carried on the other side of the kitchen, and Kaitlin led the way up the narrow staircase. The room was dirty like the rest of the place, with two windows along the back wall.

Tripp walked around studying the floor, ceiling and corners while Charlie ran to the window and looked out.

"Are we gonna have this room, Papa?"

Kaitlin stood in the center of the room watching Tripp circle around her. "It's plenty big enough for you both."

"I like it, Papa." Charlie bounced on his toes.

"If you don't want it, you can look at the room downstairs." Kaitlin pushed a lock of hair behind her ear. Gracious, this man took forever to decide anything. She felt her patience slipping away. "Mr. Callihan, do you like the room, or not?"

Tripp continued to pace. How could a room this dirty, closed up for this long, smell so sweet? His gaze landed on Kaitlin. She was how, of course.

The room that appeared so large only a second ago seemed to shrink around him. Tripp headed for the staircase. "The room's fine. I'll get the wagon unloaded."

"Good idea," Kaitlin muttered as she followed him down the steps. "I wish I'd thought of that."

Tripp was already lifting items from the wagon when she reached the back boardwalk. He held up his hand.

"You go inside. I'll take care of this."

She reached for another chair. "It will go faster if we work together."

"No, you might hurt yourself."

Tripp reached for the chair and his hands brushed hers. He jumped back. God, she was soft.

Kaitlin moved away, carrying the chair. "I'll be fine."

But she wasn't really fine. Kaitlin hurried into the store, her stomach in jitters. What was wrong with her?

She put the chair in the corner and drew in a deep breath. Something about Tripp Callihan put her on edge. At first she'd thought it was only that he was helping her reach her long sought after dream, but now...

Kaitlin squared her shoulders. This wasn't the time for such thoughts. Too much needed doing.

Outside, standing in the wagon, Tripp focused all his energy and thoughts on his work. But it was so damn hard. Time after time Kaitlin appeared, bending over, stretching, lifting. It just wasn't right that a woman could smell so sweet and look so pretty while working. How was he supposed to concentrate?

"Hello, neighbor!"

Rafe and Julia Beaumont stepped out the rear entrance of their millinery shop next door, waving.

"Could you use some help?" Rafe asked.

"Sure could." Tripp leaned against the bedsprings. "Things slow down at the livery?"

Rafe inclined his head toward the west. "I was down looking at the widow Smith's mare when I saw you drive by. Figured you could use some help."

"That's a fact."

"This is the first time I've seen him so early in the day in a month of Sundays." Julia smiled sweetly at her husband and rubbed her palm up his arm.

Rafe blushed and eased away from her. "Let's get these things unloaded."

"Papa! Papa!"

Charlie ran out the back door, then slid to a stop when he saw Julia and Rafe.

"What's wrong, son?"

"Miss Kaitlin has cookies. Can I have one?"

Kaitlin stepped out of the store and smiled at Rafe and Julia. "Thanks for coming by."

"Please, Papa? Please?" Charlie hopped up and down.

A big smile spread over Julia's face and she went to Charlie. "Oh, he's adorable. Look, Rafe, isn't he sweet? Oh, I can't wait until we have one of our own."

Rafe blushed and jumped up into the wagon. "We've got work to do."

Tripp pulled off his hat and wiped his brow with his shirtsleeve. "What kind of cookies are they?"

Kaitlin ground her lips together then replied, "Oatmeal."

He thought for a moment. "Okay, Charlie, you can have a cookie. But just one. Don't spoil your supper."

"I'd like you three to eat with us tonight," Julia said. "I've got chicken in the oven."

Kaitlin nodded. "Thanks. I think Mr. Callihan is hungry already."

She gave him a smile and went inside the store. Julia followed her in and looked the place over. "You've got your work cut out for you."

Kaitlin nodded in agreement. The kitchen needed a thorough cleaning from top to bottom before anything could be unpacked or a single meal cooked.

"Let's get started," Julia said, picking up a broom.

"But don't you have work to do in your shop?"

She shrugged. "Nothing that can't wait."

Kaitlin smiled. "Thanks."

"So," Julia asked as she swept, "you and Tripp are partners?"

Kaitlin pumped water into a wooden bucket. She'd known questions of this nature would come up. "Business partners. Strictly business."

"That's right." Tripp's voice sounded from the doorway.

He walked into the kitchen carrying another crate. Rafe followed him inside.

"We're just running the store together," Tripp said. "That's all."

"Papa?" Charlie pulled on Tripp's trouser leg. "How come ladies' underwear has bows on it?"

A stunned silence fell. All eyes riveted Tripp.

He gulped. "What?"

"See?" Charlie pointed into the bedroom. "Miss Kaitlin's underwear has pink bows. How come?"

Without wanting to, Tripp gazed into her room at the white garments piled in the middle of the bed. Soft, delicate, womanly things.

"Uh, well, uh..." Tripp pulled at his shirt collar. "We'll talk about that later."

Tripp took Charlie's hand and hurried out the door, Rafe on his heels.

Over the next several hours they unloaded the wagon, cleaned the upstairs bedroom and moved the furniture in, a bureau and washstand, a small bed in one corner, a double across the room. The kitchen was half done when hunger overcame everyone and they went next door to Julia's to eat.

The back room was small but cozy, with a lace tablecloth, fresh flowers, and the delicious smell of roasted chicken in the air. They settled around the table.

"When do you think you'll open the store?" Julia asked as she passed the biscuits.

"Don't know, exactly." Tripp spooned peas onto Charlie's plate, then took some for himself. "I have to do some figuring on that."

"Well, it can't be soon enough to suit me," Julia said. "I'm so glad you're here. Porter needs another store—and a lot of other things."

Rafe shook his head. "I don't know. Some townsfolk were glad when the railroad changed its mind and didn't come through here. Didn't like the notion of all those new people coming in. You never know what kind of folks you'll get."

"I think it would have been good for Porter," Julia said. "It certainly would have helped my business."

Rafe chuckled. "I guess if the railroad had come through town, you two wouldn't have ended up with old man Finch's store."

Kaitlin and Tripp glanced at each other across the table.

"I wonder if he sold his other property here in town?" Rafe asked. "He owned a lot of land."

"Good riddance to him, I say. A grumpier, more hateful old man I've never met." Julia nodded. "Mr. Finch hasn't been back to Porter in months. I hope he's gone forever."

"He'll be mighty surprised if he comes back and sees how well our store is doing." Kaitlin nodded confidently.

"We'll have to see how things go." Tripp looked down at Charlie beside him. "Eat your vegetables, son."

"Things will go well," Kaitlin said. "I just know it."

"Well," Tripp said, "we'll have to see."

They finished supper, and while Kaitlin and Julia cleaned the kitchen, Tripp and Rafe went outside to check on the horses.

"Come on, Charlie," Tripp called from the door.

The boy rubbed his eyes and slid down from the kitchen chair.

"Charlie can stay with us," Kaitlin said.

Tripp shook his head. "No. Charlie stays with me. Come on, son."

Julia followed the boy to the door and closed her

hand over Rafe's arm. "You won't be out late, will you?"

He eased her fingers away. "I'll be back in a while."

The men went outside, with Charlie running ahead of them. It was dark now, with only lanterns from the back windows of the shops to light the way.

Rafe stopped a short distance down the boardwalk. "I ought to apologize for Julia."

"Apologize for what? She seems like a nice woman, a good wife."

Rafe shook his head. "She's pretty headstrong, if you get my meaning."

He'd never known a woman more headstrong than Kaitlin Jeffers, but didn't think that was exactly what Rafe meant.

"Damn…" Rafe hesitated to speak, and shoved his hands in his pockets. "Julia just won't keep her hands off of me. You know what I'm saying?"

Tripp's gut tightened. "What?"

"Every time I turn around, there she is. Every morning. Every evening. Every time I get near her, she's wanting to— Well, you know." The man blushed.

Tripp's mouth went dry. "Every time?"

"Every time." Rafe sighed heavily. "But I've got a business to run. I'm at the livery before dawn, and most times I work straight through until after dark. You know what I'm saying, don't you? I mean, seeing that you've got little Charlie, you must have been married once. Did you have this problem?"

Hell no, he hadn't had this problem. In fact, he

didn't even understand why Rafe considered it a problem.

"So you don't like making love to your wife?" Tripp asked.

"No, it's not that." Rafe shook his head. "You wouldn't believe what that woman does to get me into bed with her. Why, just this morning I was trying to shave and here she came. Took my shaving soap, and before I knew what was happening, she had her top off and the lather all over her."

Tripp gulped. "Shaving soap?"

"I told her I had to go to work." Rafe grunted. "She needs to realize I haven't got time for that stuff."

Tripp's jaw sagged. "You mean you didn't...?"

"That's the last thing I need, coming in to work late. Shoot, my brothers give me hell about Julia as it is." Rafe nodded solemnly. "Lucky you've got a business partner and not a wife. You don't have those problems."

Heat pulsed through Tripp. He dragged his hand across his forehead. Oh yeah, he felt like the luckiest man on earth, all right.

Chapter Five

At the big oval mirror in the corner of her room Kaitlin studied herself from head to toe, turned in a quick circle, and headed for the door. With all the work she had planned for today, she looked good enough.

Stepping into the kitchen, she saw Tripp at the stove tending a pan of frying bacon. She wasn't sure which was more disconcerting—seeing him first thing in the morning, or seeing him cooking.

"Looks like I got the best end of this partnership."

Tripp jumped, then ran his hand over his chest. "How's that?"

"I won't have to do all the cooking." Kaitlin smiled and walked over to the stove.

He turned his back to her. "I cook for Charlie and me."

Kaitlin peered around him. "What happened to your chin?"

Tripp touched his finger to his face, and turned

away again. "I cut myself shaving this morning, that's all."

"Oh." Kaitlin gestured to the rolled-out biscuits and the bowl of eggs on the sideboard. "What can I do to earn my share of this meal?"

Tripp glanced back over his shoulder at her. "You can—" He sucked in a quick breath. She wasn't wearing a bustle.

The fabric of her simple blue dress hung in loose folds from her waist, draping her hips with clarity. He groaned softly as an all too familiar stirring coiled inside him.

Bad enough that he'd lain awake most of the night smelling her sweet scent all the way in his room, and that he'd cut his chin just looking at his shaving soap a while ago, but did Kaitlin have to be running around this morning dressed—or hardly dressed— like that?

"Well?" Kaitlin stepped closer, her eyebrows raised. "What can I do to help?"

Putting on some decent undergarments would sure as hell help. Tripp turned back to the stove. "Nothing. I'll take care of it."

"But that's not right. We're partners. I should do my share. I'll put the biscuits in the oven."

"No!" Tripp whirled around and pulled the pan from her hand. No, she couldn't do that. She couldn't bend over right there next to him at the stove.

Kaitlin shrank back and eyed him up and down. "I'll just set the table."

"Good. That's good. You do that." Tripp shoved the biscuits into the oven and slammed the door. He reached over the pump and pushed the window all the way open. Damn, it was hot in here.

"Do you remember where the plates are?" Kaitlin asked.

Tripp turned to find her bending down, rummaging through the crates that lined the wall, her round bottom bouncing up and down, and up and down as she searched box after box. He sagged against the sideboard and mopped his brow with his sleeve.

What was wrong with him? Tripp watched her, savoring every move, every rustle of her skirt. He hadn't been so randy since—well, he couldn't even remember the last time.

Maybe it was just the things Rafe had talked to him about last night. Of course, Rafe and Julia had been the furthest thing from his mind when he'd stared at his shaving cup this morning, and nicked his own chin. And it hadn't been the two of them who had crept into his thoughts as he lay staring at the ceiling during the night.

Tripp licked his dry lips as Kaitlin lifted a stack of plates from the packing crate and carried them to the table. Maybe it was just the natural order of things, he thought. He'd not had much interest in such things since—

He spun back to the stove and scooped bacon from the pan, trying to push away the memories. Emily. His wife, Emily. Even after all this time the images still came back with such force. All the old feelings, the pain. He'd put it behind him for the most part, but sometimes without warning it all rushed into his thoughts again. And God, how he hated these moments.

"Coffee?"

Kaitlin peered around him, her brown eyes bigger and wider than usual this morning.

"Sure. Coffee's fine." He cracked eggs in the skillet and wiped his hands on a linen towel.

"I'm anxious to get started on the store today," Kaitlin said as she poured two cups of coffee.

"We need to talk about that."

"How did I know you were going to say that?" She passed him one of the white mugs. "Where's Charlie?"

"Upstairs."

Kaitlin sipped her coffee. "Did Charlie have trouble sleeping last night? Being in a new place does that."

"Charlie's used to it." Tripp turned the scrambled eggs into a bowl, then pulled the biscuits from the oven and piled them on a platter. "Let's eat. I'm hungry."

She set her cup down. "I'll get Charlie."

"No. I'll get him." Tripp went to the foot of the staircase. "Charlie! Come on, son!"

Kaitlin put the food on the table. "It was nice of Julia to give us enough to fix our meals with today. I'll pay her back as soon as I get some shopping done."

Footsteps clattered on the stairs and Charlie came into the kitchen pulling up his suspenders. Kaitlin ruffled his uncombed hair and smiled down at him. "Good morning, Charlie. Hungry?"

"Yes, ma'am." He reached up for Tripp, who gave him a quick hug, then settled him into a chair at the table. "How come you don't got no kids, Miss Kaitlin?"

She slipped into the chair across from him. "I'm not married, Charlie."

"How come?"

Kaitlin glanced at Tripp as he sat down between them. "The time's not right for me to marry yet."

"Have you got a papa?"

"My papa died a long time ago, so did my mother." Kaitlin smiled, warming at the memories. "She was a great stage actress. That's how they met. She was with a touring company, and when he saw her on stage, it was instant love."

"Well, how come—"

"Eat your breakfast, Charlie." Tripp scooped eggs and bacon onto the boy's plate, then passed the platter to Kaitlin. "You, too."

"Yes, dear," Kaitlin said, and gave him a sickly sweet smile. She took a bite. "You're a good cook."

"Papa makes the bestest cookies." Charlie wiped his chin with the back of his hand. "Papa can do anything."

"Is that so?" Kaitlin smiled across the table at Tripp.

"Uh-huh. Papa built this table, and that chair." Charlie pointed to the rocker in the corner.

Kaitlin gave the table a little shake; much more sturdy than the rickety thing left behind by Mr. Finch. "So that's your trade? You're a carpenter?"

"No, I just build things when they need building," Tripp said. "I'm a farmer."

"You abandoned your farm to come here?"

Tripp shifted in his chair. "Not exactly."

"We lived with a whole bunch of people," Charlie said around a mouthful of biscuit. "They had lots of kids."

"It was a boardinghouse," Tripp said.

Kaitlin frowned. "Why were you staying at a boardinghouse if you have a farm?"

"Me and Papa move a lot. Papa says—"

"Finish your meal, Charlie."

The boy shoved a forkful of eggs into his mouth. "Do you move a lot, Miss Kaitlin?"

"Actually, I've lived in the same town all my life."

"How come?"

Tripp laid a hand on the boy's shoulder. "It's not polite to ask nosy questions, Charlie."

"I'm sorry, Papa."

Kaitlin turned back to her plate. She certainly had plenty of nosy questions she wanted to ask Tripp, but it looked as though she wouldn't get the chance, at least not right now.

They finished their meal and cleared the table, then Kaitlin set to work washing the dishes.

"Can I go outside, Papa?" Charlie asked.

"Okay. But stay near the store. Nowhere else."

"I plan to spend the morning getting this kitchen into shape," Kaitlin said, as she poured water into the basin. "Why don't you get started on the store?"

Tripp stroked his chin. "So you'll work in here, and I'll work in the store, huh?"

Kaitlin wagged her finger toward his shirt pocket where he kept his tablet. "Would you like me to jot that down for you?"

"I got it," he said sourly, and stalked from the room.

Getting the kitchen in order was a big job. They'd only done enough yesterday so that they could fix a meal. Kaitlin set to work doing the heavy cleaning. She knocked down the cobwebs, polished the windows, scrubbed the cupboards and counters, then swept and mopped the floor. Needing a breather, and wanting to let the floor dry, Kaitlin went into the store.

She stopped at the doorway. Tripp stood in the middle of the room writing on his tablet. And nothing was done.

"What are you doing?" Kaitlin asked.

He glanced up. "I'm thinking."

"Thinking?" Her back hurt from mopping, her hands were red from scrubbing, and he was—thinking? Kaitlin flung her arms out. "Why aren't you *doing?*"

"I have to think of what to do before I can do it."

"What's to think about?" Kaitlin's eyes widened. "The room needs cleaning, shelves need building, the counter and floor need repairing."

"Yeah?" He glared at her. "And what kind of shelves do we need? How wide? How deep? How far apart?"

She struggled to hold on to her temper. "They're just shelves."

"And how much wood do you recommend I buy for *just* shelves?"

Well, she hadn't thought of that. Details were not her strong suit. Kaitlin drew in a deep breath. "All

I'm saying is, I'd like to get this store open for business before my hair turns gray.''

"Believe me, I'd like the same. But the way things are going, I think I've got more to worry about than you."

Kaitlin pinched the bridge of her nose and closed her eyes. "Do you expect to have your calculations completed anytime in the near future, Mr. Callihan?" Her eyes popped open. "Or do you need some time to figure that out, too?"

He glared down at her, his emotions boiling. "Only an idiot goes running off with no plan and expects things to turn out right."

"Well, I rather be running around than standing around."

"That figures." He inched closer. The heat from her body seeped into him. Little dots of perspiration beaded on her nose. Wisps of hair curled around her face. And, God, she smelled good.

Tripp pulled her into his arms. Her breasts, soft and pliant, spread against his chest, weakening his knees and sending hot blood pumping through his veins.

He held her there, her face upturned, her lips inches from his. Their gazes met. Tripp thought she'd pull away, as stunned by what he'd done as he was himself. She didn't.

Softly he put his lips to hers. Delicate. Pure. And so sweet. He moaned at the first touch. Gently he plied her, reveling in the taste, the intimacy of their exchange.

Eyes closed, locked in his embrace, Kaitlin couldn't think. She could only feel. And she'd never felt anything like this in all her life. His chest was rock-hard, his arms strong and powerful around her, holding her up while her legs had gone completely useless. His mouth was firm, yet soft, and so very gentle. A strange heat coiled inside her as his tongue slid across her lips.

It didn't occur to him to push his way inside, to delve deeper into the recess of her sweet mouth. Now, at this moment, when his every nerve ending already stood on edge, Tripp was content to do only this. Sample, taste and lose himself in her delicate femininity.

He lifted his head and loosened his grip. Kaitlin sagged against him for a second, then splayed her hands across his chest until she found her strength once more. Not that he blamed her. He could hardly stay on his feet, either.

A little blush covered her cheeks as she stepped back from him, her gaze locked with his. Immediately he wanted to pull her against him again, but didn't.

"I, uh..." Tripp drew in a ragged breath. What could he say? That he was sorry, when he wasn't? That he shouldn't have kissed her, when he didn't regret it for a second?

Kaitlin pressed her lips together, still tasting his kiss. Her heart thumped in her chest. She'd never been so overwhelmed by anything in her life.

"I didn't intend to..." Tripp pushed his fingers through his hair. "I mean, I hadn't planned on..."

A little grin tugged at her lips. "That wasn't on your list of things to do today?"

Tripp looked down at his tablet crushed in his fist. He shook his head frantically. "No. Hell, no."

Kaitlin smiled. "Well, that's a pleasant surprise."

A tight knot bore down on his chest. Tripp backed up a step. What had he just done? Kissed a woman— a woman who wasn't Emily? Kissed her and liked it?

"I'm going to buy that lumber now." Tripp stalked out of the store.

Hours passed before Tripp returned with the wagon full of lumber, nails, assorted tools to augment those he'd unloaded the day before, along with two crates of food. And Charlie, of course. The only thing not with him was anything vaguely resembling a civil mood.

Kaitlin stayed busy putting away the supplies as Tripp carried them into the kitchen and Charlie did his best to help. But even that found no favor in Tripp.

"Leave that alone, Charlie. You'll drop it," Tripp barked at him as he crossed the room with a sack of flour.

Kaitlin looked down at the boy from the sideboard where she emptied one of the crates, and took the basket of eggs from him. "I'll help you with those, Charlie."

His lower lip poked out as he handed it over.

"Why don't you come up here and help me unload these things?" She patted the sideboard.

Tripp stalked through the room again. "I don't want him climbing on things. He'll fall."

Kaitlin looked down at Charlie and they both shrugged helplessly.

"Where did you buy the food?" she asked as he headed toward the stockroom with another sack on his shoulder.

"Some dry goods store down the street."

"I'll stop by and check out their inventory, see what our competition is doing."

Kaitlin stared at his big back as he disappeared into the storage room again. Annoyed, she put her thumbs at her ears and wagged her fingers at him, sticking out her tongue. Charlie gasped, and she realized the boy had seen her blatant act of rebellion. But she smiled and winked, and Charlie giggled, covering up the sound with his little hands.

Tripp came out of the storage room. "Come on, Charlie. I'm moving the wagon around front to unload the lumber."

Charlie skipped out the back door behind him.

Alone in the kitchen, Kaitlin put away the rest of the supplies wondering why Tripp had turned into a bear so suddenly. Quiet and cantankerous she could deal with, but grumpy and snarling was another matter. Was it their kiss?

Stunned by the notion, she tapped her finger against her lips. Maybe she'd done it wrong. She'd been kissed a few times, but nothing more than a chaste peck on the cheek or a cold, dry press of lips. Nothing vaguely resembling what Tripp had done. Her insides quivered at the thought.

Well, if that was the case, maybe it was for the best. Kaitlin brushed her hands together. After all, they were business partners. And business partners

shouldn't kiss. If she'd done it wrong, fine. Certainly
he wouldn't try it again, and they could continue on
with the business of getting the store going.

Kaitlin ran the tip of her tongue across her lips.
She still tasted him. A longing wound through her,
something she'd never felt before. Something Tripp
had awakened.

Determinedly, she pushed the thought away. Better if they stuck to business.

Halfway through stringing the green beans she
planned to cook for supper, Kaitlin heard Tripp in
the store yelling at Charlie for the third time. Until
now, she'd never heard him raise his voice to the
child once. It wasn't a mean yell, or an abusive yell,
more frustration than anything; surely, Tripp's foul
mood wasn't helping, either.

Wiping her hands on her apron, Kaitlin went into
the store. The front door stood open, letting in a
breeze, and lumber was stacked neatly to one side
of the room. Charlie's lip poked out as Tripp
frowned down at him. The two of them definitely
needed some time apart.

Kaitlin took the boy's hand. "I need some help in
the kitchen."

Tripp's eyes blazed. "The boy stays with me."

"I'm only taking him to the kitchen, Tripp, I'm
not selling him to the Gypsies."

She gave Charlie a reassuring wink as she led him
into the kitchen, but she felt Tripp's hot gaze on her
back the whole way.

Later, when Kaitlin ventured into the store again,
Tripp was engrossed in his work. Sleeves rolled
back, a pencil tucked behind his ear, brows pulled

together in concentration, he cut through a heavy piece of lumber stretched across a pair of sawhorses.

"I'm finished in the kitchen." She held up the broom. "I'll help in here."

"Where's Charlie?"

"Napping. I told him a story and he fell asleep. Is that all right?"

"I reckon." Tripp grunted and went back to sawing.

Broom in hand, Kaitlin started in the corner farthest from Tripp, knocking down cobwebs, sweeping up the dust and dirt. How good it felt to finally be working on the store.

The store—her store. The place that would bring her dreams to life. She hummed as she worked, her mind filled with images of what the future would be like, gradually turning the simple hum into a full song.

"What are you doing?"

Tripp's gruff voice caused her to stop in her tracks. She held up the broom. "Sweeping."

"No. The singing. Do you have to do that? It's distracting."

She lifted her shoulders. "I always sing when I'm happy. Don't you?"

"Maybe if I had one damn thing to be happy about, I would." He dropped the saw onto the stack of lumber.

Confused, Kaitlin walked toward him. "You have plenty to be happy about—Charlie, your locket back from Harvey Stutz, this store, a chance—"

"This store? Oh, yeah, sure." Tripp waved his arms around the room. "This place is a sinkhole.

We'll work ourselves into the ground and never see a dime from it. You think that's something to be happy about?''

Kaitlin tightened her grip on the broom. "Yes, I do! We agreed to do this, to be partners in this deal. Have you changed your mind? Do you want to back out?''

"No, I'm not backing out. I'm fixing up the place. I'm holding up my end of the bargain.''

"Can't you at least be pleasant in the process?''

Tripp rolled his eyes. "It's not enough for you that I'm doing it? I have to *like* it, too?''

Kaitlin swung the broom at him, swatting him squarely on the chest. "Yes! Yes, you have to like it!''

Tripp fell back a step, stunned.

She advanced on him, clinching the broom in her fist. "Yes, you have to like it, Tripp Callihan! This is *my* life you're a part of now, and I won't have you griping, moaning, and complaining about everything. Life's hard enough without your own partner dragging you down! Do you understand me?''

Her words hit him harder than the broom had, more like a mule kick in the gut. He understood all right. Better than Kaitlin Jeffers would ever imagine. And why had he been in such a bad mood in the first place? Tripp gazed at her, his stomach clinching. It was his fault. Not hers. His fault that he'd kissed her. His fault that he'd enjoyed it. His fault that old memories had yanked him in separate directions all day.

"You're right, Kaitlin. I'm just—'' Tripp's gaze wandered over the floor, the ceiling, the walls before returning to her. He scrubbed his hands over his face. "Hell, I don't know what's the matter with me."

Kaitlin's anger ebbed. "It's a strain on both of us."

"Don't hit me with that broom again."

"Then don't provoke me."

Tripp grinned. "That seems fair."

"Why don't we go have some coffee?"

"Okay." Tripp reached for the broom. "I'll carry this for you."

Kaitlin handed it over. "Just don't get any ideas."

"No, ma'am. You don't ever have to worry about that."

In the kitchen, Kaitlin poured two cups of coffee from the pot simmering on the stove and they sat down across the table from each other.

"You never told me what you planned to do with your share of the profit from the store." Kaitlin sprinkled sugar into her cup. "What's your dream, Tripp?"

He rested his arms on the table; hearing her say his name sounded good. "I'm fixing up my farm, getting it running again. Well, actually, it's my pa's farm. He passed on a few years back and left it to me. It's a nice spread."

"Did you grow up there?"

"Pa bought it around the time I got finished with school. My ma had died the winter before. Farming, having a place of his own, was his dream."

"But not your dream?"

"I was young with a head full of crazy ideas back then. My pa and I didn't exactly see eye to eye on what the future should hold." Tripp sipped his coffee. "Pa got sick, though, after a while. I went there and worked the place for him. It was a long time ago. Charlie had just been born."

A painful knot twisted around Kaitlin's heart. "And then your pa died?"

Tripp stared at his coffee cup. "Yeah, he died."

"Then after that, your wife—"

"It's been just Charlie and me since he was a baby." Tripp shook his head, as if to clear his thoughts. He leaned his forearms on the table, his brow wrinkled in deep thought. "I haven't done right by Charlie—myself either, for that matter. We've been moving around, drifting from town to town. Staying a few weeks here, a month or so there. I haven't wanted to live on the farm for a long time because of memories of my father and wife. The boy deserves a home. A solid place he can call his, and I can call mine."

"So you'll do that by fixing up the farm?"

"Yep." Tripp nodded decisively. "The fellow who owns the neighboring farm has been after me for years to sell it to him. He'd take it in a minute, if I'd say the word."

"But you don't want to sell?"

"Nope. The farm will be home, forever. No more running around. There's nothing I want more than to settle down and have a real home again."

"My goodness..." Kaitlin sat back in her chair.

"So, what about you?" Tripp looked across the table at her. "What's your dream? What are you going to do with this money you're working so hard to get?"

Kaitlin tried to meet his gaze but couldn't. "I'm going to be a stage actress like my mother. I'm leaving for New York as soon as possible."

Chapter Six

"Yoo-hoo! Hello! Anybody home?"

A shrill voice reverberated through the store and into the kitchen, thankfully releasing Kaitlin from Tripp's unreadable stare. Apparently, heading off to New York to become a stage actress wasn't within the scope of his normal thought patterns.

She pushed aside her coffee cup and stood, not really sure why his reaction to her plan bothered her so.

"I'll see who that is."

Hurrying through the doorway, Kaitlin saw two well-dressed women taking in every aspect of the room. They walked slowly, speaking in whispers, nodding occasionally. Kaitlin glanced down at her soiled work dress and touched her hand to the back of her hair. She should have expected this and been ready.

Plastering on a bright smile, Kaitlin crossed the room. "Good afternoon, ladies."

The oldest, a buxom woman with graying hair

coiled neatly beneath a large, plumed hat looked Kaitlin up and down quickly, then nodded.

"Good afternoon. I'm Imogene Douglas, wife of Mayor Douglas," she said. "We've come to welcome you to Porter."

Kaitlin stretched her smile farther and ran her hands down the front of her dress. "I'm Kaitlin Jeffers."

"This is June Hutchinson." Imogene Douglas waved her gloved hand toward the heavy, dark-haired woman beside her. "She's the wife of Sheriff Hutchinson."

June Hutchinson's eyes narrowed. "Hello, Miss Jeffers. It is *miss,* isn't it?"

The sheriff's wife made it sound as if that in itself were a crime. Kaitlin held on to her smile. "Yes, it is. Nice to meet you."

"Reverend Beckman plans to pay a call also," Mrs. Douglas said.

Mrs. Hutchinson's eyes narrowed. "You are planning to come to services on Sunday, aren't you?"

"Certainly." The word popped out of Kaitlin's mouth as if she'd been poked in the ribs by an unseen angel.

"So." Mrs. Douglas folded her arms under her massive bosom and gazed around. "You've bought Mr. Finch's store."

"Yes. I'm quite excited about it."

"Good. Good." She nodded. "My husband—he's the mayor, as I said—my husband says it's just what the town needs. I agree. Nasty turn of luck when we lost the railroad. Nasty turn."

June Hutchinson raised one eyebrow. "You're opening the store all by yourself?"

"I have a partner," Kaitlin said. "Mr. Callihan."

Her other brow bobbed upward. "Mr. Callihan? Is he a relative of yours?"

Kaitlin squared her shoulders. "No. Mr. Callihan and I are business partners."

"Uh-huh." She tossed her head as if garnering some information no one else did. "I *see*."

"Afternoon, ladies."

Tripp walked into the store carrying Charlie, just up from his nap. He introduced himself and Charlie, who yawned and laid his head on Tripp's shoulder.

"So, you two are *business partners?*" June Hutchinson looked back and forth between the two of them.

Kaitlin shifted uncomfortably, knowing full well what the woman was insinuating. She glanced at Tripp and saw him bristle.

Imogene Douglas scowled at the other woman. "Really, Mrs. Hutchinson, there's certainly nothing wrong with a business arrangement of this nature in this day and age. Besides, the upstairs is a separate living area."

Mrs. Hutchinson looked down her long nose at them. "I suppose not."

"Has Miss Bailey been by yet?" Mrs. Douglas asked. "She's the schoolteacher."

Tripp drew back, closing his arms tightly over Charlie. "He doesn't go to school. He's too young."

"Nonsense," Mrs. Douglas said. "He's plenty old enough."

June Hutchinson's eyes narrowed. "Is there some

other reason you don't want him in school, Mr. Callihan?''

Kaitlin saw Tripp's jaw tighten, but thankfully, the ladies missed it.

''I'll have Miss Bailey come over right away. She's an excellent teacher. Porter is lucky to have her.'' Mrs. Douglas gave the store one final look. ''Well, good luck to you both. And welcome to Porter.''

June Hutchinson threw them one last piercing gaze before she followed the other woman out the door.

''Whew...'' Kaitlin's shoulders sagged with relief.

''That Mrs. Hutchinson thinks we're up to no good here. If she's that suspicious, I wonder what her sheriff husband is like?''

Kaitlin shrugged. ''It was nice of them to come over. Running a store requires we be on good terms with the town. We can't afford to offend any potential customers.''

Charlie lifted his head from Tripp's shoulder and rubbed his eyes sleepily. ''Am I gonna go to school, Papa?''

''You woke up too early from your nap, son. You need to sleep some more.''

''But, Papa—''

''Shh.'' Tripp eased the boy's head onto his shoulder again and patted his back gently. ''Just a while longer, then you can help me build some shelves.''

Kaitlin watched them disappear into the kitchen, Tripp's big arms holding little Charlie so tenderly. The bond between them was strong, deeper than she'd seen between a father and son. But that was probably because there was only the two of them. No wife and mother to share the burden, or stretch the bond.

For an instant Kaitlin imagined the pressure of Tripp's arms around her, remembering when he'd held her and kissed her so unexpectedly. A faint longing crept through her, and for a moment she wondered what it would feel like to be locked in those strong arms again, to have those lips on her again, to have him—

Kaitlin gasped aloud. Gracious, what was she thinking? She shook herself and grabbed the broom from the corner, sweeping the floor with a vengeance.

A short while later, Tripp came into the store and set to work on the shelves again. Kaitlin kept sweeping. She concentrated hard on the chore. She focused her thoughts on gripping the broom, making neat little piles of dirt. But over and over, her gaze strayed to Tripp.

Leaning over the sawhorses, brow wrinkled, he cut through each piece of wood with precision. Muscles rippled across his back and in his arms. He sawed through board after board, but didn't seem to tire. His hands looked strong and sure. They looked capable and skilled. Yet they'd seemed so gentle when he'd carried Charlie off to his nap. And they'd felt so reassuring when he'd pulled her against his chest and held her there.

"What's wrong now?"

Kaitlin jumped as Tripp scowled across the room at her. Heat rushed into her cheeks.

"Nothing. N-nothing."

His eyes narrowed. "You were staring a hole in my back."

Kaitlin's chin went up. "I was not." Of course, she was, but she certainly wasn't going to admit it.

He waved his hand toward the neat stack of freshly cut boards. "Something not suiting you?"

"No, everything's fine." Kaitlin ventured closer, feeling pressured to come up with an excuse for her blatant ogling. "I couldn't help noticing that you measure a lot."

"If I don't measure right, it won't fit together right."

"Well, yes, but do you have to measure each thing three times?"

"I want to be sure I'm cutting on the right line. If it's done wrong, there's no going back. Everything's ruined." Tripp nodded. "It's called being *careful.*"

Annoying was the word that popped into Kaitlin's head.

"If you say so." She turned back to her sweeping.

They spent the afternoon working in the store, with the door and windows open, the fresh breeze mingling with the sweet smell of sawdust. Charlie woke up from his nap and managed to get into everything. Despite Tripp's patient efforts to keep him occupied, the boy was a handful.

Finally, Tripp wiped his brow with his shirtsleeve and dropped the saw onto the stack of lumber. "I think we've done enough for today."

Kaitlin glanced outside to see dusk falling, stretching shadows across the floor of the store. "That's a good idea."

Charlie jumped up and down. "Can I help feed the horses tonight? Can I, Papa?"

Tripp grinned down at him. "Sure. Let's get supper fixed first." He swatted Charlie on the seat of the pants. The boy laughed and ran into the kitchen.

The smile faded from Tripp's face as he looked at Kaitlin standing next to him. "I know you're not used to having kids around. This must be tough for you."

"Honestly, Tripp, you worry too much." Kaitlin waved away his concern. "Believe me, after some of the children I've seen, little Charlie is a saint."

"I don't know that I'd go that far."

"Well, I would. I worked several years as a nanny. Four children, all under age seven."

Tripp stared down at her. "You didn't like that job?"

"Actually, it was fun."

Kaitlin went into the kitchen, tied on her apron and set about making supper. Tripp did the same, with Charlie getting underfoot at every turn.

After they'd eaten and cleaned the kitchen, Kaitlin packed up some food in a crate.

"I need to take this next door to Julia, to repay her."

Tripp straightened the chairs around the table, making certain each was spaced properly. "I'll go with you. Charlie? Come on, Charlie, let's go."

"Can I feed the horses, Papa? Can I?"

"Sure." Tripp patted his little shoulder as the boy scooted by, picked up the crate and followed Kaitlin out the door.

Julia answered their knock wiping her hands on a

linen towel. Behind her, Rafe sat at the table, pushing away his empty plate.

"Come inside." Julia stepped back from the door. "We were just talking about you. How is the store coming?"

Tripp sat the crate on the sideboard. "Real good."

Rafe rose from the table. "I need some air. Tripp, let's talk outside."

"Papa saided I could help with the horses." Charlie beamed proudly.

"Okay, let's go do that." Rafe ruffled the boy's hair as the three headed for the door.

Julia stopped him with an arm on his shoulder. "You're not going to be late, are you Rafe?"

"I'll be back in a while," he muttered.

Tripp breathed in the cool evening air, pretending not to notice the look on Rafe's face as they stepped onto the back boardwalk. But they'd only gone a few steps when Rafe stopped and shook his head.

"I don't know what I'm going to do with that woman."

In the pale light, Tripp spotted Charlie running ahead to the barn. "Wait right there, son. Don't go inside until I get there."

"Okay, Papa." Charlie climbed onto the corral fence, looking at the horses.

Rafe sighed heavily and slid his hands deep into his pockets, gazing out at the alley. "I never thought being married could cause these kinds of problems. Did you? I mean, when you were married?"

Tripp lifted his shoulders. "Learning to get along with somebody isn't easy."

"Yeah, well, if it was just a matter of getting

along I could handle that. But—'' Rafe turned to Tripp. ''Do you know what Julia did when I came home tonight?''

Tripp shifted from one foot to the other. If it was anything like the shaving soap incident, he wasn't sure he wanted to know.

''I'll tell you what she did.'' Rafe leaned closer and lowered his voice.

Tripp tensed.

''I came home from work and there she stood in the middle of the kitchen, wearing her apron.''

''That's not unusual, Rafe, most women—''

''That's all she had on. Just her apron. Not another stitch of clothes.''

''You mean, she was…?'' Warmth flooded Tripp's belly, spiraling downward.

''Yep.'' Rafe shook his head. ''Naked as a jay-bird.''

Fire clawed its way through Tripp. He swallowed hard. ''So you must have—''

''Hell, I hadn't even had my supper yet.''

His jaw lackened. ''You mean…?''

''I don't know what I'm going to do with her.'' Rafe plowed his fingers through his hair, then drew in a deep breath. ''Well, we'd better tend to your horses.''

Tripp groaned softly and followed him across the alley.

Kaitlin pinned her hat in her dark curls and stared hard at herself in the bedroom mirror. She turned left, then right, and finally nodded. Green was a good color, and this was her favorite dress. And, more importantly, appropriate for her first day at church in the town of Porter.

She practiced her smile, as she intended to do upon arrival at church this morning. Everyone would stare at her, as the newcomer to town. She wanted to make a good impression. These people were more than potential friends. They were potential customers. And that, by Kaitlin's way of thinking, was of greater significance.

Entering the kitchen, she was surprised to see the stove cold, the room empty. Tripp hadn't prepared breakfast. They hadn't discussed it last night, but she'd assumed he'd go to services this morning. Surely he'd take Charlie to church.

Kaitlin touched her finger to her lips. She glanced at the back door, then at the staircase that led to his bedroom. Finally, she crossed the room and climbed the steps.

The door stood open. Kaitlin stopped on the top step as the sound of laughter floated out. Soft giggles. Deep chuckles. Both so infectious, a smile spread across Kaitlin's face as she leaned into the doorway.

Across the room Charlie sat on the bureau wearing his nightshirt. Tripp leaned over him, his arms braced on either side of the child, their faces close together, both laughing.

The humor they shared—whatever it might have been—was lost on Kaitlin. Her breath went out of her in a long, slow wheeze. Tripp was half naked.

His bare back rippled with muscles, the long expanse tapering to a lean waist. Dark trousers rode low on his hips. His arms bulged. Kaitlin's heart hammered.

"Look, Miss Kaitlin! Look what I did!"

A stunned second passed before she realized Charlie had spotted her. She tried to draw a breath, but the narrow staircase was airless and her lungs didn't seem to be working quite right. She knew she should turn away, but her feet wouldn't budge.

"Look what I did." Charlie waved a small shaving brush, his hands covered with white foamy soap. He giggled. "See? I'm helping Papa shave."

Tripp straightened and turned toward her. Strength left Kaitlin's legs. She latched on to the door casing.

Dark, crisp hair curled across his chest and arrowed straight down the center of his washboard belly. His navel appeared in a swirl of hair above the unfastened top button of his trousers.

Heat rushed into her cheeks as Kaitlin forced her line of vision upward, locking on to his face. Suddenly a little giggle bubbled up. She laughed again and covered her hand with her mouth.

"See? I'm helping Papa." Charlie waved the shaving brush again, laughing.

Tripp's face was covered with white shaving soap. Not just his cheeks and jaws. Dots of soap clung to the tip of his nose and both eyebrows. He looked so comical, Kaitlin couldn't hold in her laughter.

She expected Tripp to be embarrassed at being caught looking so ridiculous. After all, both she and Charlie were having a good laugh at his expense. But Tripp just smiled and laughed with them.

"Yeah," Tripp said to Charlie. "You're a help all right."

He scooped a fingerful of soap from his jaw and touched it to the tip of Charlie's nose. The boy giggled wildly as Tripp picked up the towel and wiped the shaving soap from his own nose and eyebrows.

Their laughter died and Kaitlin suddenly realized that here she stood looking at him and his bare chest. She cleared her throat and straightened her shoulders.

"I just came up to see if you two were going to church this morning."

"'Course we are," Charlie said. "Papa says folks gotta go to church on Sunday to make up for the bad things they did all week."

Tripp leaned his hip against the bureau and looked down at his son. "Have you been bad this week, Charlie?"

His big blue eyes grew even bigger. "Oh no, Papa, I've been good. Real good."

Tripp grinned. "Is that so?"

"Uh-huh." Charlie nodded so hard his hair bounced against his forehead. "You been bad this week, Miss Kaitlin?"

Her gaze collided with Tripp's. His eyes darkened, stealing away the last ounce of her strength, and leaving in its place the seed of an idea of just how bad she really could be.

Kaitlin swallowed hard. "Well…"

Tripp pushed away from the bureau and crossed the room. She watched him draw nearer, his chest growing wider with each step. Slowly he wiped the last of the shaving soap from his face.

"How about it, Kaitlin? Have you been bad?"

He gave off a potent physical energy. Heat rolled

off him. Kaitlin's gaze dipped to his chest, fighting the overwhelming urge to press herself against him.

He leaned down and captured her gaze. "Well?"

Kaitlin backed away, breaking the tension between them. "No. Of course not."

Tripp nodded slowly. "I see."

She tilted her head. "What about you? Have you been bad?"

His chest swelled as he drew in a big breath and his gaze ran the length of her for only a fleeting second. "Not as bad as I could have been."

"Oh." Kaitlin gulped and latched on to the stair railing. She eased down a step. "I'm going to church now."

"We'll be along in a few minutes. I don't think you and I ought to arrive together."

"That's a good idea…I suppose."

Tripp edged closer to the stairs. "We don't want people to get the wrong idea about us."

"We certainly don't want that." Kaitlin dragged her gaze up to his face. She felt dizzy. She felt her own skin warming. "Do we?"

"Well…"

They gazed at each other for a long moment, a phantom warmth binding them together, pulling them closer.

Tripp's chest swelled as he drew in a deep breath and backed away. "You'd better go."

"Yes, I'd better."

Kaitlin yanked up her skirt and flew down the staircase.

Chapter Seven

The first friendly face Kaitlin spotted in the church-yard wasn't that friendly, really, but at least it was one she recognized. June Hutchinson left the group of women standing under the elms and gave Kaitlin what passed for a smile as she approached.

"There you are, Miss Jeffers, we've been expecting you."

Kaitlin smiled pleasantly and noted the other women heading her way. "Good morning, Mrs. Hutchinson."

"Where's Mr. Callihan? He is coming too, isn't he? He does attend services, doesn't he? He does bring his son?" Her eyes narrowed. "You *have* seen him this morning, haven't you?"

The other ladies gathered closer, watching and listening intently. Kaitlin sensed they'd been talking about her. But she refused to let June Hutchinson's questions unnerve her, unwilling to give her something else to gossip about. She'd known this would happen. Questions about her relationship with Tripp were bound to come up.

She steeled herself mentally, reinforcing her decision to let the people of Porter think what they chose. In a very short time she intended to be on her way to New York, Porter and everyone in it forgotten. Still, it made her feel a bit better that Tripp had the foresight to arrive later.

Kaitlin kept her smile in place. "I imagine Mr. Callihan will be along later."

Mrs. Hutchinson eyes narrowed. "But you're not sure?"

The other women leaned closer.

"Actually—"

"Good morning, Miss Jeffers."

Imogene Douglas elbowed her way into the tight circle of ladies, planting herself at Kaitlin's side.

"I see you're getting acquainted. Good, very good. The mayor and I are so pleased to have you in town. Pleased, very pleased, indeed. Aren't we all pleased?"

The other ladies nodded and murmured a welcome.

"And," Mrs. Douglas said, "we're equally pleased to have your business partner, Mr. Callihan, here also. I think it's wonderful you two have come to town. We all hope your partnership will be a success, don't we, ladies?"

They all quickly nodded, unwilling, it seemed, to disagree with the mayor's wife's decree.

Mrs. Douglas latched on to Kaitlin's arm. "Let me introduce you to everyone."

Kaitlin made the rounds of the churchyard, smiling and nodding as Mrs. Douglas made introductions, ending at the foot of the church stairs. There,

Reverend Beckman shook her hand kindly. He was young and slender, with a quiet way about him.

"I'd like you to meet my wife." The Reverend gestured inside the open door of the church. "Lorna? Come here, dear, and meet Miss Jeffers."

A young, dark-haired woman appeared in the doorway holding a baby in her arms while three more children swarmed around her; the fullness of her dark dress indicated another baby would make its appearance very soon.

"Hello, Miss Jeffers. Welcome. I'm so sorry I haven't been able to get by and meet you yet." Lorna grabbed the hand of one of the children racing past her.

"That's fine, really. We're a long way from settled, anyway."

Mrs. Douglas squared her shoulders. "Miss Jeffers and her business partner, Mr. Callihan, have taken over the old Finch store."

The Reverend and his wife exchanged a look, then smiled pleasantly.

"And we're all very pleased to have them here," Mrs. Douglas said.

"We're glad to have you in Porter, Miss Jeffers," the Reverend said.

"Of course we are," Mrs. Douglas declared.

"Please, come inside."

Reverend Beckman directed them into the church and stood by the door, greeting the congregation as they filed inside. His wife busied herself rounding up their children and settling them into the front pew.

Kaitlin sensed that Imogene Douglas had made it her mission on this Sunday morning to see that she was welcomed into the church. She sat in a pew near the front next to Mrs. Douglas and her husband.

The church was small, but tidy and well kept. Windows lined both sides of the room, and in front was the pulpit, a piano and choir loft. Above it was a stained glass window.

Kaitlin kept up with the mayor's small talk as the congregation filed into the pews, but found herself glancing back toward the door. While she could have told herself it was just to become familiar with the faces of Porter, she knew it was one particular person she watched for.

At the last minute, Tripp and Charlie came into the church. Both looked quite handsome, dressed in white shirts, Tripp with a string tie around his collar. Charlie saw her and waved. Tripp looked up, but only nodded as the two of them sat in a pew near the back.

The Reverend Beckman opened the service with well-wishes for the sick, then introduced the newcomers, Kaitlin, Tripp and Charlie, and Mrs. Matilda Shaw, a tiny, silver-haired woman sitting next to Sheriff and Mrs. Hutchinson.

At the first hymn, Lorna Beckman left her brood and made the awkward climb up the few steps to the choir loft. Although obviously uncomfortable at the piano, she played and sang along with the eight member choir as the congregation came to its feet and joined in "Onward Christian Soldiers."

Midway through the sermon the church grew warm, despite the open windows. After several more hymns, the offering plate made its rounds, the Reverend gave the closing prayer and the congregation quickly made its way outside.

Reverend Beckman and his wife stood at the door shaking the hands of everyone who filed past, their children fidgeting next to them.

"So good to have you with us, Miss Jeffers," the Reverend said. "And good to have a new voice in the church."

Kaitlin almost blushed. "Sorry. I love to sing so much that sometimes I get carried away."

"Don't apologize," Lorna said, lifting her baby higher in her arms. "The choir appreciates the help."

Kaitlin moved to the churchyard. People gathered beneath the trees while children played. Mentally she calculated the number of people here, estimated how many would likely shop at her store, how much they'd spend. She smiled to herself. New York wasn't so far off, not at all.

Julia waved as she came down the church steps, bringing Kaitlin out of her daydream.

"Good morning," Kaitlin said. "Where's Rafe?"

Julia waved her hand across the churchyard. "Off talking to the men, of course."

"Sorry I couldn't get over to say hello to you earlier."

Julia fell in step beside her as they strolled. "I saw Mrs. Douglas had you firmly in hand. Which was good, if you don't mind my saying so."

"What do you mean?"

"There's been talk about you and Tripp. Some people thought it improper, you know. They didn't understand that yours was simply a business arrangement.''

Kaitlin felt her cheeks flush. ''I'd suspected that.''

''You can thank Mrs. Douglas for putting an end to all that this morning. She's firmly in your corner. I don't think you'll have any problems now.''

Kaitlin gazed across the churchyard at Mrs. Douglas standing in a circle of women. ''That was kind of her.''

''Oh, Imogene Douglas isn't all that kind. She wants your business here, Kaitlin. And for your business to succeed, *you* must succeed.'' Julia smiled at her. ''You should have seen how upset she was when we lost the railroad last year. She wants Porter to grow and thrive.''

''You mean *her husband* wants the town to grow?''

Julia leaned closer and lowered her voice. ''We all wonder who's really the mayor of Porter.''

They both stopped short as three little boys raced in front of them and crossed the churchyard, weaving between the adults. Charlie was one of them.

''It didn't take him long to make friends,'' Kaitlin said.

Julia smiled. ''He's such a dear. Tripp has done a fine job raising him. I wonder how long his wife's been dead?''

''He's never mentioned her.'' Kaitlin spotted Tripp standing with a group of men, keeping an eye on Charlie.

''Didn't you ask?'' Julia asked.

''No,'' Kaitlin said. ''It's really none of my business.''

"Aren't you at least curious?"

She knew she should say the noble thing and declare that she wasn't, and if it had been anyone other than Julia who'd asked, she probably would have.

"Of course I'm curious," Kaitlin said. "But we really don't know each other well enough."

Julia's eyebrows raised. "So you two really are just business partners?"

"Strictly business."

"Well, a lot of women in Porter will be glad to hear that. An eligible man always causes a flurry of interest."

Kaitlin clamped her mouth shut. Tripp Callihan had the most annoying habits she'd ever encountered in her entire life. In the short time she'd known him, he'd managed to anger her to no end nearly every time they were together. Once the young women of Porter saw those things too, that flurry of interest would certainly be short-lived.

"We should welcome Mrs. Shaw," Julia said.

Kaitlin followed her across the yard to the frail-looking woman who'd been announced in church this morning as the other newcomer to Porter, and they introduced themselves.

"It's so nice to be here," Mrs. Shaw said, and nodded across the churchyard to a woman holding a small child. "I'm living with my daughter now, since my husband passed on."

"Please come by and visit when you can," Julia said. "I own the millinery shop on Main Street, and Kaitlin is opening a store right next door."

"A store?" Matilda's smile broadened. "I'm sure

I'll be by, dear. My daughter's given me a room and I need a few things for it.''

Kaitlin could almost hear the clink of coins in her cash box. "I'm sure I'll have just what you're looking for."

Matilda Shaw nodded and moved on as a man Kaitlin had never seen before stopped at Julia's side. He was near forty, with brown wavy hair, handsome and well dressed.

"Good morning, ladies. You look lovely this morning." Though his comment included them both, he looked at Julia.

Julia introduced Kaitlin to Drew Holden.

"I own the feed store here in Porter. Been in business for over twenty years." Drew hung his thumbs in the pockets of his brocade vest. "Built the place myself, from nothing. And doing good, too. Business has never been better."

Rafe appeared, pushing between Julia and Drew Holden. He latched on to Julia's arm and gave Drew a curt nod.

"We're leaving."

"But, Rafe," Julia said. "I was going to invite Kaitlin to have supper with us."

"Not today. We're going out to Ma's for supper."

A frown wrinkled Julia's forehead. "Your mother's?"

"Then I've got to get down to the livery."

"On Sunday? But Rafe, you promised we could—"

"Let's go. I've got work to do."

Rafe hurried Julia across the churchyard and down the dirt street toward town. From the corner of her eye Kaitlin saw that Drew watched them, too.

Chapter Eight

"**S**mells good," Kaitlin said, walking into the kitchen the next morning. She hadn't seen Tripp since church yesterday; they'd each had supper with different families.

She took two mugs from the cupboard and poured. "How was supper at the mayor's house last night?"

Tripp shook his head. "Mrs. Hutchinson was there. I swear, that woman never took her eyes off me all night. She's probably got her husband going through Wanted posters this morning looking for my face. Gave me indigestion."

Kaitlin leaned around him and handed him the steaming cup. "So that's why you look so tired this morning?"

"Yeah, I reckon."

He took the mug and turned back to the stove. While June Hutchinson and her suspicious looks had made him exceedingly uncomfortable at the mayor's house last evening, it really had nothing to do with why he'd slept so little. The woman standing at his elbow right now, smelling sweet and looking entirely too fresh for so early in the morning, had given him yet another night of tossing and turning.

"I had supper with the Beckmans," Kaitlin said.

Tripp looked down at her. "With all those children?"

"They were wonderful."

Tripp grunted and turned back to his pancake batter.

"Morning, Charlie." Kaitlin dodged the boy as he bounded down the stairs and hopped across the kitchen floor.

He smiled up at her. "Papa's gonna let me help today."

"Good. We can use some help." Kaitlin reached for the plates in the cupboard as a soft knock sounded at the back door. "I'll get it."

A young woman waited on the boardwalk dressed in a plain skirt and blouse.

"Good morning. I'm Miss Bailey, the schoolteacher. The mayor's wife suggested I come by."

"Yes, Mrs. Douglas mentioned you might be by. Please come in." Kaitlin waved her inside.

Miss Bailey picked up her satchel and stepped into the kitchen. "I'm on my way to school. I understand you have a son who will be attending?"

"No—yes—I mean—" Kaitlin cleared her throat and gestured to Tripp. "Mr. Callihan has a son."

Miss Bailey looked momentarily confused, but managed a smile. "Good morning, Mr. Callihan."

Tripp's face hardened. He pulled off his apron and swung the boy into his arms.

"Charlie?" Miss Bailey asked. "Ready for school?"

"School?" Tripp's frown deepened. "Who said anything about him going to school?"

Charlie scrunched up his brows. "Do you got kids there?"

"Yes, Charlie, we have lots of children there." Miss Bailey gave Tripp a reassuring nod. "Don't worry. He'll do fine. Charlie can walk over with me, if you'd like."

"Now?" Tripp clamped his arm around Charlie and backed up a step. "You mean, take him to school now? Today?"

"Well, yes."

Charlie's eyes brightened. "Can I, Papa? Can I—"

"Hush, Charlie." Tripp tightened his arms around the boy. "Look, Miss Bailey, Charlie is too little to go to school. Maybe next year, but not now."

"Mr. Callihan, other children Charlie's age are already in school. You don't want him to fall behind, do you?"

"Papa, can I?"

Tripp shook his head. "I appreciate your coming by, Miss Bailey, but Charlie's not going anywhere."

"It's your decision, of course, Mr. Callihan."

Miss Bailey gave Kaitlin a weak smile as she left.

Charlie squirmed in Tripp's arms. "Papa, how come—"

"Never mind about school, Charlie." Tripp touched his finger beneath the boy's chin and tilted his face up. "You can help me in the store today, and tonight you can feed the horses all by yourself."

"Papa—"

Tripp smothered his words with a big hug, then

set him on the floor and kissed the top his head. "Let's get breakfast ready. I'm making pancakes. Your favorite."

"Okay, Papa."

Kaitlin drew in a deep breath as Charlie scurried back to the table, then turned to Tripp. He was watching the boy with an intensity she'd never seen before.

Tripp turned to her, then scowled. "Have you got something to say?"

Kaitlin opened her mouth, then thought better of it. Though she was tempted to speak her piece, this clearly was not the time. Tripp was in no frame of mind to listen. And besides, it was none of her business.

Kaitlin brushed past him and picked up the plates. "We've got a lot of work today. We'd better get started."

But by midafternoon, little had been accomplished. Charlie spilled the bucket of nails, pushed over the stack of lumber and scattered sawdust across the room.

Kaitlin had never seen anyone as patient as Tripp. Not once did he raise his voice, let alone lose his temper. But gradually the situation began to wear on everyone.

Kaitlin dropped the scrub brush into the bucket of dirty water and wiped her hands on her apron. "Come on, Charlie, we're running an errand."

"Okay." He skipped across the room and took her hand.

"I'll be back in a minute," Kaitlin told Tripp.

Stunned, Tripp just stared at her, and when he

didn't say anything, she headed out the door with Charlie.

Kaitlin took the boy next door to Julia's millinery shop. She answered at the first knock holding a half-finished bonnet in her hand.

"I was hoping Charlie could visit with you for a while," Kaitlin said. "Would it be all right?"

Julia beamed down at him. "Of course. It's so quiet in here during the day."

Kaitlin knelt in front of Charlie. "Can you stay with Miss Julia for a little bit?"

"We'll make cookies," Julia offered.

"My papa makes the bestest cookies," Charlie said.

Julia laughed. "Maybe we'll exchange receipes. Come on in, Charlie."

"Thanks. I'll come back for him in a bit."

"Don't rush." Julia stepped closer and lowered her voice. "Maybe you and I could…talk…later?"

The tone in Julia's voice alarmed Kaitlin slightly. "Is something wrong?"

She glanced down at Charlie standing between them. "Nothing serious, but— Well, maybe it is, I don't know."

"How about after supper tonight?"

"Sure. Thanks." Julia took Charlie's hand. "And don't worry about us. We'll have great fun."

Warmth swelled in Kaitlin's stomach at the look on Julia's face gazing down at Charlie. She knew those feelings herself. Lonely afternoons. Quiet evenings. Long nights. Each day blending seamlessly into the next.

Pleased with herself, Kaitlin went back to the

store. But those feelings evaporated abruptly when she walked into the kitchen and saw Tripp glaring at her.

"Where is he?"

"Next door with Julia. They're baking cookies." Kaitlin stood her ground as Tripp's jaw tightened and his shoulders squared. "Don't worry. He still thinks yours are the best."

"What's that supposed to mean?"

"Isn't that what this is all about?" Kaitlin asked. "*You* being the center of Charlie's world? You don't let him out of your sight. You don't want him talking to anyone. You don't want him going to school."

"I know what's best for him."

Kaitlin shook her head. "I think you're afraid he'll learn to love someone other than you."

"You don't know what the hell you're talking about."

"No? Then explain to me why you move around so much, why you never stay long in one place. I think it's because you don't want Charlie getting attached to anyone else."

"That's a goddamn lie!"

"No, it isn't. You're afraid he might care for someone other than you. You can't stand the thought, can you?"

Tripp's hands curled into fists at his side. "I'm protecting Charlie!"

"From what?" Kaitlin looked up at his tense, angry face. "From companionship, from friendship, from—"

"From someone walking out on him! From someone loving him, caring, then leaving!" Hot, angry words poured out of him. "That's not happening to Charlie. Not again."

His words crashed down on Kaitlin, catching her breath in her lungs. She'd stumbled onto something she wasn't prepared for, something that was truly none of her business. But the pain in Tripp's features twisted her stomach and wound around her heart as she'd never imagined before.

"This is about your wife, isn't it?" Kaitlin said.

Fresh pain crossed Tripp's face. He turned away. "Don't talk about her."

Kaitlin pressed her lips together. As much as she wanted to pursue it, she didn't. The past was gone. Things that had happened couldn't be changed. She knew that all too well herself.

But Charlie wasn't the past. Something needed to be done, and there was no one else to do it but her.

"Tripp, please…"

He winced as if his emotional pain were now physical. Wearily, he sank into a chair at the table and covered his face with his palms.

Kaitlin slid into the chair across from him. A long, tense moment passed before she reached out and strummed her knuckles along the back of his hand.

He jumped and glared at her. Then his face softened and he relaxed his arms on the table.

"I've had Charlie by myself since he was a baby. At first, I didn't know what to do with him. I didn't know how to take care of a baby. Everybody told me to give him up, to let someone else raise him who could give him a real home." Tripp's face hardened. "But I wasn't giving up my son."

The deep, determined love that showed in Tripp's

I never cared for him. At least, not after
."

what's wrong?"

hed heavily. "It's Rafe. We're not getting
well."

fighting?"

othing like that." Julia shrugged as she
ipping bowl to Kaitlin. "We've only been
months, and things were fine at first. But
Rafe hasn't been…a husband to me in a

bowl slipped from Kaitlin's grasp, but she
before it hit the floor. "You mean, he

ook her head miserably. "No."

hought men always wanted to…"

said, things were fine at first. Then Rafe
end all his time at the livery. All he does
hardly ever see him. And when he comes
tired. All he wants to do is sleep."

" Everything Kaitlin had heard in her life
en shattered. Could some men not care as
such things as she had been led to be-

y, it seems as if I might never have a
nd to Miss Bailey's school. Not if Rafe
ing so hard." Julia sighed dejectedly.

Rafe have brothers to help out at the
aitlin had met them the day they'd arrived

d Wade. They work their pa's farm to-
look after their ma." Julia's shoulders

face settled over Kaitlin like a soft blanket. She laid her hand over his forearm; it felt tight beneath her fingers.

"I figured out how to bottle feed him, how to diaper him. I did it all myself." A little smile tugged at Tripp's mouth. "I held his hands when he learned to walk. I taught him to feed himself. I read to him and rocked him to sleep."

Kaitlin slid her hand into his and squeezed his fingers gently. "You're a good papa. Charlie loves you so much."

Tripp looked down at the table, then lifted his gaze to lock with hers. "I guess you're right when you say I don't want anybody else in Charlie's life. But it's not for selfish reasons. It's because I can keep him safe. I can watch over him and protect him from everything bad that's out there in the world. I can keep him from being hurt."

"You have to let him go, Tripp." Her words, hardly more than a whisper, echoed in the room. "Just a little."

He shifted in his chair, but didn't pull his hand from hers. Suddenly he looked vulnerable, accessible, as she'd never seen him before.

"Charlie has to go to school." Kaitlin stroked Tripp's hand with her thumb. "Didn't you see how quickly he made friends at church yesterday? He's lonely and bored."

Tripp drew in a big, ragged breath.

"He needs friends his own age." Kaitlin gave him a light smile. "Everybody needs friends their own age."

He pulled away from her, and Kaitlin knew she'd

hit on another sore spot he didn't want to talk about. This one, even harder to face than Charlie.

"All right." Tripp planted his palms on the table and pushed himself out of the chair. "All right, he can go to school. But I'm checking into that teacher and that school before Charlie sets one foot in the place."

Kaitlin wagged her finger at his shirt pocket. "We'll make a list."

He yanked the tablet from his pocket. "Damn right we'll make a list. And if one thing bad happens to Charlie—one thing—there'll be hell to pay."

The determination etched in Tripp's face sent a flood of heat swelling through Kaitlin that settled in her chest with a dull ache. How must it feel to be loved that fiercely?

"We didn't get much done on the store today," Kaitlin said as she accepted the dripping supper plate Julia passed to her. "Tripp was checking on the school. Honestly, he must have canvased the entire town."

"Miss Bailey is a wonderful teacher."

"Be sure you tell Tripp." Kaitlin leaned around Julia's sideboard and peered at Tripp and Rafe standing outside the back door of the millinery shop in the fading light. "I'll bet he's asking Rafe about it now."

The men certainly looked deep in conversation, their heads bent together. Then Tripp leaned forward slightly as if he'd been kicked in the gut, and steadied himself against the roof support column. Rafe

shrugged and ambled aw
Tripp followed.

Kaitlin shook her head.
a discussion about the sch

"Miss Bailey was hired
ago when the town though
through. We expected so
Porter, and the mayor—the
wanted an excellent teache
coffee cup in the basin and
tell you the truth, everyone
stayed when the railroad d
lucky to have her. She's alw
with the children, like holdin
on plays."

"Plays?" Kaitlin asked. "

Julia laughed gently. "E
been holding their breath, ho
get married."

"Maybe she'll still be aro
have children to send off to

The smile dissolved from
Goodness, but she'd had
people today. First Tripp, no

"I'm sorry. I didn't mean

Julia shook her head. "No
to talk to you about it anyw

"Is this about Drew Hold

"Drew?" Julia uttered a
not."

"After seeing you two
thought maybe…"

Julia shrugged. "Drew

while, bu
I met Ra

"Then
Julia s
along ve

"You

"No,
passed a
married
now, w
long ti

The
caught
hasn't-

Julia

"Bu

"Li
began
is wor
home

"Sl
had ju
much
lieve?

"A
child
keeps

"D
livery"
in Por

"N
gether

face settled over Kaitlin like a soft blanket. She laid her hand over his forearm; it felt tight beneath her fingers.

"I figured out how to bottle feed him, how to diaper him. I did it all myself." A little smile tugged at Tripp's mouth. "I held his hands when he learned to walk. I taught him to feed himself. I read to him and rocked him to sleep."

Kaitlin slid her hand into his and squeezed his fingers gently. "You're a good papa. Charlie loves you so much."

Tripp looked down at the table, then lifted his gaze to lock with hers. "I guess you're right when you say I don't want anybody else in Charlie's life. But it's not for selfish reasons. It's because I can keep him safe. I can watch over him and protect him from everything bad that's out there in the world. I can keep him from being hurt."

"You have to let him go, Tripp." Her words, hardly more than a whisper, echoed in the room. "Just a little."

He shifted in his chair, but didn't pull his hand from hers. Suddenly he looked vulnerable, accessible, as she'd never seen him before.

"Charlie has to go to school." Kaitlin stroked Tripp's hand with her thumb. "Didn't you see how quickly he made friends at church yesterday? He's lonely and bored."

Tripp drew in a big, ragged breath.

"He needs friends his own age." Kaitlin gave him a light smile. "Everybody needs friends their own age."

He pulled away from her, and Kaitlin knew she'd

hit on another sore spot he didn't want to talk about. This one, even harder to face than Charlie.

"All right." Tripp planted his palms on the table and pushed himself out of the chair. "All right, he can go to school. But I'm checking into that teacher and that school before Charlie sets one foot in the place."

Kaitlin wagged her finger at his shirt pocket. "We'll make a list."

He yanked the tablet from his pocket. "Damn right we'll make a list. And if one thing bad happens to Charlie—one thing—there'll be hell to pay."

The determination etched in Tripp's face sent a flood of heat swelling through Kaitlin that settled in her chest with a dull ache. How must it feel to be loved that fiercely?

"We didn't get much done on the store today," Kaitlin said as she accepted the dripping supper plate Julia passed to her. "Tripp was checking on the school. Honestly, he must have canvased the entire town."

"Miss Bailey is a wonderful teacher."

"Be sure you tell Tripp." Kaitlin leaned around Julia's sideboard and peered at Tripp and Rafe standing outside the back door of the millinery shop in the fading light. "I'll bet he's asking Rafe about it now."

The men certainly looked deep in conversation, their heads bent together. Then Tripp leaned forward slightly as if he'd been kicked in the gut, and steadied himself against the roof support column. Rafe shrugged and ambled away, and after a moment, Tripp followed.

Kaitlin shook her head. *What an odd reaction to a discussion about the school.*

"Miss Bailey was hired to teach here about a year ago when the town thought the railroad was coming through. We expected so many people to move to Porter, and the mayor—the mayor's wife, actually— wanted an excellent teacher here." Julia washed a coffee cup in the basin and passed it to Kaitlin. "To tell you the truth, everyone was surprised that she stayed when the railroad deal fell through. We're lucky to have her. She's always doing special things with the children, like holding spelling bees, putting on plays."

"Plays?" Kaitlin asked. "Really?"

Julia laughed gently. "Everyone in Porter has been holding their breath, hoping Miss Bailey won't get married."

"Maybe she'll still be around when you and Rafe have children to send off to school."

The smile dissolved from Julia's face. "Oh…"

Goodness, but she'd had a knack for upsetting everyone today. First Tripp, now Julia.

"I'm sorry. I didn't mean to say the wrong thing."

Julia shook her head. "No, it's all right. I wanted to talk to you about it anyway."

"Is this about Drew Holden?"

"Drew?" Julia uttered a quick laugh. "Of course not."

"After seeing you two at church yesterday, I thought maybe…"

Julia shrugged. "Drew was courting me for a

while, but I never cared for him. At least, not after I met Rafe.''

"Then what's wrong?"

Julia sighed heavily. "It's Rafe. We're not getting along very well."

"You're fighting?"

"No, nothing like that." Julia shrugged as she passed a dripping bowl to Kaitlin. "We've only been married six months, and things were fine at first. But now, well, Rafe hasn't been…a husband to me in a long time."

The wet bowl slipped from Kaitlin's grasp, but she caught it before it hit the floor. "You mean, he hasn't—''

Julia shook her head miserably. "No."

"But I thought men always wanted to…"

"Like I said, things were fine at first. Then Rafe began to spend all his time at the livery. All he does is work. I hardly ever see him. And when he comes home he's tired. All he wants to do is sleep."

"Sleep?" Everything Kaitlin had heard in her ' had just been shattered. Could some men not c much about such things as she had been l lieve?

"Anyway, it seems as if I might neve child to send to Miss Bailey's school. Not if Rafe keeps working so hard." Julia sighed dejectedly.

"Doesn't Rafe have brothers to help out at the livery?" Kaitlin had met them the day they'd arrived in Porter.

"Ned and Wade. They work their pa's farm together and look after their ma." Julia's shoulders slumped. "I think Rafe cares more about that livery than he does me."

"Have you discussed it with him?"

"I've tried discussing it, I've tried— Well, I've tried a lot of things. Why, just this evening when Rafe came home, I—" Julia turned back to the dishes. "Anyway, Rafe just won't listen to me."

"What are you going to do?"

"I don't know. But marriage isn't turning out like I thought it would. In fact, I hardly feel like I'm married at all." Julia smiled weakly at Kaitlin. "I guess that's hard for you to understand. You don't plan to marry, do you?"

The comment stunned Kaitlin. She'd never thought of her future in such definite terms before. For as long as she could remember, her only plan was to become a great stage actress like her mother. Go to New York, entertain audiences with songs and dramatic plays, hear the roar of applause, feel the glow of the footlights. Her mother had told the stories endlessly. Kaitlin hadn't thought much past that.

"I haven't considered marriage. I'm going back East to become an actress as soon as the store is established."

"Really?" Julia's eyes widened. "My goodness, that sounds exciting."

"Please don't tell anyone," Kaitlin said. "I don't want people in Porter to think I'm not serious about the store."

"With a future like that planned," Julia said, "a husband and children must seem rather dull to you."

At that moment Kaitlin caught sight of Charlie

running through the alley, and Tripp swinging him into his arms, lifting the boy high over his head, then both of them laughing. A knot caught in her chest and rolled through her like ripples in a pond. Charlie, small and fragile. Tripp, big and powerful, tempering his strength, holding his son with such exquisite care.

Kaitlin turned away from the window, furiously drying the skillet. "I've wanted to be an actress since I was a child. That's what I'm going to do."

Chapter Nine

"All set?" Kaitlin placed the breakfast plates on the sideboard as Charlie and Tripp came down from their bedroom.

Charlie hopped up and down. "I'm gonna go to school now, Miss Kaitlin. And Papa says I can stay there all day."

"Yes, I know. Won't that be fun?"

The boy threw out his arms and whirled in a circle. Kaitlin laughed at his excitement, then glanced at Tripp, who was considerably less enthusiastic about the whole idea.

He'd broken the news to Charlie last night, sitting with the boy on his lap in the rocker, and patiently answered all Charlie's questions.

"You look mighty handsome for your first day of school," Kaitlin told him.

And how could he not, when Tripp had fussed over him all morning, ironing his little shirt, wetting down his hair and combing it into place, making certain he'd scrubbed behind his ears.

Charlie scurried to the back door. "Can we go now, Papa?"

"Don't forget your lunch." Kaitlin handed him the lunch pail Tripp had prepared. She couldn't imagine how the boy would possibly eat all the food Tripp had provided.

Reluctantly, Tripp crossed the kitchen and took his hat from the peg beside the door. "I might be a little late getting back."

She laid a hand on his arm, stopping him as he opened the back door. "None of the other parents will be there, Tripp," she said softly.

His expression tightened. "It's his first day. He might be scared."

"Do you *want* him to be made fun of?"

Tripp's scowl deepened. "Of course not."

"What do you think the other little boys will do when they see Charlie's papa waiting around the school, looking out for him?"

He shuffled from one foot to the other, then pulled at his neck. "All right."

Tripp yanked open the back door. "Come on, Charlie, let's go."

"Bye, Miss Kaitlin."

She stood in the doorway watching them head down the boardwalk, Tripp holding Charlie's hand while the boy skipped along beside him. Emotion swelled in her chest and she said a silent prayer that, for the sake of everyone in Porter, Charlie would be all right in school today.

When Tripp returned a short while later, Kaitlin was in the store with buckets of water and a scrub brush. He looked a little pale.

"Did everything go all right?"

"Yeah, I reckon."

"Were there other boys his age there?"

He dragged his hand down his face. "More kids than I'd like to look after."

"He'll be fine." Kaitlin gave him a reassuring smile.

Tripp turned away. "Let's get some work done."

He busied himself sorting through his toolbox, getting out nails, trying to remind himself of where he'd left off the day before. But his thoughts drifted from the shelves that needed building to the woman working behind him. And that perplexed him. Charlie should be uppermost in his mind.

Leaving his son at school this morning—after talking with the teacher and making certain he was playing with the other children—Tripp had found himself anxious to get back to the store. Back to Kaitlin.

Being near her brought him a comfort he hadn't felt in a long time. He stole a glance at her working by the front windows and his chest tightened a bit. He'd forgotten how nice it was to have a woman around—a decent woman. To hear the swish of skirts and petticoats, catch a glimpse of white lace stockings, see tiny shoes peeking from under hems. To have someone to talk to, someone to listen to. Someone who cared.

Tripp's chest constricted. He forced himself to turn away and concentrate on the job at hand. He couldn't do it.

"I talked to that teacher, and—"

Tripp turned and found Kaitlin standing in the

window on an overturned wooden crate with a bucket of water at her feet.

Kaitlin glanced over her shoulder. "Yes?"

Of all the times for him to turn around and look at her. Tripp gulped, feeling the tension building in his body. Standing on the crates, she was outlined by the sun's rays through the windows, highlighting the line of her waist, the curve of her hips. And if that weren't enough, she was scrubbing the window, her arm stretched high over her head, her bottom swaying back and forth.

She stopped and turned sideways, looking at him expectantly. "Did you say something?"

Did he? At the moment he wasn't sure. The only thought blazing through his brain was how high her breasts swelled, outlined by the light behind her.

"Tripp? Tripp, are you all right?"

Hell no, he wasn't all right. He shifted uncomfortably, trying to stave off the sensations growing within him.

"I talked to Julia last night about Miss Bailey. She sounds like a wonderful teacher. You shouldn't keep worrying about Charlie." Kaitlin smiled and waved her arms around the store. "I'm sure he's having a lot more fun than you are."

That was for damn sure. Heat and its urgency twisted tighter inside him, robbing his strength. He plopped down on a low stack of boards. "I need to rest a minute."

"That's a good idea."

To his dismay, Kaitlin climbed down from the crate and wound her way behind a taller stack of lumber to stand beside him. Now, not only could he see her, he could smell her, too.

She dried her hands on the towel she'd brought with her, working the fabric between her fingers, over her palms, up her delicate wrists. Tripp cringed at his body's reaction to those movements. What was it about this woman that caused this to keep happening? And over the simplest things?

Hurriedly, Tripp reminded himself that it had been a long time since he'd availed himself of female comfort. He didn't like leaving Charlie even for a short time, and whores didn't hold much appeal. But the intensity of his reaction to Kaitlin and the frequency of his dilemma were something he hadn't expected and couldn't explain.

"Julia and Rafe are nice, don't you think?" Kaitlin gazed down at him.

Why did she have to bring up them? Especially after what Rafe had told him Julia had done with the butter at supper last night when he'd asked her to pass the biscuits.

Tripp squirmed on the boards. "They're good neighbors."

With a swish of skirts, Kaitlin sat down on the lumber a few feet from him. "I'm concerned about them."

Tripp tried to focus his thoughts on the tiny furrows between her brows, but his gaze dipped to her lips, puckered in a little pout.

"What's wrong with them?" he asked.

She leaned closer and her sweet scent washed over him.

"I think they're having some problems." Kaitlin lowered her voice. "Marital problems."

Hot flames clawed at his middle and he leaned forward, draping his arms across his thighs. He knew exactly what kind of problems she meant, and he couldn't—*couldn't*—talk about them now.

Kaitlin pressed her lips together. "Julia says Rafe's not very…attentive."

"Attentive?" Delicate an explanation as it was, it didn't keep visions from popping into Tripp's mind, visions that had nothing to do with Julia and Rafe.

"They don't spend much time together." She leaned closer. "Has Rafe mentioned it to you?"

What Rafe had mentioned wasn't fit to repeat, certainly not to Kaitlin. Tripp inched farther down the board, closing the gap between them. "No, nothing like that."

"Really?" Kaitlin touched her finger to her lips. "Julia is quite upset about it. She's lonely, I think."

Tripp moved a little closer, drawn to her by some unseen force. "They're both busy, running two businesses."

Kaitlin nodded. "Two very different businesses."

Tripp sat only inches from her now, close enough to feel the warmth of her body, a warmth that tugged at him, pulled him even closer. Lord, she was a pretty thing, in her plain day dress, her hair twisted in a loose knot, errant strands curling around her face. She looked as pretty to him now as when he'd seen her all dressed up the first day they'd traveled to Porter together. Prettier, actually, because today she looked…touchable.

And that's what he did. Touched his finger to her

chin, tracing the line of her jaw. She turned, her brown eyes intent upon him. Not questioning him, or shocked by his action, but watching expectantly.

Tripp lowered his head until his lips hovered above hers. Her hot breath fanned his mouth, and he could taste her already. An ache of longing, of need, settled in his chest. Time stopped, stretching him taut.

Kaitlin's heart pounded against her ribs, banging its way upward until it lodged in her throat. She couldn't breathe. Expectation, anticipation—something—cut off her airway. Her senses crackled to life, flew in a thousand directions, only to be captured by the force of the man sitting at her side.

Need she'd never imagined sprang up in her. She trembled, caught in his gaze, caught in the spell he'd cast over her. He smelled clean, like soap and water, but muskier somehow. A potent energy radiated from him.

Minutes, hours, days—she wasn't sure how much time—dragged by while she sat tingling at his side, waiting. And she wasn't sure what she was waiting for until...

He kissed her. He brought his lips down on hers, blending them together softly, gently. But instead of finding relief from the anticipation humming in her body, he only made things worse—or better. She didn't know which. And didn't care to know.

A little whimper vibrated in her throat announcing the surrender of all thought. She leaned closer, lost, mindless as his mouth moved over hers. His lips were firm but soft, sure but gentle. He'd kissed her before. He felt familiar, not foreign or intrusive. Comfort countered by bone-melting excitement.

Sweetness. Hot, pure sweetness flowed from her, swelling Tripp's chest, driving his pulse faster. She was like molasses, thick and sweet, and he was hopelessly caught.

Tripp splayed his palm along her jaw, fanning his fingers to touch the soft flesh of her neck. Lose strands of her silken hair brushed his skin, setting it aflame. He moaned softly and urged her closer.

She responded willingly, tilting her head back, offering more of herself. Tripp deepened their kiss, gliding his tongue across her lips. She shuddered and pulled back, but not enough to break their kiss. Seconds ticked by and he waited, giving her time, choices. Then she leaned close again and he covered her lips fully with his.

Looping his arm around her, he drew her closer until her breasts brushed his chest, sending a wave of urgency rushing through him. He slid his tongue over her lips and this time she didn't pull away. Instead, she parted them for him.

She felt the heat, the fullness of his tongue against hers. Never had she imagined something so scandalous, so intimate, could be this wonderful. Kaitlin matched his movements in an exquisite private exchange. Heat rolled off him. His arms tensed around her. His hand slid deeper into her hair, kneading her neck with his long fingers.

He couldn't get enough of her. Like a man lost in the desert, Tripp drank from her greedily, sure he'd never find fulfillment, sure—

A voice. The click of a doorknob.

Tripp lifted his head from Kaitlin as two women stepped through the front door. Several seconds ticked by before his befuddled brain made the connection. June Hutchinson and Imogene Douglas.

"Hello? Miss Jeffers? Mr. Callihan?"

Half-hidden as they were by the larger stack of lumber, the ladies hadn't spotted them yet. But once they did, there'd be no denying what they were seeing.

Cursing under his breath for his stupidity—kissing her in broad daylight, for God's sake—Tripp pushed Kaitlin away. Her head wobbled, her eyes wild and unfocused. But instead of jumping to her feet as he'd expected, she tumbled out into the floor in a flurry of skirts and petticoats.

The pleasure of knowing that his kiss had robbed every ounce of her strength brought only panic to Tripp as the two women walked farther into the store. Good Lord, he certainly couldn't let the women find them like this.

Using the larger stack of lumber for cover, Tripp dropped to his hands and knees over Kaitlin, crushing the fullness of her skirt beneath him. He grabbed her shoulders and pulled her up.

"Kaitlin," he whispered frantically, "you have to get—"

"*Well.*"

Tripp looked up to find June Hutchinson glaring down her long nose at them, her lips pinched, her arms folded tightly across her middle.

And who could blame the woman? Here they were, Kaitlin's skirts and petticoats going everywhere, him straddling her hips, holding her up by her shoulders while her head lolled back and forth.

Mrs. Hutchinson's lips drew even tighter. "So, how is your *business partnership* going?"

Tripp gulped and gazed up at her, sure he looked as guilty as he felt.

Imogene Douglas pushed ahead of her. "She's fainted."

Mrs. Hutchinson's mouth curled downward. "I rather think she's—"

"Look at her," Mrs. Douglas insisted. "Her cheeks are flushed. So are Mr. Callihan's."

And that wasn't all that was flushed. Tripp surged to his feet, pulling Kaitlin up with him.

She wobbled for a moment, then came to her senses. She tried to move away but Tripp grasped her upper arms, holding her in front of him, facing the women.

Kaitlin touched her hand to her forehead, feeling her cheeks glow. "I—I don't know what happened."

"Ventilation," Mrs. Douglas announced, waving her arms around the room. "Proper ventilation is needed for good health. You must keep windows and door open when working."

Mrs. Hutchinson's eyes narrowed. "Unless there's some reason you don't *want* the windows and doors open."

Kaitlin glanced over her shoulder at Tripp, desperate to put some distance between the two of them. But when she tried again to move away, he held her firmly in front of him.

"Can we get you something, Miss Jeffers? Water?

A cool towel?'' Mrs. Douglas asked. ''Maybe you should lie down.''

''No, thank you.'' What she really needed was to get away from Tripp, but he still held her as if his life depended on it. What was wrong with him? He held her like a shield—

Kaitlin's cheeks flamed as she realized exactly what she was shielding from the view of the ladies. A strange sensation pulsed inside her.

''Thank you ladies so much for coming by.'' She pulled away from Tripp, shepherding the women toward the front door. ''It's so good of you to visit.''

''Please let me know if you need anything,'' Mrs. Douglas said. ''The mayor and I want you to feel welcome.''

Kaitlin fought the urge to glance back at Tripp. Of all the things she was feeling at the moment, welcome may have been among them. She wasn't sure.

Outside on the boardwalk, Kaitlin smiled and waved as the two women headed down the street, as if that might erase from their minds what they had just witnessed. Mrs. Hutchinson glanced back at her, suspicion wrinkling her brow, and Kaitlin smiled and waved harder.

The morning breeze washed over her cooling her cheeks and brought relief to the rest of her as well. A myriad of emotion swirled inside her. Embarrassment and relief that the ladies hadn't realized what they'd walked in on. The passion of Tripp's kiss and the warmth of his arms. The excitement of their intimacy.

A longing sprang up inside her, pushing aside all the other feelings. A longing to be with Tripp, to share with him what they'd just been through. She'd never felt it so strongly before.

Kaitlin hurried back into the store, urgency nipping at her heels.

"The ladies must—"

Kaitlin stopped, disappointment deflating the knot in her stomach.

Tripp was nowhere to be seen.

Chapter Ten

Kaitlin pushed back the new curtain that hung in the doorway of the kitchen and looked with pride at the store. Beautiful new painted shelves, all waiting to be filled with merchandise. Merchandise that would propel her onto the stage in New York.

The past weeks had been hard, but everything was finally finished. Gleaming white shelves and counters, varnished floors, sunny yellow storefront. Kaitlin had picked the colors; nothing dull or dreary for her store.

Of course, working with Tripp had been the most difficult part. He spent way too much time thinking. He measured endlessly—even things he'd already measured. He braced and supported. Watching him drive a nail was tedium to the extreme. Kaitlin had been tempted to rip the hammer from his hand and do it herself more than once.

But now the store stood ready. And somehow, she and Tripp had lived to tell about it.

"Good night, Miss Kaitlin."

Charlie, dressed in his white nightshirt, held up

his arms. Tripp waited at the stairs that led to their bedroom.

"Sweet dreams, Charlie." She knelt and gave him a hug. He mashed his lips against her cheek in a wet kiss that always made her smile.

Rising slowly, she watched Charlie hurry to Tripp, who swung the boy into his arms and carried him upstairs. A contentment settled over Kaitlin as it usually did in the evening. After supper Tripp sat the boy on his lap and had him tell everything that had gone on that day at school.

Charlie was a talker, too. He loved school, his teacher, his friends. Kaitlin usually sat at the table doing mending or whatever chore needed her attention, listening to them. Tripp's patience and thoroughness, which drove Kaitlin to distraction, was a big hit with Charlie. He listened to every word the child said. At those moments, everything Tripp had done to annoy her during the day vanished.

Tripp came back downstairs. Despite the long days they put in, the heavy work that Tripp did, as well as his help with the cooking and cleaning and his attention to Charlie, he never looked tired. Strong. Always strong. Always capable.

And for all his maddening ways, Kaitlin had to admit that he certainly knew what he was doing. The shelves, the counters, all the repairs had turned out beautifully. And for all her own grumbling about him, he'd never uttered one discouraging word.

"We'd better get the inventory list done." Tripp pulled sheafs of paper and his ledger book from the cupboard.

"I've been thinking about a name for the business,'' Kaitlin said as they sat across from each other at the kitchen table. ''Any suggestions?''

He stacked the paper neatly in front of him and positioned the lantern strategically. ''I don't know. How about Porter Dry Goods?''

Kaitlin frowned. ''Porter Dry Goods? That sounds sort of…dry, don't you think?''

He shrugged. ''What do you want to call it?''

She sat a little straighter in the chair and lifted her chin. ''How about The Emporium?''

''What the hell is an emporium?''

''A grand store. A place of unusual and unique items gathered from across the country, around the world.'' Kaitlin gestured with her hands. ''Doesn't that sound exciting? Wouldn't you just die to shop in a store with that name?''

''Not really.'' Tripp looked across the table at her and grinned. ''But we can call it that if you want.''

''Wonderful.'' She bounced in her chair. ''I'll have the sign painter start on it right away.''

''Nothing too big,'' Tripp cautioned. ''We have to watch—''

''—expenses. Yes, I believe you've mentioned that. A few thousand times.''

''The money has to come from—''

''—somewhere. I know. You've mentioned that, too.'' Kaitlin smiled sweetly at him. ''And it doesn't grow on trees, or fall from the sky, or sprout up out of the ground. I understand that.''

Tripp opened the ledger book. ''If you'll look at these figures, you'll see that…''

He frowned at the page, then pushed the ledger toward her. ''Is this a three or a five?''

Kaitlin leaned closer. "It's a three. Or maybe it's a five."

"Well, which is it? There's a big difference between a three and a five."

"Yeah, two." Kaitlin rolled her eyes. He'd not been overly thrilled when she'd sat down to do their journal entries last night, tracking their expenses. Hopefully, one day, they'd have some income to record as well.

He drummed his fingers on the ledger and drew in a big breath. "Kaitlin, we have to keep track of our money. Look at this. I can't read half your figures. And you're not staying in the lines."

"I guess I'm just not an in-the-lines person." Kaitlin pushed the ledger back toward him.

"That settles it," Tripp said, pulling the ledger back to his side of the table. "I'll keep the books from now on."

"I am more than capable of doing it."

"What good is writing down figures that nobody can read?" Tripp shook his head. "You stay away from the ledger."

Kaitlin sighed. "Fine."

"Let's get the inventory list worked out," he said, closing the ledger.

"Did you talk to Rafe yet?" Kaitlin asked.

He took out a pencil and sheaf of paper. "It's all set. His brother Ned is coming, too. That gives us three wagons."

"That should be plenty." Kaitlin clamped her lips together, holding in the desire to demand that she go along. Of course it was completely out of the question. The trip up to Ferman would take several days and she couldn't possibly travel that far, unescorted, with the three men. Even Mrs. Douglas couldn't save her from that kind of gossip.

"Are you sure about this warehouse?" Tripp asked.

"Of course. My friend Isabelle's employer gets all her stock from there."

Tripp began to write. "First off, we'll need a couple sets of scales, a half dozen glass jars, four scoops."

"That sounds fine," Kaitlin said.

"Next, there's tools. Saws, hammers, nails, shovels. A dozen of each ought to do it. Then we'll need lanterns, fuel oil, a couple dozen plain wool blankets. Cigars—"

"Plain blankets? Cigars?" Kaitlin wrinkled her nose. "Those aren't the kind of things we want in the store."

"We don't?"

"No. We want fabrics and lace, colorful crockery and pottery, kitchen utensils, scented soaps and—"

"Hold it right there." Tripp reared back in his chair. "I'm not standing in the store and selling scented soaps."

"They'll be very popular. Women will love them."

"Women? The men are who we'll be selling to."

Kaitlin waved away the notion. "Women do most of the shopping. We need to stock the items they want to buy."

"Men need things, too. And they don't need scented soaps. They need tools and cigars."

"Do you honestly think a display of hammers and

nails in the windows will draw people into the store?''

"Sure."

Kaitlin huffed impatiently. "Well, believe me, it won't. Lamb's General Merchandise is the only other store in town and that's exactly the kind of items they carry. If we want people to come to our Emporium, we'll have to offer something better."

"Sounds risky to me." Tripp shook his head. "Lamb's has been in business for a lot of years. Seems to me he knows what he's doing."

"We don't have years. We need to make a quick profit and clear out of here. That's our deal. Remember?"

"Yeah, I remember." Tripp grumbled, then leaned over his paper again. "All right. Fabric. What kind?"

Kaitlin touched her fingertip to her lips. "An array of colors. Blue, green—"

"How many bolts?"

"Two, maybe three."

"Well, which? Two or three?"

She sighed heavily. "Two."

He wrote that down. "What color?"

"Blue, green, some yellow—"

"What shade of blue?"

"Something pretty."

He looked up from his paper, his pencil gripped in his long fingers. "How the hell am I supposed to buy that? 'Something pretty.' What does that mean?"

"It means to use your imagination. Look at what they have and buy what looks best."

Tripp tossed down his pencil. "Forget it. Forget the fabric, the crockery, the scented soaps. We're buying the same thing old Mr. Lamb has in his store."

"We are not." Kaitlin reached across the table and yanked the paper away from him. "I'm a partner in this and I get a say in what happens."

He leveled his gaze at her. "You're a partner, all right. You get half a say. I get the other half."

"Fine. Then you pick out half our inventory, and I'll pick out the other half." Her jaw jutted out. "And we'll see whose merchandise sells the best."

"That suits the hell out of me. Half the store will be yours, the other half mine." Tripp jerked up another sheaf of paper. He pointed his finger at her. "Just be sure I can read what you write down."

"You just be sure you bring back what I write down," she told him.

They wrote furiously in tense silence for a long time. Finally, Tripp laid his pencil aside and folded his list.

"All that fabric and soap—are those the kinds of things you carried in your store?" he asked.

She kept writing. "What store?"

"The store you owned."

"I never owned a store." Intent on her list, she didn't even spare him a look.

"Okay, then, the store you worked in."

Kaitlin's hand froze and her gaze came up slowly to meet his. She shifted in her seat.

"I never worked in a store…exactly."

His shoulders stiffened. "Then what…exactly…did you do in a store?"

Kaitlin cleared her throat. "Well, nothing."

His jaw tightened and his chest expanded. "You never owned a store, or worked in one?"

"Well…no."

"You told me you knew all about running a store. Before I ever agreed to this deal, I asked you and you told me you knew what you were doing." Tripp's voice rose, taking his temper along with it. "And now you're saying that was all a lie!"

"No, not exactly."

"Do you know how to run a store or not?"

Kaitlin flung out her hands. "What's to know? You put merchandise on the shelves and people buy it. How hard can it be?"

"Oh, my God…" Tripp pushed himself out of his chair, paced across the room, then spun back on her. "You let me put my money into this deal! You let me work like a dog fixing up this place! You let me bring my son here, and all along you'd never worked one single day in a store?"

"I've shopped at dozens of stores. I've—"

"Shopping at a store and managing a store are two entirely different things." Tripp slapped the back of his hand into his open palm.

"What's so different?"

He clamped his hand over his forehead. "Oh, my God…"

Kaitlin rose from her chair and rounded the table. "Tripp, please listen. Everything is going to be fine. We've got the store ready, the inventory picked out. People have been stopping by here for days. You've seen them. They're all anxious for us to open so they can come in and buy. Everything will be all right."

"You should have told me the truth."

"I told you the truth, sort of. Besides, if I'd told you I'd never owned a store, you'd have never agreed to our deal."

"Exactly!"

"It's a chance we had to take," Kaitlin told him. "Have you ever taken a chance on anything in your life?"

He backed away from her, waving her off with both hands.

"Tripp, please—"

"Don't. Just don't talk to me right now."

Kaitlin planted her hands on her hips. "You worry too much."

"And you don't worry near enough!"

"There's no need for me to worry! You worry enough for eight people!"

He glared down at her, then spun away and headed out the back door, closing it with a thud.

Kaitlin pulled her shawl closer around her shoulders, warding off the cool of the predawn. Darkness had lifted, settling a gray over the back alley. The sun would climb over the horizon shortly and chase the chill from her bones.

But it would do nothing to ease the chill in Tripp's demeanor.

Pacing the boardwalk, Kaitlin watched as Tripp, Rafe, and his brother Ned checked the harnesses and the wagons for the journey up to Ferman. Rafe and Ned had spoken to her. Tripp hadn't.

Since the incident in the kitchen two nights ago, he'd kept his distance. That had suited Kaitlin all right. She wasn't all that anxious to talk to him, either.

During the night, though, lying awake, she'd wondered if she was at fault for not telling him she had no experience running a store. She'd pushed that notion away. After all, if she had been willing to jump into the endeavor under those circumstances, why shouldn't he?

The alternative was their dreams never would be fulfilled. Unacceptable to Kaitlin's way of thinking. She leaned her shoulder against the roof support column and watched Tripp's hands moving over the horses, the harness. He was capable, intelligent. But reluctant. Wary.

Well, she was neither reluctant nor wary. She had enough determination for them both.

Kaitlin straightened and drew in a big breath of the crisp morning air. She'd have her dream, and consequently, Tripp would have his—even if it meant dragging him kicking and screaming every inch of the way.

"Papa?"

Kaitlin turned to see Charlie standing in the doorway in his nightshirt, rubbing his eyes.

"Gracious, Charlie, what are you doing out of bed so early?"

Kaitlin removed her shawl, wrapped it around him and lifted him into her arms. The boy was heavy; it always looked so easy when Tripp lifted him.

"I wanted Papa."

Kaitlin stroked her hand through his hair. Tripp had discussed his leaving with Charlie for several days and they'd said their goodbyes last night, not wanting to wake the child so early in the morning. It had surprised Kaitlin that Tripp had agreed to leave the boy behind. And in her care, to boot. Even if it was the only sensible thing to do.

"Tripp?" Kaitlin called to him softly. As soon as he saw Charlie, he walked over.

Without a word he gathered Charlie in his arms, cradling him against his shoulder, resting his chin against the boy's soft hair. Charlie nestled closer.

Kaitlin felt a little sigh vibrate in her throat. How good it felt to be held in those strong arms, against that powerful chest. Visions of the times Tripp had kissed her oozed into her thoughts.

Tripp touched Charlie's chin and he sat up. "I'll be back soon. Miss Kaitlin will take good care of you."

"Okay, Papa."

Seeing the two of them together like this, Kaitlin wasn't sure which of them was taking the separation the hardest.

"We'll have lots of fun together," Kaitlin said. "I have something special planned for after school today."

"Really, Miss Kaitlin?" Charlie's sleepy eyes widened.

"And the day after that, too." She smiled and held out her arms. "Come on. We'll snuggle by the fire together and get warm."

Tripp held on to him, staring hard at Kaitlin, then finally kissed Charlie's cheek and passed him to her.

"Don't forget the list I made," he said. "I put it by the cupboard."

Kaitlin settled Charlie onto her hip. "Yes, I know where it is."

The only time they had exchanged more than a few words in the past several days was last night when Tripp showed her the list he'd made. It was an itinerary of their journey, where they would stay on which days, both going and coming, in case she needed to telegraph him. He'd also written down the name of the town doctor and where he lived, noted the time school started and dismissed, Charlie's bedtime, and his favorite foods.

Of course Kaitlin already knew all these things. But it seemed to make Tripp feel better to write them down for her, so she'd listened intently while he explained it to her, and nodded when he'd nailed it prominently to the kitchen wall.

"Have a good journey." Kaitlin offered him a smile. No need to ask if he'd remembered the inventory list, the directions, the money. She was certain he'd already checked it dozens of times himself.

Tripp stood there watching them both. "I'll be back as soon as I can."

"Don't worry, we'll be fine."

Tripp just nodded. Then he leaned close and kissed Charlie's cheek.

"You mind Miss Kaitlin."

"I will, Papa."

Still, he didn't go. He shuffled from one foot to the other. "Well, okay, I'm leaving."

"Be careful." She knew he would, but felt she had to say so.

Tripp nodded and turned away, then spun around.

His brows pulled together. "You really were a nanny, weren't you?"

A knot of hurt and anger jerked in her chest. Did he really think she would lie about her ability to take care of Charlie? Charlie, of all things?

The initial reaction to lash out at him dissolved. Of course he'd think that. And she deserved it. It wasn't a very good feeling.

"Yes, Tripp, I was a nanny. I'll follow your list, and I'll contact you if I have any problems. I'll take good care of Charlie." She laid her hand on his arm; he felt tense beneath her touch. "I promise."

He studied her for a long while, then nodded briskly. "All right."

Tripp leaned in and kissed Charlie again, this time bracing his hand against Kaitlin's shoulder to steady himself. He smelled clean and musky, his face so close his smooth-shaven cheek brushed hers. A little tremor passed through her.

"Take him inside. It's too cold out here," Tripp said.

The need to stay put overwhelmed her. Suddenly she wanted to watch until the last sight of him disappeared down the alley into the rising sun.

But she couldn't ignore his instructions on Charlie's care. Kaitlin went inside and watched out the window as Tripp climbed onto the wagon and headed out behind Rafe and Ned. She felt some tiny piece of her being pulled along with him, stretching farther and farther. He looked back over his shoulder and waved, then disappeared from view, but still the bond didn't break.

A heaviness settled in Kaitlin's chest. She didn't want him to go.

Pressing her palm against the windowpane, she stared outside until gradually, the coldness of the glass seeped into her skin.

What was she thinking? The man drove her absolutely crazy with his peculiar ways. Kaitlin shook her head and turned away.

Chapter Eleven

Kaitlin stepped through the curtain into the store and waved her hands. "Well, what do you think?"

"I can't believe my eyes." Julia shook her head in wonder. "It's beautiful."

"It turned out even better than I'd hoped." Kaitlin walked into the store.

Julia admired the tall shelves that lined both walls, the shorter ones running the length of the room, the counter that crossed the back. "Tripp built the shelves?"

Though she preferred to have the man out of her thoughts for the few days he was gone, a break she dearly deserved, in her opinion, Kaitlin had to give him credit for his hard work.

"Yes, Tripp did it all."

Julia's brows bobbed. "You're so lucky to have him."

Lucky? Off all the things she'd felt about Tripp, lucky was not among them.

"I've been after Rafe to build me one little shelf in my storeroom, and he hasn't done it. Look what

Tripp has done in only a few weeks. If it had been up to Rafe—or most of the other men in town—your shelves wouldn't be finished.''

"Tripp likes building things. He made the kitchen table and chairs, and the rocker in the corner."

Julia sighed heavily. "You're lucky, all right."

"Well, anyway, we're having our grand opening as soon as we get the merchandise in."

Julia smiled. "Old Mr. Finch never had the place looking so good. He'll certainly be surprised when he comes to Porter again and sees what you two have done here."

"Do you think he'll come back?"

"Someday, I suppose, if he still owns other property here." Julia ran her hands over the pink curtains draped over her arm. "Ready to put these up?"

"You bet," Kaitlin said. "I've got a lot to do before Tripp gets back."

"Is Charlie all right with Tripp away?"

"So far. We had breakfast together and I walked him to school."

"Tripp's done a good job with him. You have to admire a man who loves his child so much." Julia sighed heavily.

A pang of guilt stung Kaitlin. "I appreciate Rafe going with Tripp to get our inventory. I know it must be hard on you having him gone."

"To tell you the truth, it hurt me that Rafe would take so much time off from the livery to make the trip. He won't even come home an hour early to be with me." Julia shrugged. "Anyway, I'm glad he can help. That's what neighbors are for. I'm sure Tripp would do the same for him."

"How are thing going between you and Rafe? Better?"

"Nothing's changed."

"Nothing?"

"Absolutely nothing."

Kaitlin's heart ached at the troubled look on Julia's face. "What are you going to do?"

"I don't know." Julia shook herself and drew in a big breath. "Let's get these curtains up while Becky is watching my shop. I want to see how they look."

They set to work installing the hardware and hanging the curtains at the two front windows. Clinging to the ladder, fumbling with the tools, Kaitlin admitted it looked much easier when Tripp did the work. And she quickly realized why he measured things. After three tries she finally got the rod straight. Luckily the fullness of the priscillas covered the extra holes she'd pounded into the wall.

Kaitlin stood back and admired their work as Julia tied the last drape, fashioning a big bow. Both sets of curtains hung perfectly, framing the windows, drawn back to allow full view of the store. She dabbed at her forehead with the hem of her apron.

"Looks good," Julia said. "What's next?"

Kaitlin looked around. "These, I think."

Tripp had built two sets of shelves to fit just under the windows for merchandise display. The women maneuvered them into position and stepped back to assess them as the face of Imogene Douglas appeared at the front door.

"Please come in," Kaitlin said.

Mrs. Douglas planted her large frame in the center

aisle and nodded her approval. "It's lovely. Just lovely. The mayor will be so pleased."

"Thank you, Mrs. Douglas."

"Just what Porter needs. Commerce, more commerce. Maybe we'll get the railroad in here after all."

"It would certainly help all our businesses," Julia said.

"Exactly." Mrs. Douglas turned to Kaitlin. "We've another newcomer in town, you know. A Mr. Alister Dorsey. From New York, I understand."

Kaitlin's heart tumbled. "New York?"

"What's he doing in Porter?" Julia asked.

"I don't know—yet. He's only just arrived. We can surely hope he's here on business."

Porter didn't get many visitors, mostly people just passing through on the stage.

"Well, I'm off." Mrs. Douglas headed for the door. "Everyone is anxious for you to open. The whole town's buzzing. Be sure you let the mayor's office know if you need anything."

Julia followed them to the door. "I've got to go, too."

"Thanks for your help today. I'm taking Charlie to supper at the Red Rose Café. Will you come with us?"

Julia gave her a wicked smile. "With the men gone, we don't have to cook, do we?"

"Actually, Tripp does most of the cooking."

"He *cooks?*" Julia rolled her eyes. "You'd better watch it, some woman will snatch him right from under your nose."

Kaitlin forced a little laugh and closed the door, unsure why that idea bothered her so.

At the exact moment indicated on Tripp's instructions, Kaitlin walked to the school house at the edge of town. Red with white trim, the little building sat beneath spreading shade trees, amid a neat lawn.

Kaitlin paced restlessly, mentally reviewing the things she needed to get done over the next few days. When Tripp arrived with their merchandise, she wanted to stock the shelves and open the doors immediately.

Gradually she noticed several other women arriving. Most were young, some with babies. They laughed and chatted among themselves. She recognized most of them from church. Future customers. She put on her best smile and walked over.

"Where's Tripp today?" Elsa Donnley asked.

"Is he sick?" Clara Hadley shifted her baby from one arm to the other.

"He must be sick," Elsa said.

"Why else wouldn't he be here?" Frances Morgan asked.

Elsa nodded wisely. "He's always the first one here."

"Always," Frances agreed.

"Tripp's not sick," Kaitlin said. "He's gone to get the inventory for the store."

All three young women nodded broadly.

"Of course there would be a good reason for him not being here to pick up Charlie," Clara said. "I've never seen a man set such a store by a child before."

Frances huffed. "My husband could learn a thing or two from Tripp Callihan, that's for sure."

"Couldn't they all," Elsa said.

Frances giggled. "Why, I never had such a good time picking up little Ralph from school until Tripp was here."

All the women laughed together. Then Clara turned to Kaitlin, smothering her giggle with her hand.

"Oh, but listen to us go on. You already know all these things, don't you?"

No, she didn't. She'd never even imagined them. Kaitlin forced herself to smile while the other ladies prattled on about what a wonderful man Tripp Callihan was. Apparently, these ladies didn't know Tripp like she knew him.

Elsa leaned closer to the other women. "I heard Imogene Douglas talking to Mr. Lamb in his store today. Seems like there's another newcomer in town."

Kaitlin's attention piqued. "He's from New York, I understand."

"What's he doing here in Porter?" Frances asked.

Clara nodded wisely. "Mrs. Douglas will find out soon enough. Mark my words."

"I wonder if he's got a wife?" Elsa pursed her lips. "Every man needs a wife."

Frances looked at Kaitlin. "Tripp needs a wife, wouldn't you say?"

"He'd make a good husband," Clara said.

"Excuse me, please."

Anxious to escape these obviously delusional women, Kaitlin backed away and joined Reverend

Beckman and his wife as their carriage stopped at the edge of the schoolyard. Two children were crowded in with them, one on Lorna's lap.

"Miss Jeffers, I'm glad to see you." The Reverend jumped to the ground. "Lorna and I want to talk with you."

"Is something wrong?"

"Not at all." The Reverend and his wife exchanged a smile. "The Lord spoke to us a few nights ago and your name came up."

"My name?" Kaitlin's eyes widened. "The Lord spoke to you about me?"

"Yes, He did. You see, my wife hasn't been feeling very well lately, what with the new baby on the way."

The woman did look miserable. Kaitlin couldn't argue with that.

"And it's getting more and more difficult for her to keep up with everything. So, the Lord told us that you'd be perfect to take over the church choir for a while."

Kaitlin let out the breath she'd been holding. What a relief. The Lord could have spoken to the reverend about far worse things.

"It would only be for a few months." Lorna shifted the wiggly baby on her lap.

"But what about the other choir members? Doesn't one of them want the job?" Kaitlin asked.

"We've talked it over," the Reverend said, "and agreed you'd be best at it. Someone fresh, so to speak."

"Mrs. Autrey will play the piano. All you'll have

to do is run the rehearsals and direct the choir on Sunday mornings,'' Lorna said.

She could hardly say no. Especially since the Lord had requested her specifically.

''I'll be happy to help out.''

''Wonderful,'' Reverend Beckman said. ''Rehearsals are Thursdays at the church after supper.''

The school door burst open and children streamed down the steps into the yard. Charlie was the last one out, juggling his lunch pail, slate, reader and the jacket Tripp had made Kaitlin promise to send with him every day.

''Hi, Miss Kaitlin.'' His eyes were wide. ''We haded fun today. Our teacher letted us make pictures.''

Kaitlin took his belongings. ''Sounds like you had a good time. Miss Bailey is a nice teacher.''

''Uh-huh. Just like Papa said.''

Miss Bailey walked out onto the steps keeping an eye on the children.

''How was Charlie today?'' Kaitlin asked.

''Just fine, of course.''

''His father is gone.''

Miss Bailey smiled. ''Yes, Charlie gave me the note Mr. Callihan wrote explaining everything.''

''I promised him I'd ask.'' Another of Tripp's instructions.

''You can assure Mr. Callihan that Charlie is doing well, despite his father's absence.'' Miss Bailey smiled. ''Hopefully, we'll all survive it.''

Kaitlin turned to leave, but was cut off by several little boys staring up at her.

''Is that your mama, Charlie?'' one asked.

"Yeah, is that her?" asked another.

Charlie's brow wrinkled. "No, she's Miss Kaitlin."

"Then where's your mama?"

"You do got a mama, don't you?"

Clara Hadley hurried over and caught the boys by the shirt sleeves. She shooed them away. "You boys just get on home now. Your own mamas will be worrying after you."

Clara gave an apologetic look to Kaitlin, then left.

Charlie watched the boys leave, then turned his big blue eyes up to Kaitlin.

"Where is my mama, Miss Kaitlin?"

"Do you mean Charlie doesn't know?"

"I don't think so."

Kaitlin kept an eye on Charlie as he skipped down the boardwalk ahead of Julia and her.

"How could he not know?" Julia asked. "Hasn't Tripp told him?"

"All I know is what I told you happened at school this afternoon."

"What did you say to him when he asked?"

"What could I say?" Kaitlin shrugged. "I changed the subject."

"Maybe Charlie just doesn't understand. He was a baby when his mother died. Death is hard to explain to a child."

Kaitlin pulled her shawl closer around her shoulders. "You're probably right. But I think I should talk to Tripp about it."

"Well, good luck."

"Thanks." Kaitlin knew she'd need it.

At the corner they crossed the street and went inside the Red Rose Café. They found a table along the back wall.

"This is the bestest surprise in the whole world, Miss Kaitlin. Can I really have chocolate cake?" Charlie asked.

She smiled. "Of course you can."

"Even if I don't eat all my supper?"

Kaitlin slid her arm around his shoulder and gave him a little hug. "That's when chocolate cake tastes the best."

"Can I have two pieces?"

"You can have as much as you want."

"Gosh…"

Julia frowned across the table at her. "If you let Charlie get a tummy ache, you'll never hear the end of it. Tripp will—"

"Tripp worries too much."

They ate supper, then sipped coffee while Charlie worked on his cake. Julia's brows suddenly shot up over the rim of her cup.

"What's wrong?" Kaitlin asked.

"A man I've never seen before." Her cup hovered at her lips. "I'll bet he's that man Mrs. Douglas mentioned. The one from New York."

"New York?" Kaitlin swung around. "Gracious…"

Tall, with handsome features, the dark-haired man wore a well-cut suit with an elegant waistcoat and cravat. He looked to be no more than forty.

"What was his name?" Julia whispered.

"Dorsey, or something. Wasn't it?"

A low murmur went through the Red Rose Café as other patrons took notice of the man's arrival.

Julia leaned across the table. "Mrs. Douglas didn't mention how handsome he was."

Kaitlin tucked her napkin under her plate. "I should go talk to him."

Julia clamped her hand around Kaitlin's wrist. "You can't just sashay over and do that."

"But he's from New York."

"I know you intend to go there yourself, Kaitlin, but it's not proper for you to approach him. What will people say?"

"They'll say I'm a good neighbor welcoming a visitor to town."

"No, they won't." Julia's eyes narrowed. "And you know it."

Her shoulders slumped. She'd evaded the gossip about her living arrangement with Tripp thanks to Mrs. Douglas. She might not be so lucky again.

"Don't worry." Julia patted her hand. "In a town as small as Porter, you'll have your chance to talk to Mr. Dorsey before you know it."

"Goodbye, Charlie. I'll see you after school."

Kaitlin patted his little shoulder, expecting him to hurry across the schoolyard to catch up with his friends as he did yesterday. But Charlie only stood there, frowning.

She knelt down. "What's wrong?"

His bottom lip poked out.

"You're not sick, are you?" Gracious, maybe she shouldn't have let him eat two pieces of cake for supper last night. "Does your tummy hurt?"

"Uh-uh."

"Then what's wrong?" Kaitlin touched her finger to his chin. "Do you miss your Papa?"

"I don't know."

She smiled. "I've got something special planned for us after school again today. Just like yesterday."

After they'd finished supper, while it was still daylight, she had taken Charlie down to the narrow creek that flowed a half mile behind the store. Under the shade of the willows they'd dangled their feet in the water, staged a sword fight with tree branches, and played in the woods.

Charlie didn't answer, just gazed at the ground.

"Come on. I'll walk you inside." Kaitlin rose and took his hand, leading him across the schoolyard.

Miss Bailey stepped outside and yanked on the cord of the big bell mounted in the corner of the porch. The clanging brought the children racing toward the schoolhouse.

"Good morning, Miss Bailey." She and Charlie walked up the steps. "We seem to have a reluctant student on our hands this morning. I think he misses his father."

Miss Bailey smiled down at him. "Charlie, it's your turn to pass out papers. You don't want to miss that."

Charlie considered it for a moment, then said, "Bye, Miss Kaitlin." He went inside the schoolhouse with the other children.

"Don't worry," Miss Bailey said. "He'll be fine once class starts."

"Thanks."

Miss Bailey gave her a confident nod and headed into the school, but turned back at the doorway.

"Oh, Miss Jeffers? I understand Mr. Callihan is something of a carpenter."

How had word of that gotten all over town?

"Yes, that's true," Kaitlin said.

"Do you suppose he'd help out the school by putting together some sort of draw curtain? Something simple for our spring pageant. The children perform songs, put on a play, have a spelling bee. We have games, and a social for the parents."

The whole idea sounded wonderful, and delightful memories of her own school days filled Kaitlin's thoughts.

She smiled. "Of course he'll do it. Why, he could make you a whole stage."

"That would be wonderful. Thank you."

Kaitlin pressed her lips together, reluctant at first, but unable to hold herself back. "Miss Bailey? Would it be all right if I helped, too? I mean, I don't have a child here, or anything, but if there's something I can do…"

"You're a schoolteacher's fondest wish, Miss Jeffers. We'll talk after class today."

Kaitlin left the schoolyard with a newfound warmth glowing in the pit of her stomach. So many years had passed, she'd forgotten. Until now. And now all the memories were wonderful.

Her mother's experience on the New York stage had lent itself to every Christmas play, Easter sunrise service and May Day festival Kaitlin had ever been involved in. She'd staged lavish productions—lavish, at least, by schoolhouse standards—and all the children had loved performing.

Especially Kaitlin. She would stand on the stage, saying her lines, singing her song, and know that her mother was nearby watching, praising her words and her notes, sharing the joy of the moment.

Kaitlin couldn't wait to get more details from Miss Bailey this afternoon. She would make Porter's spring pageant every bit as wonderful as her mother would have done.

On the way back to the store, Kaitlin stopped by the newspaper office and checked on the advertisement she'd planned for their grand opening. It looked perfect. All she needed was for Tripp to get back with their inventory so she could give the editor the okay to run the ad.

Julia waited outside her millinery shop, sweeping her way down the boardwalk when Kaitlin got back to the store.

"Looks like you're getting your wish," Julia said.

Kaitlin stopped on the boardwalk. "What do you mean?"

"That Mr. Dorsey we saw at supper last night?" Julia gave her a wicked smile. "He asked about you."

Chapter Twelve

"Sleepy already?"

Kaitlin wiped her hands on the linen towel and sank into a kitchen chair. Charlie rested his arms on the table, his hands pillowed under his cheek.

"I don't know," he said.

Outside in the darkness, rain pattered against the window and tapped on the tin roof. "Sorry we couldn't go out after school today. I missed us playing down by the creek. Did you?"

Charlie planted his elbows on the table, propping up his chin with his palms. "I don't know."

The boy had been listless all afternoon. No matter what Kaitlin tried, he moped. She'd even offered to make cookies after supper, but that hadn't pleased him, either.

Her brows pulled together. "You're not sick, are you?"

She pressed her hand to his forehead, then relaxed. No sign of fever.

"I guess it's the rain." She'd felt a bit blue herself

most of the day and figured the weather was the reason. What else could it be?

"When's Papa coming home?"

Kaitlin's heart sank. The boy looked forlorn, his eyes sad. No matter how much chocolate cake she allowed him, or how many games they played or books they read, he still missed his papa.

"Tomorrow, probably," she said.

Tripp had made out his schedule and, of course, it was accurate. He'd allowed time for the journey, the possibility of the wagons breaking down, delays in Ferman, and a slower pace heading home with the heavy wagons. He'd been gone three days. Tomorrow afternoon was the earliest she expected him, but now with the rain, it could take longer.

Charlie's bottom lip trembled. "I want my papa."

"Oh dear."

Kaitlin lifted him from the chair and carried him to the rocker in the corner. She snuggled him against her, swaying gently.

"I know," she said softly against his hair. "He'll be home as quick as he can. He misses you, too."

Charlie sniffed and gazed up at her, his eyes shinning with tears. "Do you miss Papa, too?"

"Of course I do." Her chest tightened as she realized it was true.

The respite from Tripp's peculiar ways she'd thought she so desperately needed, and deserved, hadn't been nearly as welcome as she'd thought. The store felt strangely empty without him. As if some vital piece were missing.

She hadn't expected to feel this way, any more than she'd expected to hear the young mothers at the schoolyard praise Tripp for his concern over Charlie, or the other women in town marveling at the work he'd done in the store. Nor had she expected to feel her annoyance at his strange ways soften. Now, she wasn't sure why the things Tripp had done had upset her so.

"I have an idea," Kaitlin said brightly. "Let's make a picture for your papa. We'll surprise him when he gets back. Doesn't that sound like fun?"

Charlie sniffed. "I guess."

They settled at the kitchen table. Charlie chewed on his tongue as he worked diligently creating a picture of all the things he and Kaitlin had done together in the past few days. She kept him talking and drawing, focusing on Tripp's return home, not the long wait until he arrived. Charlie had learned to print his name, so he signed the bottom corner and Kaitlin wrote "To Papa" at the top.

By the time they'd finished, Charlie's spirits had lifted, as had Kaitlin's. They shared an apple, went over Charlie's school lessons and got ready for bed.

Dressed in the nightgown and wrapper, Kaitlin went upstairs to tuck Charlie into bed. In his nightshirt, he sat atop his covers, his eyes wide.

"What's wrong, Charlie?" Kaitlin placed the lantern on the night table and sat on the edge of the bed.

He plastered his palms against his ears.

Kaitlin smiled. Raindrops pelted the windowpanes and hammered the roof. The storm did seem louder up here, probably because the room was so quiet.

"How about if I stay up here with you for a while?"

Charlie nodded eagerly and scrambled off the bed.

"Where are you going?"

He climbed into Tripp's bed and wiggled under the covers. "Let's sleep in Papa's bed."

Kaitlin gasped. She heard it herself even over the rumbling of the storm. No, she couldn't lie down in Tripp's bed. It was far too personal—almost indecent.

"Please, Miss Kaitlin? Papa lets me." Charlie shook his head hard. "Me and Papa don't like storms."

Kaitlin carried the lantern to Tripp's bed and placed it on the table. What difference did it make, really? Tripp wasn't home. Charlie was upset, and sleeping here would comfort him. In fact, Tripp would probably be displeased with her if she didn't.

"All right. Move over." Kaitlin turned down the flame on the lantern and tossed her wrapper onto Charlie's bed. "You don't snore, do you?"

Charlie giggled and scooted to the middle of the bed. "No, but Papa does."

"Just what I wanted to hear."

Kaitlin's body tingled as she settled in, acutely aware that Tripp had also been in this bed. The linens smelled vaguely of him, a deep, masculine scent. Did he sleep in his long johns? In his socks? Naked?

Images flashed in her mind, and she gasped aloud. Gracious, what was she thinking?

"Tell me a story, Miss Kaitlin."

She pulled the quilt over her and rolled onto her side. Charlie sprawled on his belly and she tucked the covers around him.

"All right. I'll tell you about a wondrous adventure."

"Is that a story?"

She grinned. "Yes, Charlie, it is."

Halfway through, his eyelids sank. He tried valiantly to keep them open, but he fell asleep. Kaitlin's heart warmed at the sight. Charlie was a beautiful little boy. She saw so much of Tripp in him.

But what did Tripp see when he looked at his child? His wife, surely. How could he not? Even though Charlie looked just like his father, certainly Tripp saw more than that.

Kaitlin saw it too, sometimes, reflected the pain that flashed across Tripp's face. He always pushed it aside and went on. She supposed he'd had to learn to do that. But it was still there. Tripp's wife still claimed part of him.

An ache rose in Kaitlin's chest. Maybe that's the way it should be.

The rain slacked off a bit, but the wind was high. The storm would blow itself out by morning. Kaitlin knew she should get up and go to her own bed. Charlie was sleeping soundly, and didn't need her.

But the chilly air and the warmth of the little body snuggling near kept her where she was. Kaitlin gently touched Charlie's hair. She'd stay just a little longer, to make sure he didn't wake.

A sprinkle of rain and gust of cold wind followed Tripp inside. He pushed the kitchen door closed and heaved a deep sigh. It felt good to be home.

The room was pitch dark, but easily his gaze traveled to Kaitlin's bedroom door. His heart pumped a little faster, forcing heat into his chilled body. Instinct urged him to go inside, see her snuggled in bed. She'd want to know he was back and that their inventory was stashed safely inside Rafe's livery stable.

Tripp moved across the room, then stopped. Indecision seesawed through him. He wanted to see her, talk to her, tell her everything that had happened. She was his business partner. She'd want to hear it all.

His chest constricted. No, it wasn't strictly business on his mind. It'd be better if he talked to her in the morning.

Tripp shrugged out of his wet hat and coat, then pulled off his boots and set them beside the cookstove. Silently he went up the stairs to his bedroom.

Lantern light took the edge off the darkness, and he went immediately to Charlie's bed. He'd missed his son, and worried about him, too. He froze at the bedside. Where was Charlie?

Tripp spun around and saw the lump in his own bed. He smiled and pulled off his shirt. Charlie was safe.

Anxious for the warmth of his bed, Tripp stripped off his damp clothes and, because he was cold, put on another pair of long johns. He circled the bed and pulled back the covers.

Kaitlin.

The lantern light from the night table cast her in shadows. Dark hair fanned out over the white linen pillow. Lashes brushed her pale pink cheeks. Her delicate features were relaxed with sleep, her lips slightly parted. She was beautiful.

Yes, beautiful. Tripp stood beside the bed watching her, his breath quickening. He'd thought about her during his whole journey. At first he told himself it was his concern for Charlie that kept his thoughts on Kaitlin. But after a while, he knew he was lying to himself. He'd missed her, plain and simple.

But of all the times he'd thought of getting home, he'd never imagined finding her like *this*.

She lay on the opposite side of the bed, with Charlie sleeping on his belly beside her. The decent thing to do would be for him to go climb into Charlie's little bed in the corner. Tripp ran his hand over his chest. Yes, that would be the decent thing to do.

Or, he could wake Kaitlin and give her the chance to get back into her own bed. He could do that. In fact, he probably should do that.

But Tripp did neither. He cautiously slid under the covers. Charlie's bed was too small for him, and what kind of man would he be, anyway, waking Kaitlin in the middle of the night? She was probably tired. And the store was cold. Why, she could catch a chill.

Tripp rolled on his side to face Kaitlin, Charlie separating them. He'd been miserable driving the wagon through the rainstorm, thinking he'd never get warm again. Now he was plenty warm. And comfortable, too. Content.

He watched Kaitlin sleeping, watched his son. Somehow everything seemed right, the three of them snuggled together like this. It felt very right.

Her scent brought him awake, a fragrance with no name that reminded him of nothing but Kaitlin. It had hovered in his semiconscious state, flirting, tickling, tantalizing before rousing him completely. And when Tripp did open his eyes, the realization that it wasn't a dream stunned him.

Kaitlin lay facing him, her hair tousled, her face stilled with the contentedness of sleep. Between them, Charlie had scooted down the bed during the night, his head now barely visible above the quilt. Tripp relaxed against the pillow, watching them both.

Somewhere in the back of his thoughts it occurred to him that he should get up now, before Kaitlin woke. But he couldn't bring himself to leave the warmth of the bed, despite the bright morning sunlight beaming through the window, chasing away the chill.

Kaitlin's lips smacked together and she snuggled deeper into the pillow, sighing contentedly. Her eyes fluttered open, then widened until he saw the whites above the deep brown. Tripp held his breath, sure she'd bolt, or at least hit him with something. But she did neither.

"Good morning."

Tripp's heart beat harder, bringing a fullness to his chest. "Good morning."

"I wasn't expecting to find you—" her cheeks pinkened "—here."

Tripp grinned. "I wasn't expecting to be...here."

She pushed a stray lock of hair off her cheek, but made no move to rise. "What happened?"

How could he answer her? How could he explain that he'd been so anxious to get back home that he'd changed his schedule and driven straight through? He wasn't completely sure of the reason himself.

Tripp shifted on the bed, bringing himself a little closer to Kaitlin. Their faces inches apart on separate pillows, a warmth somehow bound them together, despite Charlie's little body between them.

A strange joy welled inside Tripp, saturating his parched senses. Kaitlin hadn't looked shocked at finding him beside her, nor had she looked indignant or angry.

How long had it been since he'd awakened with a woman beside him who'd looked at him the way Kaitlin did?

Years.

And how long had it been since he'd awakened with a woman beside him who really wanted to be there, with him?

Years longer.

"Kaitlin—" His heart rose in his throat, aching and pounding. Tripp eased closer. "Kaitlin, I—"

"Papa!"

Charlie sprang from beneath the heavy quilt and threw himself onto Tripp's chest. He wrapped his little arms around Tripp's neck and smashed his lips against his cheek.

"Papa, I misseded you so much!"

Tripp chuckled and put his arms around his son. "I missed you too, Charlie."

"I misseded you the most." Charlie flung out his arms, stretching as far as he could. "I misseded you *this much.*"

Tripp cuddled him closer and kissed the top of his head. "I hurried home just to be with you."

Charlie sat up on his knees beside Tripp, his tiny hands curled around Tripp's big fingers. "Miss Kaitlin misseded you too. Didn't you, Miss Kaitlin? You did, huh."

Tripp turned his gaze to Kaitlin, his heart warming. "Did you?"

An ache of need washed through Kaitlin as she watched the two of them together. She wished she could throw her own arms around Tripp, around Charlie, snuggle with them, revel in the love they shared. The want to be part of it engulfed her.

Kaitlin coiled her fists into the quilt, pulling it taut against her. The look on Tripp's face was so hopeful; she knew she looked the same.

"Yes," she whispered. "I missed you."

A smile lit up Tripp's face, warming her all over again.

"Papa, guess what me and Miss Kaitlin did." Charlie bounced on his knees beside Tripp. "She took me to the creek, and she told me stories about knights and soldiers."

Tripp glanced at Kaitlin, then back at his son. "She did?"

"Yeah. And she let me have two pieces of cake, and she said I could have all I wanted—even if I got a tummy ache."

Tripp's brows pulled together as he turned to Kaitlin. "She *did*?"

"Let's save some of our stories for later, Charlie." She sat up quickly. "I'd better go fix breakfast."

Tripp's frown dissolved as his gaze fell on her breasts, loose and molded to the front of her nightgown. The pressure that had swelled his chest and heart arrowed downward with powerful and predictable force.

Tripp sat up clutching the quilt over his lap with one hand, holding on to Charlie with the other. He glanced at Kaitlin. She looked uncomfortable suddenly, holding the covers in front of her.

"Go ahead," he said, turning his head away. "You can get up."

She'd left her wrapper all the way across the room on Charlie's bed. Her skin prickled at the thought of Tripp watching her retrieve it.

"No, it's fine. You can get up first."

He looked back over his shoulder at her. "No, I can't."

"It's all right, Tripp, I'll wait until—"

"I *can't,* Kaitlin."

She gasped as the extent of his dilemma dawned on her. Without meaning to, her gaze strayed to his lap, then bounced up to his face. Heat flooded her cheeks and she sprang off the bed.

Kaitlin grabbed her wrapper and dashed down the stairs, her nightgown billowing behind her. But not before Tripp got an eyefull of her curves outlined by the sunlight from the windows. He groaned and fell back on the bed.

In front of the big mirror in her room, Kaitlin took one last look at herself and the pale-pink dress she'd selected for today. Surely it was a poor choice, much too nice to wear on a day when she would be unpacking crates and inventorying merchandise. But she felt like fixing up today.

She went into the kitchen and saw Tripp at the

cookstove, as if he'd never left. Charlie sat on the
sideboard, talking nonstop. What a welcome sight.

"Coffee," Kaitlin said as she sidled up next to
him at the stove. "I've really missed your coffee."

He looked down at her. "Just my coffee?"

She felt his gaze bathing her with warmth. "Your
biscuits are pretty good, too."

He grinned. "Wait until you taste my corn
bread."

Kaitlin helped him with breakfast while Charlie
talked. He had lots to tell, and Tripp listened to every
word.

She tried to concentrate on the cooking, and Charlie's stories, but Kaitlin's mind kept wandering. She
wasn't sure what she was thinking about, but she was
constantly drawn to Tripp. Without realizing it, she
found herself standing next to him, brushing arms,
his leg swishing against her skirt, bumping into him
at the stove. Neither of them spoke, or even acknowl-
edged their nearness, but it kept happening. As if
they were drawn together like magnets.

After breakfast they stood side by side washing
the dishes. Such a simple chore, but this morning it
seemed almost entertaining.

Charlie bounced around the kitchen, talking, giggling, clinging to his father while he got ready for
school. Kaitlin half expected Tripp to keep the child
home with him, but he packed his little lunch pail
and they headed out the door together.

A short while later when the door opened again
and Tripp walked into the kitchen, Kaitlin's heart
lurched. He paused in the doorway. Their gazes

caught. The moment froze them both. Her heart pounded faster.

Tripp stepped inside and pushed the door shut. "Charlie was tickled with everything you two did while I was gone. He couldn't quit talking about you."

Kaitlin squirmed uncomfortably. "About the chocolate cake…I wouldn't really have let him—"

"I know." Tripp fumbled with his hat for a moment, then hung it beside the door. "I don't leave Charlie with just anybody. I knew you'd take care of him."

"I didn't give you much reason to believe in me." Kaitlin stepped closer. "I did lie about being Harvey Stutz's widow, about being…pregnant."

A wanting pulsed through Tripp at the memory her words evoked. The first time he'd seen her, belly swollen as if a baby were really tucked safely inside her. Now, as then, the same feelings surged in him. He crossed the room, unable to hold himself back.

Kaitlin gazed up at him. "And while I didn't exactly lie to you about owning a store, I did give you the wrong impression about my ability. I shouldn't have done that."

"Any more confessions?" Tripp touched his finger to her cheek.

Her skin warmed at his touch, and left her struggling to think clearly. "Well, yes. One other thing."

He eased closer, his gaze locked with hers. "Yes?"

"I volunteered you to build a stage for the school pageant."

Tripp grinned and wound his finger around a loose

strand of her hair. "Is there no end to your conniving ways?"

A well of emotion bubbled deep within Kaitlin. She laid her hand on his arm; he was tense and taut beneath his shirt.

"What about you?" she asked. "Anything you want to get off your chest?"

"Oh, yes." He lowered his head. "Ever since the day I left for Ferman, all I could think about was doing this…"

He covered his lips with hers, sinking into the kiss. He groaned softly and worked his mouth over hers, drinking in her taste. She was softer than he'd remembered. Sweeter than he imagined. And everything he wanted.

Looping his arms around her he pulled her against him. Her breasts melted into his chest, her thighs caressed his legs. He tightened his grip on her, pulling her even closer, losing himself in the taste and feel of her.

Kaitlin threw her arms around his neck, pressing herself harder against him, hungry for the feel of him. Her body hummed with a tension she'd felt only a few times before. The few times Tripp had held her and kissed her. It grew inside her, demanding more.

Every muscle, every fiber of him tensed with wanting. Tripp slid his hands around her waist and upward to cup her breast. She moaned, her breath hot against his mouth, driving his need further. He wanted her—all of her.

Frantically, he fumbled with the buttons of her dress, opening them. Her skin was hot. He pushed his fingers inside, closing them over the flesh of her breast. She was so soft, so warm, so tender. He shifted, desperate for her touch, settling himself intimately against her. She leaned into him, caressing with the sway of her hips. Then her hand slid downward and captured him.

Tripp's knees nearly gave out. Blindly, he kissed her, raking his lips over her throat, her cheeks, her lips. His hands covered her every curve, burning his palms. Need overwhelmed him. He had to have her.

One tiny thread of common sense slithered through his thoughts. Yes, he wanted her—wanted her now. But did Kaitlin want the same?

Tripp lifted his head. Her eyes were glassy, her lips wet and swollen, her breath warm and rapid.

"Kaitlin, I—"

She grabbed a fistful of his hair and pulled his mouth down on hers.

He groaned helplessly, struggling to hold on. He didn't know if he could wait until he carried her upstairs. The floor, then? The kitchen table?

No, no, neither of those. Her fingers tightened against him, testing his control further. Tripp gulped. Maybe the table.

He eased her back toward it, then stopped himself. No. Not here in the kitchen. He wanted her in his bed.

Tripp lifted her into his arms and headed across the room. Her lips burned into his neck, hurrying him onward. He reached the stairs and—

A man passed the window. A fist pounded at the back door.

"Hey, Tripp! Open up!"

Tripp froze on the bottom step as the icy wall of reality crashed over him. Ned Beaumont. He knew the voice; he'd listened to the man talk nonstop for the past four days.

A fist banged at the door again.

"Let's get this wagon unloaded!"

"Damn." Tripp placed Kaitlin on the step above him. She clung to his shirt and swayed for a moment. Color was high in her cheeks, but not from embarrassment.

Neither spoke. They just looked at each other, want and need throbbing between the two of them.

Kaitlin pulled her blouse together, working the buttons closed with trembling fingers. Tripp stood only inches from her, their bond still strong.

She wasn't sure how it had happened, only that it had. She'd have gone willingly with Tripp upstairs to his bed. Willingly she'd have lain with him. An odd sense of abandonment and loss swept over her as their bond dissolved.

"I'd better..." Tripp jerked his chin toward the kitchen door behind him.

She nodded quickly. "Yes, you'd better..."

He didn't leave, though. A lingering heat held him in front of her, turned his eyes a deeper blue. The knock sounded at the door again, and finally, he left.

Kaitlin hurried up to Tripp's bedroom, but couldn't stay. The scent of him hung in the air. His clothing lay draped on the chair, his hairbrush and shaving razor rested on the bureau. She splashed water in her face, straightened her hair and her dress, and went back to the kitchen.

The back door stood open, letting in the crisp air

and the sunshine. Outside a wagon and team waited at the boardwalk, loaded with crates. Ned and Tripp walked out of the store and headed toward the back door.

"Morning, Miss Kaitlin." Ned touched the brim of his hat. "Sorry to come to call so early, but Rafe needed the room in his livery."

She glanced outside. "He's at the livery already?"

"Yep. He was down there working before first light this morning." Ned shook his head in disgust. "That boy's got to learn about priorities."

Tripp's gaze collided with Kaitlin's as he walked outside; she had no doubt what *his* priorities were.

It was nearly noon before all three of the wagons were brought over and unloaded. The store was filled with big wooden crates stacked in every possible inch of space.

Ned rocked back on his heels, surveying the store. "How about if I give you a hand unpacking this stuff?"

Tripp and Kaitlin looked at each other; both knew what the answer would be. After what had happened in the kitchen this morning, if they were left alone again, the store might never open.

"Appreciate the offer," Tripp said, and passed Ned the claw hammer.

Ned stayed until all the crates were opened, then begged off. He had work at his own place to see to. Tripp thanked him and Kaitlin promised him supper some night soon, and Ned disappeared out the door, leaving Kaitlin and Tripp alone.

Kaitlin feared their conduct this morning might somehow strain their relationship, but just the opposite happened. As when they'd prepared breakfast together this morning, she felt drawn to Tripp. She couldn't get enough of him. He seemed to feel the same, as they pried open the wooden crates and pulled out the packing straw.

"Oh, Tripp, this is beautiful," she declared as she unwraped bolts of cloth. "You got just the right thing."

He grinned at her from the other side of the crate. "I tried hard to get what you wrote on your list. You wanted to go yourself, I know, but you stayed and looked after Charlie for me."

She ran her fingers across the dark-blue linen. "Charlie was a delight. We had no problems at all, except—"

Tripp's hands still and he frowned. "What happened?"

She waved away his concern. "Nothing serious, I don't think, but when I picked Charlie up at school, some of the children thought…"

His frown deepened. "Thought what?"

"They thought I was Charlie's mother," she said softly.

For a moment he simply stood on the other side of the crate while the color drained from his face. Then he clamped his palm over his forehead and spun away.

Darn it, how foolish she was. Kaitlin hurried after him winding through the maze of crates. Why had she brought up his wife? Especially now, after he'd been ready to carry her up to his room only a few hours ago? She should have waited, told him about it later.

In the kitchen she found him gazing out the window, his arms braced against the sideboard. The angles of his body were rigid, his jaw set. Kaitlin approached him slowly, his stance warding off any closeness.

"Charlie was upset," she said softly. "But that's understandable. I'm sure you did everything you could to explain it to him. Death is hard for a child to understand."

His head sank lower between his sagging shoulders. "Kaitlin—"

"It's especially difficult when it involves a parent. And Charlie was so young when she died."

Tripp winced and swung away.

She threaded her fingers together, wanting desperately to touch him, but too afraid to move closer.

"You shouldn't feel you've done something wrong, Tripp."

He glanced back over his shoulder at her. Deep lines cut through his forehead. His lips met in a tight line. Tripp turned away again.

"Charlie's mother isn't dead. I'm still married to her."

Chapter Thirteen

Married.

He was a married man. He had a wife.

Kaitlin pawed to the bottom of the packing crate, tossing straw over her shoulders.

He had a wife. A wife who had bore his son.

A light sheen of perspiration damped her face and bits of packing straw clung to her as she pulled boxes of phosphorous matches from the crate. Her pink dress was ruined now, smudged with dirt and dust. The dress she'd selected so carefully this morning, with Tripp in mind.

And all along he was married.

Kaitlin placed the matches on the stack of other items she'd unpacked and dived to the bottom of the crate again.

At first she'd been too stunned to speak, standing there in the kitchen with Tripp. It was only an hour or so ago, wasn't it? Kaitlin wasn't certain. It felt as if a lifetime had passed since Tripp had told her Charlie's mother was actually alive.

He'd said no more. He hadn't even turned to look at her.

Kaitlin had sensed his pain, heard the hurt in the words as he spoke them. She wanted to take him in her arms and hold him. She wanted to make his hurt go away.

But she'd been too stunned to move, too shocked to say anything. And what could she have said? The obvious questions rushed into her mind. Where was the woman? Why wasn't she here? Why hadn't she been with her husband and son all these years?

Tripp hadn't said anything, either. He'd just stood there, staring out the window with his shoulders hunched, and offered no explanation. His silence had hurt as much as the words he'd spoken.

After a moment when she'd gathered her wits a fraction, she'd taken a step toward him, then frozen in place as the realization of what she'd nearly done sapped her strength.

Tripp was a married man. And she'd nearly given herself to him.

Bad enough that she'd been tempted to do such a thing, not married to him herself. But with him already married?

Kaitlin pulled a stack of wool blankets from the crate, heat flushing her cheeks at the memory.

"Do you need some help?"

Kaitlin's head snapped up at the sound of Tripp's voice coming from across the room. A maze of opened, but unpacked crates separated them. He'd followed her into the store shortly after she'd turned on her heels and fled the kitchen and buried herself in the packing crates. But he hadn't spoken until now.

Tripp took a step toward her. "Can I give you a hand?"

She realized then that she'd been struggling with the armload of hot, scratchy blankets, trying to pull them from the deep crate.

"No."

She shot the word at him like a shell from a cannon, and he fell back to a defensive position behind a row of crates. Still, the opening salvo had been fired, shattering the cocoon of silence Kaitlin had retreated into.

"Why did you get all these plain, ugly blankets? I specifically asked you to get colorful ones. I put them on my list." Straw scattered across the floor as she moved, and she knew it was driving him crazy that she was making such a mess. But he said nothing about it.

"I got some of both." Tripp spoke evenly, with no emotion in his voice. "Men don't want colorful blankets."

"Oh, *men*..." Kaitlin spat the word as she plopped the stack of blankets on the floor beside her. "Women will do the shopping in this store. I told you that."

She heard the anger in her voice, but couldn't stop herself. She didn't want to. It felt good.

"And what is this?" Kaitlin lifted a humidor of cigars from the crate. She wrinkled her nose. "There will be no smoking in this store."

He just looked at her, then nodded. "Fine. If that's what you want."

"It certainly is what I want." She moved to the next crate and dumped an armful of straw on the floor. "More tools? What, for goodness sake, do you think is going to be built here in tiny little Porter that will require the dozens of tools you bought?"

"That's from my list," Tripp explained patiently. "My half of the inventory."

"Half?" Kaitlin flung her hand across the sea of opened crates. "It seems to me that your half is more than *half*."

"I'll show you the list. I divided it right down the middle."

She was certain he had. But he was being so darn calm and considerate that it irritated her to no end. In the space of only a few short hours she'd been confused, hurt, and humiliated. The only emotion left was anger.

"Then take your half of the inventory." Kaitlin grabbed an armload of blankets, matches and cigars and dumped them in front of the shelves on the other side of the room.

"Take all your *men's* inventory and keep it to yourself," she told him. "This is your side of the store."

He raised an eyebrow. "We're dividing up the store?"

She was being unreasonable and she knew it. Why didn't he yell back at her? If only he would, she could scream at him. Scream until her anger went away, or until she cried, which she desperately wanted to do, but couldn't. Her hurt was too great to let tears fall.

"Yes. This is your side." She pointed. "That's mine."

"All right. If that's what you want, Kaitlin."

She wished he hadn't said her name, with his voice so rich it stirred a well deep within her, bringing recollections of the times he'd breathed the word against her neck, hot with passion.

Kaitlin forced away the weakness that lightened her bones and pointed to the side of the store she'd just claimed for herself.

"I don't know what use those shelves will be to me," she said. "You made them so tall I can't even reach them."

Tripp looked at the shelves he'd built into the wall, then at her, and she saw his cheeks flush, just a little. "I guess I didn't think—"

"Of anyone but yourself?" she demanded.

He winced, and she knew she'd hurt him, as she had intended. But now that she'd done it, it hurt her too, just as much.

Kaitlin drew in a deep breath and turned to another crate. For weeks she'd looked forward to this minute, when she would unpack her merchandise, her future. Now, there was no joy in it.

A few minutes later Tripp spoke again. "I've got to go get Charlie from school now."

Kaitlin kept her back to him and didn't answer, just listened as his boots scuffed across the floor and the door closed. Then she sank into the packing straw and cried.

By the time Tripp returned with Charlie, Kaitlin had cried enough tears that she could continue with

her work, washed her face and plucked the straw from her hair. She had also changed her dress, the bright pink one no longer appealing, and slipped into a dark one.

He was longer than usual returning from school with Charlie. Obviously Tripp was no more anxious to get back to the store than she was to have him there.

Charlie didn't notice anything wrong as he ran between the packing boxes, played in the straw and chattered about his day at school. He didn't let Tripp get too far from his sight; he'd missed his papa too much for that.

Kaitlin kept herself on the other side of the store, tending to her half of the merchandise, but couldn't help overhearing them talk.

Couldn't help but be envious.

Couldn't help but wonder where the woman was and how she could bear not seeing the child she'd created.

Couldn't help but be jealous.

Tripp fixed supper, and Kaitlin let him with no offer of help. When the meal was ready, the three of them sat at the table. Charlie ate while Kaitlin and Tripp went to great lengths to avoid making eye contact. Kaitlin pushed the food around her plate and managed to get down a few bites. It was the first time she'd seen Tripp uninterested in food. Afterward, they went into the store again and resumed their work on opposite sides of the room.

Just as the sun was going down, Rafe and Julia smiled and waved through the front door, breaking the tedious silence.

"Would you just look at this?" Julia said as she walked inside. "So much merchandise! My goodness, I can't wait to shop here!"

"I hope everyone in town feels that way," Kaitlin said, placing a box of candles on the shelves.

"They will," Julia said. "Don't worry. They will."

Rafe turned in a circle, taking in the half-filled shelves. "Sure looks like more stuff when it's spread out like this."

"It's just like one of those fine stores back East. The kind you see in magazines," Julia said. "Why, I'll just bet our Mr. Dorsey will think he's in New York again when he sees this place. He'll be so tickled, he'll forget what he wanted to talk to you about, Kaitlin."

Tripp's brows furrowed. "Who's Dorsey?"

Rafe grunted. "Some uppity fella from back East."

"He's not uppity," Julia said. "He's a gentleman."

Tripp's gaze bored into Kaitlin. "What does he want to talk to you for?"

The intensity in his eyes startled Kaitlin and it took a moment to find her voice. "I—I don't know."

"It's my fault," Julia said. She looked at Kaitlin. "I'm sorry, but I let it slip that you wanted to go to New York. I know you didn't want anybody to know about your plans and get the idea that you weren't serious about the store. Mr. Dorsey promised he wouldn't tell. He's a patron of the arts, he says. He knows all about the theater."

"He does?" Kaitlin's spirits lifted a little.

"Oh, yes. He's very knowledgeable," Julia said. "Mr. Dorsey said—"

"I've got to go tend the stock," Tripp said. "Rafe, give me a hand, will you?"

He turned and left before Rafe could respond.

"Me too, Papa?" Charlie asked.

"Come on, cowboy," Rafe said, and shooed Charlie out of the store ahead of him.

"Isn't this exciting about Mr. Dorsey?" Julia asked. "He says he knows all about those big stage productions in New York. I'll bet he could get you a part in a play, Kaitlin. Isn't that wonderful?"

"Yes," she said, fumbling with the candles. "I suppose it is."

"You're going to talk to him, aren't you?"

Kaitlin watched the curtain at the back of the store that Tripp had just disappeared through and felt her heart squeeze and her chest tighten.

"Yes," she said. "I'm going to talk to Mr. Dorsey."

On the boardwalk behind the store, Tripp drew in several deep breaths of the cooling night air. He felt half sick and there were so many reasons for it that he didn't know where to start.

Those old feelings always affected him this way. The ones he'd tried hard to forget, the ones that had kicked him in the teeth today.

He deserved Kaitlin's anger. He couldn't blame her for yelling at him. Tripp dug the heels of his hands into his eyes and gave himself a shake. Problem was, he just didn't know what to do about it.

Charlie raced up and yanked on his trouser leg.

"Can I feed the horses, Papa? Please? Can I? Can I?"

Tripp smiled down at him and ruffled his hair. Seeing little Charlie always eased his worries.

"Sure, Charlie. You get the feed measured out."

"I know how, Papa. I already know how." Charlie bounced up and down.

"Okay, but don't give it to the horses until I get in there."

Charlie dashed across the dirt alley and into the stable, holding his tongue between his teeth.

Rafe came outside. The two of them stood there at the edge of the alley, taking in the dark and the quiet, looking up at the stars.

"Did you get caught up with your work today?" Tripp asked.

Rafe nodded. "Just about. Got right on it, early."

"I heard you were down there before first light," Tripp said. "Your brother mentioned it when he brought the wagon over this morning."

"My brother's..." Rafe grumbled under his breath. "Always giving me a hard time about...you know."

"Julia?"

He nodded. "She didn't want me to leave her this morning. Thought that just because I'd been gone a few days I should stay."

"And you didn't think you should?"

"Well, no. Not when I had all that work to catch up on." Rafe shook his head. "But did that stop her? No siree. She threw her leg over me and climbed right up there. Can you believe that?"

Tripp shuddered, his whole body quaking. He

didn't know how many more of these stories he could take.

"Said we could play Ride the Bull. Have you ever heard of such a thing in your life?" Rafe shook his head. "I swear, I like to never have gotten away from her."

Tripp squinted at him in the darkness. "You left? Before…?"

"Of course." Rafe slid his hands into his trouser pockets and rocked back on his heels for a moment, staring off down the street. Finally he turned to Tripp again.

"I was wondering if… Well, if Kaitlin said anything to you about what went on here while we were gone?"

Tripp shook himself; he wasn't quite recovered from the notion of the Ride the Bull game yet. "Like what?"

"You know, like, well…" Rafe looked straight at him. "Did she say anything about Drew Holden coming around?"

"Holden? The fella that runs the feed-and-grain store?" Tripp shook his head. "No, not a word."

Rafe pressed his lips together and grunted.

"Do you think something is going on?" Tripp asked.

"That Drew Holden is a fine businessman, I'll give him that," Rafe said. "Dresses in those fancy suits and slicks his hair down, even when he's working. He'd turn a woman's head."

"I've never seen Julia give the man more than a passing howdy at church," Tripp said. "And I've not seen him once over at her shop."

"He was courting her," Rafe said. "He'd have done her proud. A good-looking woman like Julia, kind and caring like she is, she deserves only the very best a man can offer. She deserves the kind of life Drew Holden could have given her."

"But she didn't marry him," Tripp said. "She married you."

"So don't you see why I have to work so hard? She chose me. I've got to prove I'm worthy of having her. I've got to give her the very best kind of life." Rafe shook his head. "I don't want her to be sorry she passed up that successful Drew Holden, and start thinking she got stuck with a nobody."

Rafe gazed off down the street. "No, indeed. I've got to make my business as successful as Drew Holden's. I've got to do everything I can to hold on to my Julia."

Kaitlin stood on her side of the store, sorting through bolts of fabric with Julia when Tripp came into the store again. She sensed him before she actually saw him, and it left her confused, wanting to run to him, wanting him to leave and never come back.

Charlie dashed around him, breaking the silence before either of them was forced to.

"I fed the horses, Miss Kaitlin. All by myself!"

She smiled at him; it was impossible not to. "Good for you, Charlie."

"Papa helped, too. But only this much." He held up his palms, an inch apart.

"Where's Rafe?" Julia asked.

Tripp nodded out back. "He said to tell you he

was going on home, and for you to take your time here and—''

''I have to go now.'' Julia pulled the bolts of fabric from Kaitlin's arms. ''I'll get started on this first thing in the morning.''

''But I wanted us to—''

''Don't worry,'' Julia said, backing toward the door. ''I'll sketch out a design and show it to you. The children will love them. It will be the best spring pageant ever. Good night.''

Julia left the store, taking with her Kaitlin's best reason to ignore Tripp. Now, with no one else to talk to, she turned back to the shelves she was stocking.

''What was that all about?'' Tripp asked.

She glanced at him. He wasn't close, but she could see the firm line around his mouth, the tightness in his jaw. The blue of his eyes that seemed to see right through her.

She looked away, straightening the tins she'd just shelved.

''It's for the spring pageant at Charlie's school. Miss Bailey said I could help. I'm staging a play with the children, and Julia is making the costumes.''

''Is that right?'' Anger crept into his voice.

Her chin went up a notch. ''Yes, that's right.''

Charlie hopped like a frog through the straw at Tripp's feet. ''Miss Kaitlin came to school, Papa. She's teaching us a song. She's gonna teach songs at church, too.''

Tripp's brows pulled together. ''You're what?''

She straightened her shoulders. ''I've been asked to take over the choir until the reverend's wife has her baby. Is there something wrong with that?''

Tripp caught Charlie's arm as he leaped past. "Bedtime, son. You go on up. I'll be there in a minute."

His bottom lip poked out. "But, Papa—"

"Go on, Charlie." Tripp laid his hand on the boy's shoulders and guided him toward the back of the store. When he disappeared through the curtain, Tripp turned to Kaitlin again.

"What the hell do you think you're doing?" he asked.

Tripp was angry and she didn't have the slightest idea why. But neither did she care. Or so she told herself.

"I don't see that it's any of your business, Mr. Callihan." Kaitlin turned back to her shelves.

"You'd damn well better know that it's my business."

Tripp stepped closer, hemming her against the shelves. She felt the heat from his body. Smelled him. And remembered.

Kaitlin's cheeks pinkened. "I'm simply getting involved in civic matters. What's so wrong with that?"

"I'll tell you what's wrong." He moved closer. "You've got no intention of staying here. You're acting like you care about this town, that you like it here. And you don't."

"Neither of us intend to stay. Have you forgotten that? I'm simply making the most of the time I'm here."

"No, you're not." Tripp glared down at her, his eyes burning. "You're setting up a lot of people to get hurt."

Anger sliced through her, then, like quicksilver,

changed to a dull ache in her stomach. Tears stung her eyes, but Kaitlin pressed her lips together, forbidding them to fall.

''People have already gotten hurt, Mr. Callihan.'' She stomped through the straw and out of the room.

Kaitlin fell across her bed in the darkness, pressing her fist into her mouth to muffle her tears. She knew of no one who'd gotten hurt since her arrival in Porter, except for herself.

She'd fallen in love with Tripp Callihan.

And he was married.

Chapter Fourteen

The place looked pretty darn good, Kaitlin decided, as she stepped back and admired the merchandise displayed on her side of the store. Bolts of colorful fabric, buttons, threads. Knitting needles and skeins of yard. Copper pots, blue-enameled dishes, pitchers—all of the items guaranteed to attract the women of Porter into her store and have them dig deep into their purses for the things they couldn't possibly live without. And there was much more in the crates, still waiting to be unpacked.

Kaitlin turned to the opposite side of the store. Tripp's side. His merchandise still lay on the floor and in crates, with only a few of the shelves stocked. Their grand opening was slated for tomorrow, and he wasn't ready.

She didn't know what he was doing this morning. She'd hardly slept at all last night, dozing off near dawn, and by the time she'd come from her room he was already gone, taking Charlie to school.

With a cup of coffee and a cold biscuit in hand Kaitlin had come into the store and set to work. Later

when she'd heard him return through the back door, he disappeared again into the room off the kitchen they used as a stockroom. He kept his tools in there, along with the wood left over from the renovations. For over an hour now all she'd heard was the grinding of a saw and pounding of a hammer.

Which was probably for the best.

Kaitlin turned her attention to her display shelves under the front window and set about arranging her most attractive merchandise: scented soaps, elegant writing paper, envelopes and fountain pens.

She admired her arrangement, and thought again that yes it was for the best that she and Tripp had seen nothing of each other this morning. She was confused and hurt, still. Her chest ached as if her heart had shriveled and was straining for every beat.

Yes, it was better that she hadn't seen Tripp this morning. Her head knew it. She only wished her heart would get the message.

"Kaitlin?"

She whirled at the sound of his voice, feeling a thud in her chest. Coming through the curtains from the kitchen, he looked tired, and she wondered if he'd slept any last night. She didn't ask. Instead, she steeled her feelings.

He approached her unsure, understandably so, of the reception he'd get. "I have something for you," he said.

He'd bought her a gift? As an apology, perhaps? An "I'm sorry" for lying to her? Her resolve softened, just a fraction.

He came closer and held it out. "For you to use."

A footstool. He'd spent the morning building her a footstool.

"I made it out of pine so it's plenty strong," Tripp said and rapped his knuckles against it. "And it's light so you can move it wherever you need it."

Kaitlin just looked at it. Had she really expected him to present her with flowers? Candy? An explanation of where his wife was?

He pushed the stool toward her. "It's so you can reach the top shelves."

She took it from him, this practical gift from a practical man.

Tripp cleared his throat. "It was…thoughtless…of me to make the shelves too high for you. I should have planned better."

She felt the grain of the wood under her fingers, and the edges he'd sanded smooth. He prized the work he'd done in the store and it was surely a difficult thing for him to admit he'd made a mistake. If nothing else, Tripp was a prideful man.

"If you don't want to use it I'll get the stuff off the top shelves you need," Tripp said quickly. "Anytime you need something, you just say so and I'll—"

"No, that's not necessary."

He looked at the stool, then at her. "Just promise me you'll be careful, with your skirt, and all, climbing up and down. I don't want you to get…hurt."

He'd already hurt her, and they both knew it.

Kaitlin drew in a brisk breath. "Well, thank you."

She dared to glance at him. They made eye contact, then both looked away.

"Are you going to start to work on your side of

the store?'' Kaitlin nodded across the room. ''To-morrow—''

''Good morning! Good morning!''

Imogene Douglas steamed through the front door bringing the morning sunshine and breeze with her. Her face shone bright with a big smile.

''Good morning,'' she said again, and planted her-self in the center of the store. She took in everything, then nodded so broadly her jowls flapped.

''Excellent,'' Mrs. Douglas declared. ''I'm so pleased—that is, *the mayor*—is so pleased to have your store here in Porter. It's just what we need.''

Kaitlin joined her in the center of the store, still clutching her footstool. ''I'm very excited about our grand opening.''

''Of course.'' Mrs. Douglas whipped out the newspaper tucked under her arm. ''Your advertise-ment is this morning's headline.''

With everything that had happened since yester-day Kaitlin had completely forgotten about the ad she'd placed in Porter's weekly newspaper. She leaned around Mrs. Douglas, looking at the copy.

''Excellent timing,'' Mrs. Douglas said. ''Plan-ning your grand opening a day after the newspaper is published. One thing about our newspaper, it's well read. We'll have people from all over coming to Porter. A boon for us all. Why, your grand open-ing is the only thing in town being talked about more than the arrival of our Mr. Dorsey.''

From the corner of her eye, Kaitlin saw Tripp tense.

''Have you learned anything about Mr. Dorsey?'' Kaitlin asked. ''Why he's here?''

Mrs. Douglas leaned closer and lowered her voice, though it still carried across the room. "He's a businessman from New York. A *wealthy* businessman. We're left to wonder exactly why he's here in Porter."

"He hasn't said?" she asked.

"Only that he's touring this part of the country." Mrs. Douglas nodded wisely. "He will reveal his intentions in due time, which, we can only hope, will benefit Porter."

"I can't imagine he'd be here for any other purpose," Kaitlin said.

"We shall see, Miss Jeffers." Mrs. Douglas refolded her newspaper, then stopped suddenly and rapped it against the footstool in Kaitlin's arms. "And where did this come from?"

Kaitlin glanced back at Tripp. "Mr. Callihan made it."

Mrs. Douglas squinted at it. "Excellent. Mr. Callihan, could you build another? For the mayor, you see."

Tripp shrugged. "Yes, ma'am."

"Porter needs a good carpenter. We need so many things, and would have had them if the railroad hadn't let us down." Mrs. Douglas's brows rose. "I understand, Mr. Callihan, that you have a friend working for the railroad."

"A relative, actually," he said. "My brother-in-law."

"Is he a man of influence?" Mrs. Douglas asked. "Could he do something to help Porter get the railroad here?"

Tripp shook his head. "No, ma'am. Russ is the

foreman of the track crew. He knows where the railroad is going once it's decided on, but that's about it.''

"Too bad." Mrs. Douglas pressed her lips together for a moment, then turned sharply and headed for the door. "Carry on with your work. I'll spread the word of your grand opening. And don't be surprised if our Mr. Dorsey isn't your first customer—right after the mayor, of course.''

Tripp moved alongside Kaitlin as Mrs. Douglas disappeared out the door. His jaw was set and his brows were furrowed. Kaitlin sensed that he wanted to say something about Mr. Dorsey.

Whatever it was, she didn't want to hear it. Kaitlin took her stool and retreated to her side of the store.

Townsfolk streamed past the store all day, gazing in the windows, craning their necks to catch a peek through the door. Kaitlin kept the shades down to discourage lookers; she didn't want people to glimpse her merchandise and spoil tomorrow's grand opening.

The drawn shades didn't discourage Mrs. Matilda Shaw, however. She walked right through the front door without so much as a knock.

Kaitlin paused behind the counter where she was shelving tins of coffee and tea. She'd met Mrs. Shaw at church, a sweet little gray-haired lady, Porter's newest resident.

"Good morning, Mrs. Shaw," Kaitlin said, coming out from behind the counter. "So nice to see you again.''

"Oh, yes, good morning, dear." Mrs. Shaw clutched her handbag and gazed around the store.

"I'm sorry, but we're not open until tomorrow," Kaitlin said.

Mrs. Shaw sighed wistfully. "Yes, dear. I know."

Kaitlin glanced at Tripp, busy stocking his shelves. "Is there something I can help you with, Mrs. Shaw?"

"No, dear." A breathy gasp slipped from her lips. "I just wanted to take a look at the place before…"

At a loss now, Kaitlin hadn't the foggiest idea what Mrs. Shaw wanted. Had the little lady been out in the sun too long?

"Before you moved in completely," Mrs. Shaw went on. "While there was a little bit of Everette still here."

"Everette?"

"Yes, dear. Everette Finch."

"Oh, yes, Mr. Finch," Kaitlin said, surprised to hear the store's former owner mentioned. She thought of the place as her own. Hers and Tripp's.

Mrs. Shaw touched Kaitlin's hand. "I've been to Porter several times over the years visiting my daughter. I met Everette. He was quite the gentleman, you know. Of course, I was married then."

Mrs. Shaw drew in a trembling little sigh. "And now here I am living in Porter. Funny how things work out, don't you think?"

Kaitlin glanced at Tripp, the weight of Mrs. Shaw's words sagging her shoulders a little. "Yes, very funny."

Mrs. Shaw straightened herself and looked around the store, as if seeing it for the first time. "Well,

everything here does look marvelous. I'll be back first thing in the morning.''

Kaitlin walked to the door with her. "That's wonderful, Mrs. Shaw. See you bright and early tomorrow.''

"What was that all about?" Tripp asked as she closed the door.

"Nothing." Kaitlin could hardly talk to him about Mrs. Shaw's lost love, when her own feelings on the subject threatened to explode into tears and angry words.

"I'm going next door." Kaitlin left.

She hoped when she returned that Tripp would have finished stocking the shelves on his side of the store. He'd worked on them all morning, meticulously arranging the merchandise, squaring off corners, lining up rows. He made a slow job of it, unnecessarily so to Kaitlin's way of thinking. When she returned an hour later, he was still at it.

Kaitlin ignored him. It was either that or scream at him to hurry up. Julia was with her, and they had their hands full, anyway.

Standing in the open doorway, Kaitlin grasped her end of the small settee she and Julia had dragged down the boardwalk from Julia's shop. It blocked the entrance, with Kaitlin inside pulling, and Julia outside pushing.

"All right," Kaitlin said, digging her fingers into the padded arm. "On three. One…two…"

"What are you doing?"

Tripp's voice boomed and he was beside Kaitlin

before the echo died. He caught her arm, pulling her away from the settee.

"What are you two doing?" he repeated. He looked back and forth between Kaitlin and Julia. "Are you out to hurt yourselves purposely? You can't be moving this heavy furniture around. What's the matter with you?"

Kaitlin opened her mouth, but before she could get a word out, Tripp grabbed hold of the settee arm.

"Stand back out of the way," he said to Julia, and with a tug, pulled it into the store. "Where do you want this thing?"

Kaitlin pointed to a spot near the front window where the shelves ended, on her side of the store. "There."

She could do nothing but keep out of the way as Tripp pulled the settee into position along the wall with little more than a flip of his wrist. He was so strong. She and Julia had worked themselves to the point of nearly perspiring, just inching the settee from next door.

"Is this where you want it?" Tripp asked. "Exactly?"

"That's fine," Kaitlin said.

He stepped in front of it, eyed its placement, then scooted it to the left a fraction of an inch. "There, that's better."

Satisfied, he stepped back, then looked at Kaitlin and scratched his head. "Why have we got a settee sitting in the middle of our store?"

"Because Kaitlin is a genius," Julia declared.

One of Tripp's eyebrows rose. "What's that got to do with the settee?"

"It's for the ladies," Kaitlin said. "Shopping is tiring. So is carrying packages. They'll have a nice spot to rest when they come here, so, naturally, they'll come here more often."

Tripp looked as if he wanted to say something more, but didn't. He just looked at her, then went back to his side of the store. Julia didn't notice the tension between them, had no reason to suspect anything was wrong. Kaitlin hadn't told her about Tripp's wife. She couldn't bring herself to say the words.

"I have to get back to the shop," Julia said. "Let me know if you need anything else."

"Thanks," Kaitlin said. "And don't forget, I'll pay you for the settee as soon as I can."

"It was just taking up space in the storage room." Julia wrinkled her nose. "Rafe's mother gave it to us."

While it certainly wasn't the most attractive settee she'd ever laid eyes on, it fit her purpose, and cheaply. After Julia left, Kaitlin gave it a thorough cleaning and spread out a small rug in front of it, one she'd brought from home that was of no use to her in her tiny bedroom off the kitchen.

Abandoning his side of the store, Tripp moved all the empty crates out back, and Kaitlin spent hours cleaning up the straw that littered the floor; she wished now that she hadn't made such a mess.

Night had fallen and Charlie was tucked into bed before they finished their work in the store. Tripp's shelves were finished, at long last, and standing at the counter Kaitlin had to admit they looked neater

than hers. Taking ten times longer to do the job, how could they not?

"I guess we're all set," Kaitlin said, and wiped her hands on her apron.

Tripp pulled a metal container from under the counter. "Not yet. We still have a few things to go over."

Kaitlin sighed. She was tired. The strain of the work and ache in her heart she'd carried since yesterday had taken its toll.

"Can't it wait?" she asked.

"We ought to cover this before tomorrow morning when folks show up."

"Fine." She moved to the counter where he'd spread out his ledger books, a tally pad, and the box.

Tripp slid the lantern closer, catching them both in its pool of yellow light.

"We need to fill out one of these for every item we sell," Tripp said, and pushed the tally pad toward her. "That way we can keep track of our inventory."

"Can't we just look at the shelves and see what's missing?" Kaitlin asked.

He frowned at her. "No, it won't work like that."

"Why not?"

"Look right here and you'll see." Tripp opened one of the ledgers.

Kaitlin moved closer and was captured by the energy he always gave off. It soaked into her. She curled her fingers into a fist and focused on the ledger he opened.

Tripp ran his big finger across the page heading. "I'll enter our sales in here at night."

"Is that how you want to spend your nights?"

Kaitlin asked. Immediately, she wished she'd phrased her question differently. She felt his gaze searing her cheek, and glanced up at him. Kaitlin gulped.

Tripp eased closer. Every other time they'd been this close, he'd kissed her. Wrapped his arms around her. Pressed his lips against her neck. Moaned her name. Run his hands...

Kaitlin stepped away from the counter. Away from him. Away from temptation.

"I mean, wouldn't you rather spend your evening with Charlie, rather than tracking our inventory?" she asked.

"I can do it after Charlie goes to bed. Not much to do after that, anyway."

The notion of all the things that could be done in that time spilled onto Kaitlin, flowing from Tripp like a river current.

Kaitlin touched her hand to her forehead. "What—what else did you want to talk about?"

Tripp stretched his neck, as if his collar had suddenly become too tight.

"When I got Charlie from school today I went by the bank and opened an account for us. I'll put our receipts in at the end of every day. I got us some change for our transactions tomorrow." He tapped his finger against the metal cash box. "It should be enough to—"

"I'm sure it's fine," Kaitlin said.

She didn't want to see the coins in the box, or the figures tallied in the neat columns in the ledger he kept. She didn't want to be standing this close to him, in the quiet store, in the lantern light.

The only thing Kaitlin knew for certain she wanted was for her heart to stop its aching.

Tripp put the ledgers beneath the counter, placing them just so on the shelves, then set the tally pad on top, squaring them up. Neat and orderly. Meticulous and careful.

How could he seem so unaffected when she was falling apart? Kaitlin bit her bottom lip, feeling the press of tears in her eyes again. How would she get through tomorrow—her grand opening—when her heart was so heavy, so filled with doubts? And questions.

She would ask him. In that moment, Kaitlin knew what had to be done. Just come out and demand that he explain to her about his wife.

He'd kissed her. Touched her. He'd gathered her in his arms. Carried her up the steps toward his bedroom. If that didn't entitle her to the answers to her questions, what did?

Kaitlin drew in a deep breath. The words formed in her mind, but along with them came troubling memories.

Yes, Tripp had kissed her, touched her, headed up to his bedroom with her in his arms. But had he done anything else? Had he said he loved her? Cared for her? Had he once indicated that he intended anything more than the moment they shared?

The answer to those questions, plain and simple, was no. He hadn't led her on, made promises, or offered anything. And that, Kaitlin realized, entitled her to nothing.

Besides, what if she did, somehow, dare to ask him about his wife? How would she bear it if he told

her how much he still loved the woman, cherished her, lived every breath for her?

Kaitlin had her dream. Tripp had his dream. Reaching their goals brought them together. Once they'd achieved those goals, they would go their separate ways. As business partners always did.

Tripp blew out the lantern on the counter leaving them in darkness, with only the light from the kitchen seeping into the store.

"I guess tomorrow is the big day," he said softly.

Kaitlin pulled her shoulders higher, summoning her strength...her pride.

"We'll know tomorrow if our partnership will pay off."

The heat of his body washed over her as he eased around her. He stood behind her for a moment, then moved to the kitchen door.

"Well, good night...partner," Tripp said.

He disappeared through the curtained doorway before she could answer, leaving Kaitlin alone in the quiet store.

The shelves were filled to overflowing. The new sign was up. The newspaper ad had run. The public was waiting.

Tomorrow morning she would be on her way to earning the money she needed. To going to New York. To having her dream. It was all spread out before her.

Kaitlin turned away and watched the kitchen door curtain swaying in the night, and listened to Tripp's footsteps disappearing up the stairs.

Chapter Fifteen

Grand opening.

Up and dressed early, Kaitlin buzzed through the kitchen, helping with breakfast and getting Charlie ready for school.

"Can I be in the store today, Miss Kaitlin?" Charlie asked, as Tripp helped him with his jacket. "Can I?"

"Of course, Charlie." Kaitlin knelt in front of him and the child threw his arms around her neck and smashed a kiss against her cheek, the part of their morning ritual that never failed to bring a smile to her heart.

"I'll do my school lessons really fast today, so I can come home quick." Charlie looked up at Tripp with big eyes. "Can I, Papa?"

He smoothed a lock of the child's hair into place. "You just mind Miss Bailey."

"I will, Papa. I promise."

"Goodbye, Charlie." Kaitlin handed him his reader and the lunch pail Tripp had packed, and the two of them went out the back door.

Kaitlin flew around the kitchen, washing up the last of the breakfast dishes, wiping down the sideboard. She dashed into her room and turned in front of the big oval mirror near her bed.

While it was a bit early in the season for a yellow dress, she'd selected this one today to project a bright, cheerful image. And it wasn't too much of a stretch, even with the heartache she still felt over Tripp. Today was her grand opening and she was excited.

Kaitlin checked her hair in the mirror, practiced her shopkeepers's smile—gracious and welcoming— and hurried into the store.

Everything looked wonderful. The shelves were overflowing. The merchandise was bright and new.

Despite the personal feelings she had for Tripp, the two of them had done wonders with the store. And that much, she could certainly be happy about.

Tripp returned through the back door a few minutes later. "There're people outside already," he said.

"Isn't this exciting?" Kaitlin asked. She'd heard their murmured voices and their footsteps on the boardwalk.

He stopped beside her. "We did it, huh?"

"Yes, we did."

"To tell you the truth, I didn't think it would happen."

She nodded. "I know. But here we are."

Tripp eased closer, gazing into her eyes. "I guess this means you're on your way to New York now."

She looked up at him. "And you're on your way back to your farm."

"I suppose so." He drew in a breath. "That's what we both want, isn't it? I mean, that's why we started this whole thing. Right?"

"Yes, that's how it began."

Tripp gazed at her for a moment, then squared his shoulders. "I guess we'd better open for business before all these folks scratch down the door I took so much time to paint."

He presented her with the brass key. "Would you like to have the honor?"

Kaitlin smiled. "Yes, I would."

With a flourish, Kaitlin unlocked the door and two dozen townspeople streamed inside. The store filled quickly as they fanned out, touching, pointing, chatting.

Kaitlin stood by the door, welcoming each of them, thanking them for coming, and when they were all inside she stood there a moment longer, pride filling her heart. She'd done it. She'd turned an empty, run-down shell into a beautiful business. She'd done it...with Tripp.

She found him in the crowd, on his side of the store, talking with several men about the tools displayed on his shelves. Tripp was impossible to miss, a head taller than everyone else. And handsomer, too.

Mrs. Imogene Douglas planted herself in front of Kaitlin.

"Quite a turnout," she said. "I knew Porter would welcome a store like this."

Kaitlin glanced at her customers. "You were exactly right, Mrs. Douglas."

She latched on to Kaitlin's elbow. "Direct me

through your merchandise, Miss Jeffers. The mayor wants the honor of making your very first purchase."

"My pleasure, Mrs. Douglas."

The store stayed packed with people all morning, sometimes so full Kaitlin could hardly make her way to the counter to take their money. The crowd buzzed noisily, talking, laughing, complimenting her on the quality of her merchandise.

She passed Tripp dozens of times, but hardly had the chance to talk, they were both so busy. Ladies stopped her and asked about certain items, and Kaitlin spent much of her time helping them make purchases, pointing out other items, steering them around the store.

Some of them were friends she'd met at church and at Charlie's school. Others she'd never laid eyes on before. But all of them bought something, so Kaitlin smiled, pointed, talked, and thanked in the confusion.

Around midmorning, Alister Dorsey sauntered into the store. He was the image of a wealthy Easterner wearing a fine suit and a confident air. She met him at the display of black kettles.

"Good morning. Is there anything I could help you find?" she asked.

He swept his hat from his head and bowed ever so slightly. "Good morning. May I be so bold as to introduce myself? Alister Dorsey, at your service."

A fine-looking man he was. Tall and dark-haired with a thin mustache. Kaitlin wasn't surprised he'd been talked about all over town.

"I'm so pleased you could stop by, Mr. Dorsey."

He settled his hat on his head and his gaze on her. "And may I also be so bold as to assume you are the Miss Kaitlin Jeffers I've heard so much about?"

Kaitlin's cheeks flushed. "Yes, Mr. Dorsey. That's correct."

"I would like to compliment you on your success." Alister peered around the room, nodding thoughtfully. "From what I understand you've turned a sow's ear into a silk purse almost single-handedly."

"I had help."

"Ah, yes. Your business partner." Alister eased closer, testing the limit of what was proper. "I hope you'll understand, Miss Jeffers, when I say that it is *your* accomplishments that pique my interest."

Kaitlin flushed again and cleared her throat. "Shall I show you around the store?"

"No, thank you, Miss Jeffers." Alister backed away, smiling confidently. "I'll have a look around myself."

Kaitlin turned away and stared straight into Tripp's wide chest.

"What did he want?" he asked.

"That was Mr.—"

"I know who he was. What did he want?"

Irritated slightly, Kaitlin pursed her lips. "The same as everybody else that's here today."

"I doubt that," Tripp said, staring after Dorsey.

June Hutchinson, the sheriff's wife, inserted herself between Tripp and Kaitlin.

"Seems mighty peculiar to me, too," she said, "if you ask me."

Kaitlin realized she'd be eavesdroping on their conversation.

"That Eastern fella showing up here in Porter, just out of the blue like that," Mrs. Hutchinson said. "Makes you wonder why he's here."

"Mrs. Douglas seemed quite pleased to have him in Porter," Kaitlin said. "And I'm very happy he's shopping here today."

Mrs. Hutchinson huffed and gave a knowing nod toward Tripp. "Seems mighty strange to me," she said, then blended into the crowd again.

The hectic pace continued all day, shoppers jamming the store, Kaitlin smiling, pointing, recommending. Reverend Beckman came by and made a modest purchase and reminded her that tonight was choir practice while his wife rested on the settee near the front window. Kaitlin kept smiling and assured him she'd be there promptly after supper, her smile so well in place that she gave no indication she'd forgotten it completely.

The settee proved a popular spot, and much talked about. Mrs. Douglas held court there for quite some time before moving on. Mrs. Shaw took a turn, simply because she needed the rest. Other women tried it out, just for the novelty of the idea.

Kaitlin nearly wore the finish off her new footstool. Up and down she climbed, again and again. She didn't know how she would have managed if Tripp hadn't built it for her.

Near midafternoon Julia stopped by and offered to pick up Charlie from school.

"You're so busy here I was afraid Tripp couldn't get away," she said.

Kaitlin touched her hand to her forehead, relaxing her shopkeeper's stance for a moment.

"Don't you need to be at your own shop?" she asked.

Julia laughed softly. "Don't be silly. All the other stores in town may as well be closed today. Everyone in Porter is here."

Kaitlin smiled proudly. "The Emporium does seem to be off to a good start."

"I'll say," Julia agreed. "You and Tripp make excellent business partners."

Kaitlin caught a glimpse of him at that moment tallying up an order, listening to the customer across the counter from him. She'd seen him do that dozens of times, work and pay attention to Charlie at the same time. He made it look easy, like so many of the other things he did.

At the close of business, Kaitlin locked the door as eagerly as she'd unlocked it this morning. She pulled down the shade and fell against it, blowing out a heavy breath.

The store had been jammed all day, the crowd coming and going steadily, not letting up once. She'd wanted a successful grand opening, and it was grand, all right.

Things had been awkward between her and Tripp these past few days. But today he'd hardly been out of her sight, helping customers, working alongside her. They'd been a team. Partners.

But for all his closeness he may as well have been on the other side of the country. He was untouchable.

Kaitlin wondered if everyone else ached from seeing their partner across their place of business.

The clink of coins caught her attention and brought her to the back counter where Tripp was busy with his cash box, tally pads, and ledgers. The sound of money energized her.

Kaitlin bounced on her toes across the counter from him.

"Did we make a fortune? Are we rich? Are the two of us the most prosperous storekeepers in history?" she asked.

He glanced up from his work, and a little grin pulled at his lips. "We're the busiest, that's for damn sure."

"Wasn't that a wonderful crowd? I think everyone within fifty miles of Porter was here today."

"I hope there's somebody left to come back tomorrow."

"There will be." Kaitlin nodded confidently. "So, how much money did we make? It must have been lots and lots."

"We did pretty good," Tripp said, writing another figure into his ledger. "But don't get too excited yet. We've got a long way to go."

Kaitlin peered into the cash box. "There's a small fortune in there."

"Yeah, but all this merchandise cost a big fortune," Tripp said, and waved his hand around the store.

Kaitlin tapped her finger against her lips. "I was thinking today about all sorts of other merchandise we can get. People asked for lots of things we didn't have. So, I was thinking that if we—"

"Where are your tally sheets?" Tripp frowned as he sorted through the slips of paper. He looked up at her and his scowl deepened. "There's only a couple here in your handwriting. Where are the others?"

Kaitlin rolled her eyes. "You didn't really think I was going to take the time to fill out those things, did you?"

"But—I—" Tripp sighed resolutely. "Yeah, what the hell was I thinking?"

"Papa!"

Charlie burst through the kitchen door and launched himself into Tripp's arms. To Kaitlin's surprise Tripp had agreed to let Julia pick up the boy from school, and had allowed him to stay with her for the afternoon. Hearing promises of oatmeal cookies, the store had immediately lost its appeal for Charlie.

Tripp held him against his chest and kissed the top of his head. "Were you a good boy for Miss Julia?"

"Of course he was," Julia said as she came in from the kitchen. "We had quite an afternoon. I might just keep him for myself one of these days."

Charlie leaned across the counter and threw his arms around Kaitlin, with Tripp still holding on to him.

"We misseded you at school today, Miss Kaitlin," he said. "How come you didn't come and teach us some more songs?"

"Oh, I missed you too, Charlie," Kaitlin said, hugging him fiercely. "I explained to Miss Bailey I couldn't be there today. But I'll be back soon."

"You promise?"

"I promise."

Tripp pulled Charlie into his arms again, and put the tally sheets and ledger books under the counter. He tucked the cash box under his other arm.

"I'll get this money over to the bank, then we can eat. Hungry?" he asked.

"I'm hungrier than a bear *this* big, Papa." Charlie spread his arms wide.

"I want you all to eat with Rafe and me tonight," Julia said. "It's been such a busy day, and Kaitlin has to leave in a bit."

Tripp looked at Kaitlin. "Where are you going?"

Kaitlin stifled a gasp. She'd forgotten choir practice again. How many times could she forget her Christian duties before the Lord held it against her?

"To church for choir practice," Kaitlin said.

"What about the store?" Tripp asked. "We need to restock tonight and clean up."

"Will you teach me the song tonight?" Charlie asked. "Will you, Miss Kaitlin?"

"I won't be gone long," Kaitlin promised. "And yes, Charlie, I'll teach you the new song as soon as I get home."

She was anxious to get back to the store, get it prepared for tomorrow's business. Anxious to spend time with Charlie. And anxious to see her partner?

Yes. Though she wished she weren't.

Reverend Beckman was at the church when Kaitlin arrived, busy lighting lanterns and candles while he waited for the other members of the choir to show up. He thanked her six times for taking over the choir, as he went about his chores, and six times

Kaitlin assured him she was glad to help out. And she was, really.

Mrs. Autry proved sure-fingered at the piano keyboard, taking over for Lorna Beckman with ease. The choir seemed content to have Kaitlin there; like many organizations everybody wanted to be part of it, but nobody wanted to be in charge.

Kaitlin led the choir through the hymns the reverend had requested for Sunday. For a choir so small, the eight singers had big voices. She sang along too, unable not to.

Halfway through practice Alister Dorsey walked in. Talking with the choir, Kaitlin's back was turned and she didn't see him. The choir members did, and fell silent.

She saw him standing in the aisle, holding his hat, and was more than a little surprised at seeing him there. Hardly the sort of pastime for a wealthy Eastern gentleman.

"Good evening, Mr. Dorsey," she called from the choir loft behind the pulpit.

"Good evening," he said, and waved his hand, taking in the entire choir. "I don't mean to intrude, but I was passing by and heard your singing. Do you mind if I sit for a while and listen?"

Kaitlin glanced at the other choir members. "You're welcome to stay, Mr. Dorsey, but please keep in mind we're rehearsing, not performing."

He smiled easily. "I enjoy music, Miss Jeffers, at any stage."

They ran through several more songs and all agreed they sounded just fine. The choir turned their

hymn books over to Kaitlin as they bid her good-night and left the church.

"It's a good group. Very uplifting," Alister said.

Kaitlin smiled down at him seated in his pew. "Thank you. I've just taken over the choir."

Reverend Beckman came out of his office sliding his arms into his coat. "All finished?"

Kaitlin stacked the hymnals on the shelf under the pulpit. "I'm on my way out right now, Reverend."

"I'll walk you home, Miss Jeffers," the reverend said.

"I'd like to see to that myself." Alister Dorsey rose from the pew. "If Miss Jeffers doesn't mind."

The reverend looked at Alister, then at Kaitlin. "Miss Jeffers?"

She supposed it couldn't do any harm, except perhaps to set a few tongues wagging. But if they weren't gossiping about her living in the same home as Tripp Callihan, what could they say about her walking the public street with Alister Dorsey?

"Very well, Mr. Dorsey. If you'd like."

Evening shadows stretched across the churchyard as Kaitlin bid good-night to Reverend Beckman and glanced up at Alister Dorsey beside her. They strolled in silence for a few moments before Kaitlin spoke.

"Are you enjoying your visit here in Porter?" she asked.

"Yes, very much."

"I suppose you know everyone in town is wondering why you're here, Mr. Dorsey."

He chuckled softly. "No one has said a thing to me."

"Well, believe me. They're all wondering," Kaitlin said.

"I suppose they are." Alister stopped suddenly and touched Kaitlin's arm, turned her to face him. "What do you suppose the good folk of Porter will say when they hear I've come here for you?"

Chapter Sixteen

"Come for me?" Kaitlin pulled out of his grip. "What do you mean?"

Alister smiled. "No need to get upset, Miss Jeffers. I've come for people *like* you, not necessarily you personally."

"You'll have to explain your meaning, Mr. Dorsey."

"I'm from New York, as I'm sure you've heard by now, and I'm involved in many worthwhile causes."

"A patron of the arts, I believe I heard," Kaitlin said.

"Yes, and you're interested in a career on the New York stage. Am I right, Miss Jeffers?"

She hesitated. It was disconcerting that this stranger knew about her...about her dream.

"Yes, that's true," Kaitlin said.

"Well, I'm here to offer you that opportunity."

Kaitlin's breath caught. "You're not serious."

"Indeed I am," he said with an easy smile. "I'm offering you passage to New York. I can arrange for

your living accommodations, auditions, voice classes. Whatever you might need to launch your career.''

Kaitlin could only stare at him. "But you don't even know if I have any talent."

"On the contrary, Miss Jeffers. A man would have to be blind not to notice your pleasing looks. Classic looks, perfect for the stage. You could assume many roles. And I heard you just now singing in the church. You are quite talented, I assure you.''

Her head spun. This couldn't really be true? Was this man standing before her right now, offering her the dream of a lifetime?

"But why?" she asked. "Why would you do this?"

He shrugged. "I love the theater. It needs fresh faces and new talent to keep it alive. I believe you could do that, Miss Jeffers."

"Forgive me, Mr. Dorsey, but it's difficult to think you would give such an opportunity to someone you don't even know."

"I do this sort of thing quite often," Alister replied. "In my travels I often see people from all walks of life who dream of performing. I help them."

It couldn't be that easy. Kaitlin's chin went up a notch. "And what do you get in return, Mr. Dorsey?"

A little grin tugged at his lips. "The satisfaction that I've made someone's dream come true."

"And that's all?"

Alister shrugged. "Mr. Callihan is your business partner, isn't he? Do you suspect him of anything

underhanded, or of holding intentions that are less than honorable?''

''No, of course not.'' She'd never even considered the idea. With Tripp, it was unthinkable.

''Then why distrust me? I'm simply offering a helping hand, as one theater lover to another.''

The prospect of a benign benefactor wasn't far-fetched. It happened frequently, and not just in the theater.

''But I can't leave Porter,'' Kaitlin said. ''I have commitments here, and a business to run.''

''Don't worry, Miss Jeffers. I'm sure something can be worked out.''

''But—''

''Think it over, Miss Jeffers. I'll be leaving for New York soon and I'll need your answer by then, if you're coming with me.''

''Coming with you?''

''It's getting quite late. Perhaps we should move along.'' Alister grinned. ''I wouldn't want the town to get the wrong idea about us.''

It was dark now and they'd been standing here for quite some time. Kaitlin accepted his arm and they walked toward town, her head spinning.

When they reached the back entrance of the store, Kaitlin hesitated before opening the door. She turned to Alister, his features barely distinguishable in the darkness.

''Your offer is—well, it's breathtaking,'' she said. ''It's what I've wanted, what I've dreamed of all my life. My mother was an actress, you know. She performed on the New York stage and told the most wonderful stories.''

"Ah, I should have known," Alister said, smiling. "Talent and beauty run in your family."

Kaitlin drew in a deep breath to keep from blushing. "But I do have a commitment here in Porter, Mr. Dorsey. A commitment to run the store with Mr. Callihan. At least until we've made a substantial profit. You see, Mr. Callihan has a dream of his own to follow. I can't just walk away."

Alister lifted a shoulder. "Maybe I can solve that problem, too."

"What do you mean?"

"It's quite simple, Miss Jeffers," Alister said. "I'll buy your store."

"You want to buy the store? Just like that?" Tripp eyed Alister Dorsey standing across the kitchen table from him.

"Precisely," Alister said. "And I'm prepared to make you an adequate offer. Enough to cover your expenses and have a tidy profit for yourselves."

Tripp glanced at Kaitlin standing at his elbow. Her eyes were round and she looked slightly breathless.

His first inclination was to tell the Easterner that the store wasn't for sale. He didn't like Alister Dorsey, and for no real reason that he could pin down. Just didn't like the look of the man.

"Miss Jeffers has told me that the both of you have future plans and never intended to keep the store," Alister said.

Anger rippled through Tripp that Kaitlin was telling their personal plans to this stranger.

"I'm simply offering you the opportunity to re-

alize those plans now, rather than waiting," Alister said.

"And what are you going to do with a store way out here in Porter?" Tripp asked.

"I have business ventures all over the country. All over the world, actually. Porter is a comfortable little town, and a store here would no doubt offer a small profit, enough to make the venture worthwhile." Alister Dorsey smiled down at Kaitlin. "But, more importantly, it would free the two of you to follow your dreams."

Tripp glanced down at Kaitlin again, his chest tightening. He didn't like this—any of it. Not the idea of selling out to Dorsey, and certainly not the look on Kaitlin's face.

"Think it over," Alister said. "I'll be in town a while longer. Good night."

Alister Dorsey smiled, bowed slightly to Kaitlin, and left the kitchen.

The air in the room went with him, replaced by a palpable tension. A heavy silence draped Tripp and Kaitlin, holding them in place, silencing them.

Tripp couldn't look at her. He couldn't seem to find any words to speak. The sale of the store meant they would go their separate ways. Forever.

His thoughts scattered in a hundred directions. He wouldn't know what he would say, even if he found his tongue. Now they faced another problem, when the last one hadn't even been handled yet.

He'd been going on his gut for the past few days. Just getting by. Not thinking much. He knew that, sooner or later, he'd have to talk to Kaitlin and explain about Emily. It made his heart ache to think

about his wife. Tripp wasn't sure how he'd face Kaitlin with the truth.

He should never have held her, never have kissed her. And certainly he shouldn't have carried her upstairs to his room. Even though they hadn't made it, his intentions were crystal clear.

It wasn't right to do that to Kaitlin. Tripp gazed at her now and his chest hurt. He shouldn't have put himself—and Kaitlin—through it.

"Well, what do you think?" Kaitlin asked.

Lord, Kaitlin was a pretty woman. On the inside and out. A pure heart, a clear mind, a sweet soul. Even though she did tend to get her dander up pretty easily, and she made him a little crazy at times, that was the spirit in her that he...loved.

Tripp gulped suddenly at his own thought. Good God, he did love her.

"Tripp?" Kaitlin leaned closer. "What do you think?"

He splayed his hand across his chest, feeling it tighten, his heart swell. Yes, he was in love with Kaitlin Jeffers.

"About the store?" Kaitlin prompted, her brows raised. "About Mr. Dorsey's offer?"

"I, uh, I—" When had it happened? When had he fallen in love with her? Tripp didn't know, exactly. It had sneaked up on him and surprised him. Made his heart soar. Scared him.

"Papa?" Charlie came down the steps dressed in his nightshirt. "You saided you would tell me a story."

Tripp lifted him into his arms, grateful for the distraction. "I was on my way up."

Charlie rubbed his fists in his eyes and yawned. "Can Miss Kaitlin tuck me in, Papa. Please? She promised to teach me a song tonight. She promised."

Kaitlin smiled at the child and touched his hair. "I'd love to tuck you in, Charlie, if it's okay with your Papa."

Tripp hesitated a moment, then nodded. He needed some time to think.

He kissed Charlie on the cheek and set him down. "Not too late, now. You've got school in the morning."

Kaitlin took Charlie's hand and led him up the stairs while Tripp stood there in the kitchen, watching. Watching and aching. Wishing.

Wishing for a lot of things. None of which it seemed he could have.

Singing floated down from the bedroom. Kaitlin's sweet voice. He'd heard her sing as she worked getting the store ready to open. She'd hum in the morning sometimes before she came out for breakfast. Tripp had learned that when Kaitlin sang, she was happy.

What other secrets did she hold that he hadn't unlocked yet? Secrets that now, he might never learn.

Tripp went outside on the boardwalk and drew in several quick breaths. The night air was cool and crisp. He glanced next door to the millinery shop. No lanterns burned, but no bedsprings squeaked. Rafe was surely sound asleep; he doubted Julia was.

The night air did nothing to clear his head. After a while he went back inside. Kaitlin's singing had stopped and a moment later she came downstairs.

"Charlie's asleep," she said. "He's very excited

about the spring pageant. I'm glad you let him go to school, Tripp. He loves it.''

Tripp nodded. He and Charlie both had eased into life in Porter, thanks in part, to Kaitlin.

"How are you doing on the stage for the pageant?" Kaitlin asked.

"It's coming along." He'd been working on it in the evenings in the stockroom.

"I'd like the children to practice on it before Saturday's pageant.''

Tripp nodded. "I'll bring it down to the school on Friday. Will that do?"

"Perfect." Kaitlin pressed her lips together and looked up at him. "I think we should discuss Mr. Dorsey's offer.''

Tripp sighed heavily and sat down at the kitchen table. Kaitlin took a chair across from him.

"What do you think?" she asked.

Tripp always found it tough to think about much of anything when Kaitlin was this close, especially when she smelled so good. It was even more difficult tonight, given that he'd realized he loved her, but couldn't do one damn thing about it.

"Mr. Dorsey made a generous offer," Kaitlin said. "We can get back our expenses, get rid of the store, and make a profit for ourselves. That's what we entered into this partnership for, wasn't it?"

Yes, that's how it had started, but things had changed. Tripp wished he could tell her how much they'd changed.

"I take it you're in favor of making the sale?" he asked.

"We both wanted our dreams," Kaitlin said

softly. "You still want your farm, don't you? For you and Charlie?"

"Yeah, I want to make a home for Charlie and me." Tripp pulled on his neck. "And I guess you still want to go off to New York?"

"I've dreamed about it for so long, Tripp." Her eyes took on a faraway look. "Since I was a child my mother told me about performing on the stage. We'd put on little plays together, just Mama and me. We'd make costumes and props, we'd sing. Papa was our audience. And after Mama died, Papa and I would talk for hours about those moments. They were so special to us."

Tripp's heart ached. He didn't want her to go, but he couldn't refuse to grant her dream. She wanted to be like her mama. What was wrong with that?

Harvey Stutz had already stolen it from her once. He couldn't do the same.

Besides, what did he have to replace it with? His promise that he loved her wouldn't be enough to hold her if she really wanted to go. He already knew that. He'd learned it the hard way, the painful way.

Tripp sat back in his chair. "So I guess you want to sell?"

For a moment, she looked as if she didn't, then she nodded. "If I miss this opportunity, I might not get another. Especially with Mr. Dorsey sponsoring me. Once we get to New York he'll open doors that I—"

Tripp shot to his feet. *"What?"*

Stunned, Kaitlin looked up at him. "Didn't I tell you? Mr. Dorsey has offered to let me travel to New York with him."

Hot anger surged through him. "You're going away with that—that bastard?"

"Mr. Dorsey is a gentleman," Kaitlin insisted. "He only wants to help."

"Help himself to your—" Tripp paced across the room, then swung back to look at her. "You don't know one goddamn thing about Dorsey. How can you even consider running off with him?"

"I'm not 'running off.' It's a business arrangement."

"Like hell!"

Her chin went up. "I didn't know anything about you before we moved in together to open the store. I didn't think the worst of you, why should I think the worst of him?"

Tripp plowed both hands through his hair. She should have thought the worst of him, because he sure as hell was thinking those thoughts himself.

Tripp glared down at her. "He'll expect you to repay him, Kaitlin. And not with cash."

Her cheeks flushed. "I believe his intentions are honorable. And besides, if Mr. Dorsey should prove otherwise, I'll have money of my own. I can leave. I don't have to depend on him."

"Forget it, Kaitlin. I'm not selling. Not like this."

Kaitlin came to her feet. "But we had an agreement. We'd keep the store until we made back what we'd lost to Harvey Stutz. Alister Dorsey is simply offering a shortcut to our goal."

Tripp shook his head. "No."

"We had a deal!"

"No! I won't let you go! Not like that!"

"Fine! Then give me a reason to stay!"

Tripp glared at her angry face, her pink cheeks, and the fight went out of him. Oh, God, he wanted to take her in his arms, kiss the breath out of her, carry her to bed and show her how much he wanted her to stay. How much he wanted her. How much he loved her.

Emily's face flashed before his eyes. He couldn't say the words. The memories were too strong. They hurt too badly.

Silence crackled in the kitchen. Kaitlin faced him in the lantern light, her eyes flashing, her back rigid.

She deserved to know. She was waiting to hear. Still, Tripp couldn't tell her.

She crumbled then, her anger, her defiance. Kaitlin gathered her skirt, holding herself erect with some effort.

"Fine, then," she said. "I'll tell Mr. Dorsey we agree to the sale. And I'll leave with him next week."

She headed for her bedroom. Kaitlin didn't think she'd ever reach the door. The kitchen that had always seemed so tiny was suddenly miles long, her steps slowed by her aching heart, dragging her downward.

Tears burned her eyes, but she refused to cry here in front of Tripp. She didn't want him to know that he'd hurt her again, this last time.

If only he'd told her he wanted her to stay, for himself, for the two of them, rather than because of his fears about Alister Dorsey. If he'd just given her some hint, some small sign that he cared. Some explanation of what had happened. Some hope of what might be.

Her bedroom door drew nearer. New York drew nearer. Yet Tripp was moving farther away, Charlie disappearing, Porter gone. If only he would—

"Kaitlin..."

Tripp called her name, his voice so hoarse she hardly recognized it. She turned. He stood in the floor, anguish etched in the drawn lines of his face, clutching his chest as if he were in physical pain. He drew in a deep, ragged breath.

"She...left me."

Chapter Seventeen

Kaitlin went to him, but he backed away. She stopped, keeping the distance he seemed to want, seemed to need.

"Your wife?" she asked softly.

Tripp swallowed hard and nodded. "Emily. She...she left me."

Kaitlin's own heart hurt seeing him in such pain. It was as if he could hardly breathe. She wanted to help him, make things easier, but didn't know how.

"She was sort of wild when I married her, full of life and high spirits. And I fell crazy in love with her. Who wouldn't love that kind of spirit?" Tripp scrubbed his palms over his face and drew in another ragged breath. "It didn't take long for her to regret that she'd married me. I took her to my pa's farm when he got sick. She hated it. Missed town. Missed her friends. Missed having fun."

"You had Charlie by then?"

Tripp nodded. "I thought having a baby would settle her down. It didn't. Just made things worse. I

came home from working the fields one day and she...she was gone.''

"She just left? Without a word?''

Tripp rubbed his forehead. "She ran off with Harvey Stutz.''

Kaitlin winced. "Oh, Tripp...'' He'd never said exactly what Stutz had taken from him, besides the locket. Now she understood why.

"Stutz had come around the place a few times, claiming to be a drummer,'' Tripp said. "The two of them took what money I had, the locket that belonged to my folks, and left me with Charlie, a sick father and a farm to run.''

"And you never heard from her?''

Tripp shook his head. "The years piled up with no word. After my pa passed on, I left the farm. Charlie and I just moved around.''

"Thinking that you'd find her?''

"I don't know...maybe,'' Tripp said. "It was just easier to let people think she was dead. I was too hurt, too...embarrassed...to tell folks what had really happened.''

"What about her family?'' Kaitlin asked.

"They took it pretty much in stride. Seems they expected something like that might happen,'' Tripp said. "I stayed in touch with them for a time, just in case. Russ, her brother, worked for the railroad so he traveled. He kept an eye out for her, too.''

"You never found her, did you?''

"No, not a sign. Not until I saw the notice in the newspaper that Stutz was dead. I answered the ad, thinking maybe she was with him, but—''

"But you saw me instead,'' Kaitlin realized.

"You must have been disappointed seeing me there in the sheriff's office."

Her words seemed to galvanize him. Tripp straightened and shook his head fiercely. "No, Kaitlin, I was never sorry I found you there instead of her."

Joy touched her heart, swelled it a bit. Kaitlin went to him, gazing up into his deep-blue eyes. "Why are you telling me this, Tripp?"

"Because..." He seemed lost again as a new sadness overcame him. "Because you deserve to know."

Kaitlin eased her way through the crowded store with the two spools of thread and half dozen buttons she'd just helped Elsa Donnley select. Their second day of business was only slightly slower than their first.

At the counter she ignored the tally pads and gave Elsa her total.

"Thanks so much, Elsa," Kaitlin said, her shopkeeper's smile in place. "Come back soon."

"Oh, I will. I certainly will."

Kaitlin waded into the crowd again, helping other shoppers, though her heart wasn't really in it. All she'd thought of since last night was Tripp. And his wife, of course. A few more things made sense to her, at least.

The woman had left him, deserted him without a word. No wonder Tripp had been reluctant to go into business with her. He'd doubted her commitment to their partnership, and with good cause. Tripp had been hurt. Badly hurt. And Kaitlin was sure it had

hurt him just as much last night to admit what his wife had done to him. Tripp was a prideful man.

Yet, of all the things he'd said, all the things he'd told her, the one issue he hadn't addressed was the most important one of all: did he still love Emily?

Kaitlin could ask him. He'd broached the subject himself and told her things she was certain he'd never told anyone before. He'd opened the door, so surely she could ask him the question that burned in her heart.

The thought that his answer might be yes, kept the question locked deep inside Kaitlin.

That, and the fact that she didn't know how she'd respond if he said no, he didn't love Emily any longer.

Of course she could confess her love to him and hopefully, Tripp would say he loved her, too. But then what?

They still had separate dreams. Tripp wanted his farm. Kaitlin wanted the stage. How could they possibly reconcile the two?

Mrs. Shaw came into the store again and Kaitlin helped her select a new blanket. The older lady rested on the settee for a time, admiring the elegant stationery displayed in the window, and chatted about this and that. Kaitlin thought it more likely Mrs. Shaw was lonely, rather than that she needed another blanket.

Sometime later Clara Hadley came into the store along with her niece, Gloria Gail. An attractive young woman, Gloria Gail was nearly eighteen and worked as a cook at the Red Rose Café. They were interested in purchasing fabric. Kaitlin showed them

her stock and they discussed the dress Clara wanted to make.

"I just don't know," Clara said, pursing her lips. "I can't decide between the blue and the pink. What do you think, Gloria Gail?"

"The blue, definitely the blue," she replied.

"I don't know..." Clara's eyes brightened suddenly. "I know. We'll get a man's opinion. Let's go ask Mr. Callihan."

Clara latched on to Gloria Gail and pulled her across the store along with two bolts of fabric, and parked all three under Tripp's nose. From the giggling and fawning going on, Kaitlin decided this conference had nothing to do with fabric selection, and everything to do with Gloria Gail's status as an unmarried woman.

The thought renewed the ache in Kaitlin's heart. While Tripp didn't seem to understand the true nature of the ladies' desired consultation, Kaitlin knew full well what was going on. Since arriving in Porter, Tripp had been locked away inside the store for the most part, unavailable. Now that the store was open he was more accessible. Tripp was a handsome man. He was a good man. He adored his son. He'd make a wonderful husband.

He'd already made a wonderful partner.

Kaitlin turned away, unable to look at the women gathered around him. She wanted him for herself.

But she wanted her dream, too.

The last shopper left shortly before closing time so Kaitlin straightened the shelves as Tripp counted the money in the cash box. Charlie played in the

corner near the settee; Tripp had made him some blocks from the leftover wood and he was busy building towers.

"How did we do today?" Kaitlin asked.

Tripp entered a figure in the ledger. "Pretty good. But we've still got a long—"

"—way to go," Kaitlin said. "Yes, I believe you told me that yesterday."

Tripp looked up at her and a hint of a grin pulled at his lips. "I guess I did, huh?"

She rested her hands on the counter. "What do you think about adding a line of toys to the store?"

Tripp shrugged. "I guess that depends on whether we're going to be here to run the place."

"Oh, yes...of course." She'd surprised herself at how much she'd liked running the store, listening to the customers, thinking of ways to sell more merchandise. But the truth was that there might be no need for her good ideas. "We should talk about Mr. Dorsey's offer," Kaitlin said.

Tripp closed the ledger with a thud and shoved it under the counter. "I guess you're pretty anxious to get out of here, and go running off to New York with Dorsey?"

It was an accusation more than a question, and it annoyed Kaitlin.

"Just as anxious as you are to get your farm producing again," she told him.

"I'm not just farming. I'm making a home." Tripp snatched up a fistful of papers. "And are you going to fill out these tally sheets like I asked you to, or not?"

She glared right back at him. "I'm not."

"Fine." Tripp tucked the cash box under his arm and stalked into the back room.

Kaitlin forced down the urge to throw something after him. If Charlie hadn't been in the corner of the store, she might have done it, or at least yelled at him. Instead, she turned her energy to straightening the glass jars of candy on the counter.

The bell over the door jingled and another customer came into the store. Kaitlin turned to offer a greeting and saw a man dressed in a rumpled dark suit with a hat pulled low over his forehead. He was well into his fifties. His features were sharp, his face wrinkled, as if he'd spent much of his life frowning.

"Good evening," Kaitlin said with her ever present smile. "May I help you?"

"You certainly may," he barked.

The man hung his thumbs in the pockets of his vest and planted himself in the center of the store. Lips pinched, he turned slowly, taking in the entire store.

Kaitlin ventured closer. "What can I do for you, sir?"

"You can give me back my store, you and that thieving partner of yours."

Stunned, Kaitlin froze in place. "What do you mean?"

"I mean you stole it from me and I want it back." The man's eyes narrowed. "My name is Everette Finch, and this store belongs to me."

"What are you going to do?"

Kaitlin heard the question Julia asked but didn't

have an answer for it. No more so than when she'd asked herself the same thing over the past two days.

The two women strolled across the schoolyard carrying their donation to the food table for today's spring pageant. The afternoon was warm and sunny, and nearly everyone in Porter had turned out for the event. Like the other merchants, Kaitlin and Tripp closed early for the day.

Under the shady elms some men had set up a horseshoe pit. Children played on the swings. The girls jumped rope, and the boys couldn't resist the urge to get down on all fours in the dirt and shoot marbles.

"I don't really know what we'll do," Kaitlin said as they walked. "Everette Finch claims that the deed to the store was stolen from him."

"But you and Tripp have it now. Doesn't that make it yours legally?" Julia asked.

Considering that she'd laid claim to the deed by pretending to be Harvey Stutz's pregnant widow didn't say much for her ownership rights to the store. But she wasn't going to share that story with Julia.

Kaitlin sighed. "I'm not sure."

"What does Tripp say about all this?"

"He's not happy," Kaitlin said. And that covered a multitude of things, not just Everette Finch's sudden arrival; she hadn't told Julia about those other things, either.

Not that Kaitlin was thrilled with this turn of events. She'd lain awake last night, tossing and turning, pondering how her dream that just days ago had been within her grasp, was now even farther away.

She wondered, not for the first time, if her dearest hopes and wishes were destined to come true.

It also put off the question of whether she and Tripp should sell the store to Alister Dorsey. That whole transaction was under a cloud now. Along with their lives.

"This certainly isn't endearing grumpy old Mr. Finch to anyone here in Porter," Julia said.

The news that The Emporium might be changing hands hadn't stopped the flow of customers into the store. If anything, it seemed the townspeople were even more anxious to support the store in the face of the new adversity.

"There's not much we can do but wait," Kaitlin said. "The circuit court judge will be in town in a few weeks and he'll decide who gets ownership of the store. That's what Mrs. Douglas says, anyway."

"Try to put it out of your mind for today, at least," Julia said. "You have your big debut scheduled."

Kaitlin smiled. Most every day she'd come to the school and rehearsed the spring pageant program with the children. They had worked diligently, memorizing their lines, learning the songs, remembering where they were supposed to stand, when they were to enter and exit the stage.

They had all been delightful. The older girls had helped the younger ones. Even the older boys had joined in with few complaints.

Kaitlin loved every minute of it. From the rehearsals, to solving the problems that cropped up, to helping Julia with the simple costumes in the evenings. It reminded Kaitlin of her own school days and how

her mother directed all the pageants. Kaitlin had been so proud of her mother.

"I hope you'll be able to round up your cast," Julia said, gazing at the children scattered around the schoolyard.

"I may need your help, if you don't mind."

"I'd love to," Julia said, and sighed wistfully. "This is as close as I might ever come to having children."

"Things are no better between you and Rafe?" Kaitlin asked.

Julia shook her head. "But he's coming to the pageant today. I want him to see the costumes I made. I'm sure he'll be here. He promised."

They reached the food table and Kaitlin put her platter of fried chicken alongside the other dishes already there. Ham, sliced beef, boiled eggs and pickles, dishes of vegetables, and an array of cakes and pies, including Julia's apple cobbler.

Kaitlin checked on Tripp who, along with several other men, was busy putting the stage in place at the back corner of the school house. He'd built a large platform, with support columns on the front and back, and poles suspended between them for the curtains Mrs. Douglas had donated. Tripp had put a lot of thought and effort into it, as always. There was nothing the man couldn't build, it seemed.

"Good afternoon, Miss Jeffers."

She turned to see Alister Dorsey looking as handsome and gentlemanly as always, standing behind her.

"I didn't expect to see you here today," Kaitlin said.

"And miss the biggest stage production in Porter?" Alister grinned. "I should say not, Miss Jeffers."

"I suppose you heard the news about the store," Kaitlin said. "There's no way we can sell it to you now."

"But that doesn't mean you can't come with me to New York, does it?"

Go to New York anyway? Leave without a conclusion to her deal with Tripp? She hadn't considered the possibility.

"I have responsibilities here, Mr. Dorsey."

"Not if Finch has a legal claim to the store," Alister said. "No store, no partnership. Your deal with Mr. Callihan will be dissolved."

Kaitlin gasped. "I—I hadn't really considered that."

"You'll be free to go." Alister smiled. "Think it over, Miss Jeffers. I'm leaving at the end of next week."

Miss Bailey clanged the school bell and everyone moved toward the food tables, saving Kaitlin from responding or even thinking too much about Alister's words. Mrs. Douglas took Alister's arm and directed him to the spot she'd staked out for herself and the mayor.

June Hutchinson eased up beside Kaitlin, her eyes narrowing at Alister Dorsey and the mayor's wife.

"Seems mighty suspicious, if you ask me," she said.

"What's that?" Kaitlin asked. Everything seemed suspicious to the sheriff's wife.

"Mr. Dorsey, claiming to be here visiting, then offering to buy up businesses in Porter."

Kaitlin didn't want to tell Mrs. Hutchinson that the only reason Alister had offered to buy the Emporium was to help her get to New York.

"He's a businessman," Kaitlin said.

"Humph!" Mrs. Hutchinson jerked her chin. "And what on earth would a dandy like Mr. Dorsey want with a feed store here in Porter?"

"A feed store?"

"And a barber shop?" Mrs. Hutchinson harumped again. "Seems mighty suspicious, if you ask me."

Kaitlin watched June Hutchinson flounce across the schoolyard, and admitted to herself, that yes, it seemed suspicious to her, too.

But what other motives would Alister Dorsey have?

Chapter Eighteen

Kaitlin ate with Reverend Beckman, his wife and their noisy brood. Across the table, Julia saved a place for Rafe and had prepared a plate for him; so far, the spot was empty.

Tripp had relented and let Charlie eat with his friends in the grass under the trees, but Tripp didn't eat alone. Clara Hadley swarmed his table with her husband and family, strategically seating everyone so that Gloria Gail was next to Tripp. If he didn't notice what Clara was up to, Kaitlin certainly did.

She studied Gloria Gail for a few minutes. She was a pretty girl, quiet and soft-spoken. She'd probably fit in just fine on Tripp's farm.

Kaitlin pulled her gaze from them and determinedly turned to Lorna Beckman for conversation.

After everyone had eaten, Kaitlin helped clear the tables, including Rafe's untouched plate. He'd never arrived.

"I know you're disappointed," Kaitlin said quietly to Julia. "I'm sure he's doing something important, otherwise he would have been here."

Julia smiled bravely. "Yes, I'm sure you're right."

Once the tables were cleared, the spring pageant began. Everyone crowded on to the benches and tabletops, and sat on blankets in the grass facing the stage. Behind the schoolhouse, at the corner of the stage, Kaitlin gave last-minute instructions and encouragement while Julia and Miss Bailey helped with the childrens' costumes.

Spring, of course, was the theme of the pageant. Julia had fashioned long strips of yellow, blue and red fabric tied to the childrens' arms with yarn to look like wings, and big yellow cones that served as beaks. In class, the children had painted large flowers and glued them to sticks that they carried. All the girls wore flowers pinned in their hair.

Miss Bailey stepped onto the stage, greeted everyone, and extended special thanks to the mayor's office, Tripp for building the stage, Julia for making the costumes, and Kaitlin for coordinating this year's pageant.

"Everybody ready?" Kaitlin asked the children in a low voice.

They looked up at her nodding and smiling, fidgeting with their costumes. They were all excited, and so was she.

"Okay, then, we're almost ready." Kaitlin glanced at the tablet in her hand. "Yellow birds, you're up first. Come along now."

"Is he here yet?" Julia asked, as she knelt to retie the yarn on a costume. "Is Rafe in the audience?"

Kaitlin pulled back the edge of the curtain where it met with the corner of the school house and

searched the faces of the parents and families gathered there. Alister Dorsey sat with Mrs. Douglas and the mayor. Tripp had a seat right up front. But there was no sign of Rafe.

She closed the curtain. "I don't see him."

Julia's smile faded. "Oh…"

"But he might be in the back," Kaitlin said. "Or off to the side where I can't see him."

Julia nodded. "Yes, probably."

Reverend Beckman offered a prayer, then the yellow birds went onstage. Kaitlin stood in the wings, watching and coaching a bit as the four little girls did the simple dance she'd taught them. Next, two older girls did a dramatic reading, followed by a song performed by the red and bluebirds. A particularly gifted young boy played "Oh! Susanna" on the harmonica. There was another poetry reading followed by the grand finale of all the children onstage singing together.

The audience burst into applause, and the children bowed, some losing their beaks. Two of the older boys who'd operated the curtain pulled Kaitlin onstage and presented her with a bouquet of daisies.

Her heart soared as the children crowded around her and she looked into their bright, happy faces, and out into the audience of parents. Charlie worked his way to her side in his little bluebird costume, and Kaitlin gave him a special hug.

She couldn't imagine a reception on the New York stage would ever be as wonderful as this one. She couldn't imagine leaving all these people behind.

Children found their parents in the crowd, showing off their costumes, laughing and giggling. Tripp

stepped up onto the stage and swung Charlie into his arms.

"I did good, Papa. Huh?"

Tripp's smile was as broad as Charlie's. "You were the best singing bluebird I ever saw."

"Can I keep my costume, Miss Kaitlin? Can I?" Charlie asked, playing with his beak.

"Just for a few more minutes," Kaitlin said. She understood how he felt; she was reluctant to let go of the moment herself.

Parents stopped by and congratulated her on the pageant, declaring it the best one yet. Tripp received compliments on the stage he'd constructed.

"Didn't know you did carpentry work, Mr. Callihan," Frances Morgan said.

Tripp nodded modestly. "Anything from a box to a building."

"I have a table that's so rickety I'm afraid it will fall apart, and my Ralph just can't get around to fixing it," Frances said. "Would you consider looking at it?"

"Sure thing, ma'am," Tripp said.

"Wonderful," Frances said, and hurried away.

"Looks like we're both a hit," Kaitlin said, smiling.

Tripp grinned. "Pretty good partners."

Kaitlin's heart warmed at the thought.

Charlie wiggled down and joined his friends in the schoolyard, all of them flapping their wings and running between the trees. Kaitlin decided it was time to reclaim the costumes, while they were still in good enough condition to be used next year. She looked

for help from Julia, and spied her standing beside the schoolhouse, all alone.

In the swirl of parents and children, the laughter and fun, Julia's face was somber. Kaitlin's heart lurched. She walked over.

"Julia, I'm sure Rafe would have been here if he could. Something important must have come up," she said, but her words sounded hollow, even to herself.

"I'd like to think that was true." Julia turned a weak smile to Kaitlin. "But we both know it's not."

"Why don't we go over to the blacksmith shop and—"

"No." Julia pressed her lips together, struggling to hold back tears. She drew in a ragged breath. "It's time I faced the truth, Kaitlin. I've been trying to make a marriage where one simply doesn't exist. Seeing all these parents here with their children today made me realize that."

"But what do you mean?"

A tear splashed onto Julia's cheek. "Tonight when Rafe comes home, I'm telling him I want a divorce."

"A divorce?"

Tripp whispered the word to Kaitlin standing at the sideboard after supper. He glanced over his shoulder at Charlie bringing the last of their dishes, and leaned closer to Kaitlin.

"Julia wants a divorce?" he asked.

Kaitlin rinsed a cup and passed it to him. "That's what she told me."

"Can I go outside now, Papa? Please?"

He looked down at his son. "Okay. But don't go far."

"I won't, Papa," he called as he scooted out the door.

"Damn." Tripp shook his head as he dried the coffee cup. "I knew things weren't going too good for them, but I never thought this would happen. Do you think she's serious?"

"She seems to be."

"Damn."

They washed and dried the supper dishes and put them away, then Tripp went out back to take care of the horses for the night. By the time he finished, twilight had settled, and he'd shooed Charlie into the store to get ready for bed. Rafe came outside.

"Evening, Rafe," Tripp called. He didn't want to nose into the man's personal business uninvited, but couldn't ignore him, either. Rafe had been his first friend here in Porter.

Rafe walked over, his hands thrust into his pockets, his shoulders sagging.

"I guess you heard?" he asked.

Tripp nodded, his own stomach knotting. "Yeah, Kaitlin told me. Look, Rafe, I hate to hear this is happening to you."

"I knew it would. I never deserved a woman as special as Julia." Rafe uttered a short, bitter laugh. "I guess I just wasn't good enough for her."

"Don't be so hard on yourself," Tripp said.

"No, it's true," Rafe said. "I did everything I knew to do. I worked damn near day and night to build my business for her."

"Yes, you did," Tripp agreed. Rafe was the hardest working man he'd ever seen.

Rafe studied the toe of his boot, then drew in a deep breath. "I guess I just couldn't give her what she wanted."

Tripp's stomach pitched so hard he thought he'd been punched. "What did you say?"

"I said that hard as I tried, I guess I just didn't give Julia what she wanted," Rafe said.

The notion blazed through Tripp's mind like a runaway freight wagon. Memories of the past swept over him, crystalizing in his mind. And then the future spread across his thoughts.

Tripp strode down the boardwalk, away from the store, determination hardening in his belly like a knot. He knew what he had to do. He knew it would hurt. But it was time he faced that hurt, instead of running from it. The alternative was even more painful.

Around the corner at the express office, Tripp banged his fist on the door until the Closed sign shook, and Gabe Kingery, the senior agent, finally came out of his room in the back. When he opened the door, Tripp pushed his way inside.

"I've got to send a telegram," Tripp said.

The agent squinted up at him. "We open Monday morning at—"

Tripp slammed his fist into his open palm. "There's no way in hell I'm waiting until Monday. I want it sent now."

Kaitlin knew something was wrong. She'd felt it in the pit of her stomach for days. It clung to her

like a heavy mantle.

Whatever it was went beyond the threat that she and Tripp could lose the store. Beyond the decision she'd have to make by the end of the week, whether or not to go to New York with Alister Dorsey.

She saw it in Tripp, too. He had been different since the night of the spring pageant. He'd gone about his work in the store with gritty determination. In the stockroom every night, he banged away on the bookcases, stools and tables the folks in town had hired him to make.

He'd spoken little to Kaitlin, and that hurt her worst of all. She hadn't realized how much they talked, what a comfort he was until it was lost.

Something was wrong, all right. Something dreadful.

Her fears were realized Tuesday afternoon when Gabe Kingery came into the store and presented Tripp with a telegram.

"You had such a fit to send it out," Gabe said, smoothing down his chin whiskers, "I figured you'd want the reply as soon as it came in."

Tripp stared at the folded paper for a long moment before accepting it.

"Thanks, Gabe," he mumbled and disappeared into the kitchen.

Kaitlin watched the sway of the doorway curtain, a feeling of dread bearing down on her. This was it. The moment her intuition had told her was coming for days now.

With leaden steps she made her way through the crowded store into the kitchen. Tripp stood with his

back to her, head bent, reading. His back was rigid, his stance tense.

"Tripp?"

He whirled, the lines of his face hard.

She stepped closer, but just a little. "Is something wrong?"

It seemed a foolish thing to say, because so obviously something was terribly wrong. And, she sensed, not solely with Tripp. Whatever it was pulled her into the swirling vortex, too, along with him. She couldn't escape it.

He help up the telegram. "I found Emily."

The morning chill seeped into Kaitlin's bones, and pulling the shawl tighter around her shoulders did no good. Nothing warmed her. She'd been cold since yesterday when Tripp had received his telegram. And seeing him and Charlie in the kitchen this morning only made her colder.

"Do we gotta go, Papa? Do we gotta?" Charlie whined and clung to the chair at the table.

Tripp took down his jacket from the peg beside the door. "Yes, son, come on."

He'd told Charlie last night that they were going away this morning, and the child hadn't been happy about it. If Tripp had told him he was going to see his mother, he might have felt differently. Tripp just said it was business.

"But teacher said I'm 'posed to hand out papers today. It's my turn," Charlie said.

"We have to go." Tripp crossed the room toward him.

Charlie ran to Kaitlin and threw his arms around

her. "I don't want to go, Miss Kaitlin. Can I stay
here with you? Can I?"

Pain slashed through her, piercing her heart. Kaitlin knelt and took Charlie into her arms.

"Please, Miss Kaitlin? I'll be good. I promise."

She squeezed him tighter, holding on to this moment, while it was hers to hold.

Kaitlin swallowed the lump in her throat. "You
have to go with your Papa, Charlie."

"But I don't wanna…"

She made herself smile. "I'll miss you, Charlie,
but you'll have a good time with your papa. It will
be fun."

Charlie gazed up at Tripp standing over them.
"Are we coming back, Papa?"

Kaitlin leaned her head back to look at Tripp. His
gaze met hers briefly, then broke away.

"Come on, Charlie," Tripp said. "It's time to
go."

He guided the child's arms into his jacket and
lifted him into his arms.

Kaitlin rose and put on a brave face, for Charlie's
sake. "You two have fun."

The boy's bottom lip poked out and he clamped
his mouth shut in a pout.

Kaitlin followed them to the back door. Outside,
the gray of morning settled over the alley. Tripp's
wagon waited; he'd hitched the team and loaded
their bags earlier. Now, they were leaving.

Tripp looked at her for a moment, as if he wanted
to say something. But in the end, he simply walked
out the door.

Kaitlin's throat constricted as she stood on the

boardwalk, watching Tripp put Charlie onto the seat and climb up after him.

Her stomach knotted as he picked up the reins and called to the team.

Her heart ached as Charlie turned and waved his little hand at her.

Tears fell when the wagon pulled away…and Tripp didn't even look back.

If he'd left Charlie with her, there would have been a chance. She'd have reason to hope—slight, but still hope—that Tripp would return. Now, it seemed hopeless.

Tripp was going to his wife. And would probably never come back.

Chapter Nineteen

Waiting on customers all day kept Kaitlin busy, but hadn't relieved the anxiety that dragged her down. Hadn't kept her from thinking, either.

Now, at closing time, Kaitlin shut the lid on the cash box and shoved it under the counter. She didn't know where Tripp stored the ledgers, and wasn't in the mood to try to figure them out.

Everything she looked at, everything she attempted to do in the store reminded her of Tripp. He was everywhere. But he was nowhere.

The bell jingled over the door and Julia came inside.

"How were sales today?" Julia asked, as she came to the counter.

Kaitlin sighed. "People are still coming in steadily."

"That's good."

"I suppose so." Kaitlin sighed again and took a harder look at her friend. Julia's eyes were puffy and she looked washed out, as if no emotion was left inside her.

"Did you see Rafe today?" Kaitlin asked softly.

"No. He's staying at his mother's place."

Kaitlin shook her head. "I thought sure he'd come by and talk with you about...things."

"He hasn't." Julia drew in a ragged breath. "Have you heard from Tripp?"

The story she'd told everyone who'd asked—and nearly everyone had asked—was that Tripp had to leave on a family emergency.

"No," Kaitlin said. "I haven't heard from him."

Her own problems had weighed heavily on her, but Julia looked even more miserable than she felt.

"Why don't we go out for supper tonight?" Kaitlin suggested.

"I don't know..."

"We don't have to cook, if we don't want to," Kaitlin said.

"You never had to cook, anyway."

Tripp had done the cooking. He'd built the shelves, counted their money, paid their bills, cared for Charlie...stolen her heart. And now he was gone.

Kaitlin lifted her shoulders. "We have to do something. We can't mope around here all night."

Julia sighed. "I suppose—"

The bell jingled and Everette Finch came into the store, stopped in the center, planted his hands on his hips and eyed the place like the proprietor he fancied himself to be.

Kaitlin steeled her emotions, warning herself to keep calm and not let this man rile her.

"Good evening, Mr. Finch."

He grunted. "I'll be making a few changes around

here, when the judge settles my claim and you're tossed out in the street.''

''That remains to be seen, Mr. Finch.''

''Oh, it will happen, all right. You can bet on it.''

''Like you bet this store on a losing poker hand, just to get rid of it?'' Kaitlin asked.

He glared at her.

''Everyone in Porter knows that's what you did,'' Julia said.

''A lie! Nothing but a lie!''

''Kaitlin and Tripp have the deed,'' Julia said. ''They have all the documents, properly filed, and perfectly legal.''

''I haven't seen nothing of theirs yet,'' Everette said. ''All I know is that they're no better than squatters, sneaking in here the minute my back was turned, and taking over the place like it's a—''

''Good evening.''

Matilda Shaw came into the store, closing the door quietly behind her. She stopped suddenly when she saw Everette Finch standing beside the display of lanterns.

He stopped just as suddenly. They both stared for a moment before Everette pulled off his hat.

''Evening, Mrs. Shaw,'' he said respectfully.

She dipped her eyelids demurely. ''Why, good evening to you too, Mr. Finch.''

He rolled his hat in his hands for a minute, then shoved it on his head again. ''I got to go.'' Everette Finch stalked out the door.

Mrs. Shaw watched him go, then drew in a deep breath.

"Can I help you with something?" Kaitlin asked, coming around the counter.

"Oh, yes, dear. I need a little sugar, please."

Kaitlin measured out a pound. Mrs. Shaw never bought more than a pound of anything. It was too heavy to carry, and it gave her a good excuse to come back for more.

"Mr. Finch seemed surprised to see you," Kaitlin said.

She smiled. "Yes, I'd say so."

"In fact," Kaitlin said, "he seemed quite taken with you."

"Are you two interested in each other, Mrs. Shaw?" Julia asked. It seemed to hurt her to pose the question, her own feelings so raw.

She dipped her lashes. "Well, you just never know what might happen, now do you?"

Julia burst into tears and ran from the store.

The store was busy the next day with a steady stream of customers, but Kaitlin had never felt so alone in her life. She'd meant for the people of Porter to be only customers, a means to an end—the stage in New York. But they had become more than customers. They had become her friends. Still, they weren't enough to keep the loneliness from her heart today.

How had she managed to live alone for those years after her father died? That thought kept running through Kaitlin's head as she directed customers to her merchandise, helped them make selections, took their money. At the time, it had seemed quite natural. And acceptable.

But no more. Not after having Tripp here filling her waking moments. Not after spending weeks together building the store. And certainly not after Charlie had so easily found a spot in her heart.

How would she learn to live that kind of life again?

How would she manage if Tripp never came back from seeing his wife?

June Hutchinson came into the store around noon, eyeing the other customers, watching their shopping baskets. She even made Kaitlin nervous—and Kaitlin was quite certain she wasn't doing anything wrong. Not at the moment, anyway.

"Quite a crowd," Mrs. Hutchinson said, as Kaitlin joined her. "A very *large* crowd."

Kaitlin made herself smile. "Merchants like a large crowd."

"You can't be too careful." She jerked her chin. "I saw that Everette Finch come in here last night."

Kaitlin shuddered to think what might have erupted if Matilda Shaw hadn't walked in and headed off their argument.

"Mighty suspicious, if you ask me," Mrs. Hutchinson said.

"What's that?"

Her eyes narrowed. "Everette Finch showing up here in town just after that Alister Dorsey."

The sheriff's wife always found suspicion where no one else did, but Kaitlin couldn't see any connection between these two men.

"I don't understand," Kaitlin said.

"Humph." Mrs. Hutchinson tossed her head. "That Everette Finch might be the grumpiest old

man ever to set foot in Porter, but he's got a nose for business. He can sniff out money like a hound after a rabbit.''

"Yes," Kaitlin agreed. "He must have seen the advertisement of our grand opening in the newspaper, somehow, and realized we were making money. That's what brought him back to Porter."

"Probably saw that Alister Dorsey was in town, too. The story was in the newspaper." Mrs. Hutchinson pressed her lips together. "Everette Finch doesn't need this store, Miss Jeffers. He owns all sorts of properties—and not just here in Porter. He's smelling something bigger. Much bigger. You mark my words.''

And with that, and a final suspicious sweep of the other customers, June Hutchinson left the store.

Glumly, Kaitlin went about seeing to her customers and closing up the store at the end of the day. She turned the big brass key in the lock and pulled down the shade, wondering how many more times she could do this. Not many, surely.

Everette Finch would certainly be awarded the store when the circuit judge heard their case. The validity of her claim was a stretch, at best. If they were lucky, Everette would reimburse them for the merchandise they stocked the store with, and the judge wouldn't send her to jail.

Kaitlin pulled the cash box from under the counter and carried it into the kitchen. She didn't count it. She'd have to soon, though, and take it to the bank as Tripp did every day after closing.

Her heart sank a little further into her stomach. Tripp. Would she ever see him again? If he returned,

would it be to gather the rest of his belongings and go back to his wife for good?

Kaitlin looked at the cold cookstove and couldn't bring herself to fire it up and fix supper. Not for herself alone. How much lonelier could that make her feel? Grabbing her shawl from her bedroom, Kaitlin headed for the Red Rose Café.

The only table available was in the back corner, and that suited Kaitlin fine; she hardly wanted to sit in the front window so everyone in Porter could see that she was alone.

At least from the rear of the restaurant she could see everyone else dining, and that gave her something to concentrate on, other than her own misery.

She ordered the ham plate from the serving girl and looked over a copy of the *Porter Gazette* someone had left lying in the chair beside her. It was the issue advertising the grand opening of the Emporium.

Kaitlin determinedly folded the paper to the next page. Couldn't she look at anything without being reminded of Tripp?

Inside she noted an article detailing Alister Dorsey's arrival in Porter. So busy with the store, Kaitlin had not seen the entire paper and hadn't noticed the story before. It seemed that June Hutchinson was right. Everette Finch could have learned about her store opening and Alister Dorsey's arrival at the same time.

Looking over the newspaper, she realized that Mrs. Douglas's assessment of Alister Dorsey was, apparently, correct. A wealthy Easterner, he was touring the state and included Porter in his scheduled

stops. The newspaper reported that Alister was a businessman known to have connections in the highest seats of government and industry.

Vaguely, Kaitlin wondered why Mrs. Douglas hadn't pressed him to use his influence to get the railroad through Porter, one of the mayor's wife's biggest causes.

Alister Dorsey was also a patron of the arts, the newspaper reported. Kaitlin's stomach jumped, seeing the words on the printed page. It was also reported that Alister had purchased several paintings while on this trip.

When the serving girl brought her food, Kaitlin put the newspaper aside and occupied herself with watching the other diners. She knew some of them from her dealings at the store. Others she knew from church.

A family seated near the front of the restaurant left their table and it was then Kaitlin realized Alister Dorsey was present. He ate with three other men. They were cattle ranchers with spreads on the outskirts of Porter. Kaitlin couldn't remember their names but they had been in her store, and so had many of their ranch hands.

They made odd dining partners, Kaitlin decided, watching but trying not to be obvious about it. The three men were dressed in rough trousers and shirts, leather vests and boots, and Alister in his fine suit, white shirt and cravat.

The men seemed quite at ease with each other. Talking until they'd concluded their meal, they shook hands and departed. Turning to go, Alister caught sight of Kaitlin and walked to her table.

"Good evening, Miss Jeffers." He smiled down at her.

Kaitlin laid her fork aside. "Nice to see you."

"Have you given my proposal consideration?" he asked.

Kaitlin nodded. "Yes, but I haven't made a decision yet."

Alister looked disappointed. "You don't have much time left, Miss Jeffers. I'm leaving tomorrow."

"Tomorrow? So soon? But, I thought—"

"A change in plans." Alister Dorsey smiled. "I'll be on the ten o'clock stage. I hope you will, too."

With a troubled sigh, Kaitlin let herself in through the kitchen door and went straight to her bedroom. She lit the lantern at her bedside. The flickering light danced across the big oval mirror, illuminating her reflection. She looked terrible.

Kaitlin straightened her shoulders and put on a smile. The face in the mirror looked a little brighter, but only for a moment. Finally she slumped down onto the bed.

She didn't remember feeling so alone and lost before, even after her father died. Her dream was always her shining beacon, the one thing that pulled her along, pushed her through life. The one thing she looked forward to.

Images of herself on the New York stage skipped through Kaitlin's mind, as they had for years. The comraderie of rehearsals. Dancing, singing, delivering her lines. Laughter from the audience. Sniffles. Bursts of wild applause. The press of the other cast members crowding around her at the final curtain.

It's what she had always wanted. And it could be hers—if she met Alister Dorsey at the stage depot tomorrow morning.

Could she leave? Pack her bag and go, without telling everyone goodbye? Without knowing what would happen with Everette Finch and the store? Without helping Julia through her divorce?

Without telling Tripp goodbye?

No, she couldn't.

And suddenly, the idea of going to New York didn't seem appealing anymore. In fact, it felt lonely and empty.

Kaitlin rose from the bed, sure in her heart that nothing could feel as perfect as a life with Tripp, here in Porter, on his farm—anywhere.

In the mirror, Kaitlin saw her face brighten at the realization. Yes, she loved Tripp, and she loved the life they could make for themselves—regardless of what Everette Finch claimed or what the judge decided. She could give up her dream, if she got Tripp in exchange.

With new energy, Kaitlin undressed, bathed at the washstand, and slipped into a pink nightgown. Tomorrow, she would go to the express office and make Gabe Kingery tell her where Tripp had gone; he'd know from the origin of the telegram. And Kaitlin would go there. She'd close The Emporium, find Tripp, and tell him that he was her dream now, not New York.

Her mind made up, Kaitlin fell into bed and snuggled into the pillows, falling blissfully to sleep for the first time in days.

* * *

She dreamed of Tripp. Dreamed he'd come home, that she heard the back door open and the scuff of his boots, that she smelled his masculine scent. Kaitlin roused from her slumbers, sorry to let the dream slip away, and saw a figure move past her bedroom door.

She bolted straight up in the bed and held her scream to a tiny mewl as she slapped her hand across her mouth. The figure materialized in her doorway.

"Sorry, I didn't mean to wake you."

"Tripp?" Kaitlin sprang to her knees in the center of the bed, clutching her chest.

"Shh," he whispered. "He's sleeping."

She saw then that Tripp held Charlie against his shoulder with one hand, and carried the satchel he'd packed their clothes in with the other.

"I—I wasn't expecting you to—"

He came into the room and she made out the hard, tight lines of his face in the darkness.

"I've got to talk to you, Kaitlin," he whispered. "Let me put Charlie to bed."

"Talk? About what?"

Tripp left without another word. Kaitlin pulled on her wrapper, tying it at her waist as she hurried after him.

"Put on some coffee, will you?" Tripp asked, as he disappeared up the stairs with Charlie and their satchel.

He needed coffee for this talk? What on earth did that mean?

Kaitlin lit the lanterns and built up the fire in the cookstove. She fumbled with the pot, sloshed water on the floor, and spilled the grounds, but finally got

the coffee going. Outside the window she saw no sign of Tripp's wagon and team. He must have stabled them before bringing Charlie inside. Tripp, always so organized.

She wrung her hands, pacing, anxious for him to come downstairs, yet afraid to see him. Should she just blurt out that she loved him? That she didn't want to go to New York? She'd had no time to rehearse.

Maybe she'd have no opportunity to say any of those things. Was he about to tell her that he was heading out for his farm? Back to his wife?

Tripp's boots thudded on the stairs, and he crossed the kitchen to where she stood beside the stove. He caught her arms and turned her toward the lantern light.

Kaitlin's breath caught and her heart pounded. He looked fierce, but not frightening. Emotions swirled through her, rose from the well deep within her, matching his heightened senses.

Every nerve ending stood on end, straining, humming. Her gaze, ensnared by his, wouldn't budge from his face.

"I had to come back tonight, Kaitlin. It was dark, and too late to travel, and it looked like rain, but I had to talk to you...tell you."

"Tell me what?"

Tripp shook his head. "I've been practicing all the way here, inside my head, trying to find the right words. I even wrote something down."

She glanced at his shirt pocket where he kept his tiny tablet and made his lists, but all she saw was his big chest heaving with powerful breaths.

She searched his face. "What is it, Tripp?"

"Nothing seemed right," he said. "All the fancy words, the reasons, the excuses—there's just not but one way to say it."

Kaitlin clamped her lips together to keep from screaming at him.

Tripp drew in a big breath. "There's nothing to do but just say it flat out."

Was he about to tell her that he loved her? Or that his wife was waiting in the wagon inside the stable?

"Then just say it, Tripp, flat out."

He loosened his grip on her arms and nodded slowly. "Okay. Here goes..."

Chapter Twenty

Tripp shook his head and released her.

"No," he said. "I'd better start from the beginning. Tell it in order."

Kaitlin clenched her hands into fists to keep from shaking him. She drew in a calming breath.

"Fine, Tripp. Just take your time."

He nodded slowly and moved away from her. "All right. Well, first off— Do you want some coffee?"

No, she wanted him to tell her what had happened. Kaitlin sighed heavily. "Yes, maybe I should."

They moved around the kitchen together fixing the coffee, then settled at the table facing each other across the steaming cups.

"Did everything go all right while I was away?" Tripp asked. "Anything happen?"

Well, she'd given up her lifelong dream and was dying to tell him, and if he would just get on with this she could.

Kaitlin held her patience. Tripp had to get to

things in his own way. Or maybe she was just anxious—and afraid—of what he might say.

"Everything was fine," she said.

"Good." Tripp sipped his coffee and was quiet for a long moment. Finally, he looked at her. "Seeing what happened to Rafe and Julia got me to thinking. You know, how two people could love each other, but not make each other happy. That's why I wanted to see Emily."

"So you did see her?" Kaitlin's heart beat a little faster.

"The telegram I sent was addressed to her brother," Tripp said. "Russ is a good man. We stayed in touch for a while after…after she left. Remember I told you about him working for the railroad? He kept an eye out for her."

"The return telegram you got was from Russ, wasn't it?" Kaitlin said. "He told you where you could find her?"

"And I found her, all right."

Tripp pushed his fingers through his hair. He looked tired, but not from his journey. Weary from what he'd been through. What he may still have to go through.

Kaitlin studied his expression, trying to glean some idea of where the conversation was going. Had Tripp come back to her to stay? Or was he leaving again to go to Emily?

"She's sick, Kaitlin."

Her heart tumbled. She was ill. His wife was ill. How could he turn his back on her now?

"Emily is real sick. I talked to the doctor and…"

Tripp drew in a fresh breath. "Well, he doesn't expect her to hold out much longer."

"Oh, Tripp..." Kaitlin reached across the table and laid her hand on his. "I'm so sorry."

"Seems Russ had wanted to let me know for a while now, but didn't know where to find me until I sent him that telegram." Tripp shook his head. "The doctor didn't hold out much hope. It's only a matter of time."

She'd wanted Tripp for herself, but she certainly didn't wish Emily any harm. Kaitlin gulped, forcing down her emotion.

"Of course you'll want to go to her," she said. "Spend with her whatever time she might have left."

Tripp pulled his hand from hers and stared at his cup. "Emily...doesn't want me there."

"But...?" Kaitlin shook her head. "How could she not want you with her? You're her husband."

"Seems she was done with me the day she ran off with Harvey Stutz."

It pained him to say those words, and it showed in his face. Kaitlin felt it herself.

"But what about Charlie?" she asked. "Surely she—"

"She didn't even look at him."

Kaitlin leaned forward and clenched her hands into fists. "She wouldn't see her own son?"

"She's true to herself, right to the end," Tripp said. "I guess you've got to admire her for that much, anyway."

"I know that hurt you," Kaitlin said.

He nodded. "But it's better this way. Better to let

Charlie just think his mama is dead. She'll be dead soon anyway, the doctor says. She led a pretty wild life after she left me...and Stutz. It finally caught up with her.''

Kaitlin took his hand again. ''What are you going to do?''

''She asked me not to come back,'' he said.

''Do you think she meant it? Or was she trying to be noble?''

Tripp shook his head. ''Oh, no. She meant it. I won't go back there again. As far as I'm concerned, it's over.''

Secretly, Kaitlin had hoped to hear Tripp say those words, but now that he had, she found no real joy in them. Not when they hurt him so much.

''I've been holding on to *nothing* all these years.'' Tripp gazed across the table at her. ''Stupid, realizing it now.''

Kaitlin smiled softly. ''You have such a good heart, Tripp. Emily doesn't know what she missed.''

''Maybe...'' Tripp wrapped his fingers around Kaitlin's hand. ''But I know what I nearly missed. And I don't like it.''

Kaitlin's skin tingled as he tightened his grip on her. His gaze warmed her, set her nerves on edge.

''I nearly missed *you*, Kaitlin,'' he said. ''Hanging on to the past so tight, I almost let the present slip right through my fingers. Is it too late?''

''Too late for—''

''For you and me.''

Tripp rose from the chair and pulled her up next to him. He slipped his arms around her waist and eased her against him.

"I thought about nothing but you, Kaitlin, the whole time I was gone." Tripp threaded his fingers through her loose hair. "Even seeing Emily after all those years, all I cared about was getting back to you."

Her heart fluttered, hearing him say those words.

"I missed you, Tripp," she whispered.

He leaned down and brushed his lips against her temple, breathing in her sweet scent. One hand traveled up her back and burrowed into the hair at her nape.

Kaitlin's knees weakened. She looped her arms around his neck and swayed against him.

His chest was hard, strong. His thighs, brushing hers, were muscular. His arms wrapped her in a powerful cocoon. A deep masculinity flowed from him, seeped inside her.

Tripp lowered his head and covered her mouth with his. She parted her lips and he slipped inside to her welcoming warmth. He groaned and pulled her tighter against him.

Kaitlin rose on tiptoes, pressing herself closer, soaking up the taste and feel of him. He'd kissed her before and the memories flooded back, thick and heavy with desire.

She tasted sweet, pure, and he wanted more. He wanted all of her. Tripp deepened their kiss and pulled loose the sash of her wrapper. He slid his hand inside. His palm burned as it settled on the curve of her hip. His fingers tingled at the feel of her, even through the fabric of her nightgown.

Urgency claimed him. He'd thought of Kaitlin for weeks—her and this moment. Desire surged through

him, charging him with a want and hunger he'd never felt before. He moved his hand upward, cupping her breast.

Kaitlin gasped and clenched his hair in her fist. Her heart raced. A strange heat consumed her. She'd never felt this way before, except with Tripp. And with Tripp it could only feel right.

He fumbled with the buttons of her nightgown, opening them to her waist. Her flesh was hot, welcoming. Tripp couldn't stop himself. He touched her bare breast, and when she arched toward him, his knees nearly gave out.

"Kaitlin…" He breathed the word against her hot mouth. "Kaitlin, if we don't stop soon…"

Blinded by the sensations racing through her, Kaitlin couldn't imagine this ending. Not now. Not like this.

"Kaitlin…" Tripp pulled his lips from hers, panting heavily. "We have to stop…or…"

She gulped and gazed up at him. "Or…what?"

This was the most beautiful woman he'd ever held, the most desirable, the one—the only one—he wanted. Tripp pulled in a quick breath.

"We have to stop…or…else."

"I'll take 'or else.'" Kaitlin threw her arms around his neck and locked her lips onto his.

Tripp scooped her up and headed for the stairs, kissing her wildly. He stopped on the first step. Good God, what was he thinking? Charlie was up there. He swung around and carried Kaitlin to her bedroom.

Tripp kicked the door closed and set her down, her feet touching the floor lightly. He grabbed a

straight-back chair from the corner and wedged it under the doorknob.

Looking at her in the lamplight, she was the most exciting thing he'd ever seen. Tussled hair, wrapper thrown off one shoulder, nightgown unbuttoned. And smiling. Oh, yes, she was smiling.

He wanted to sweep her into bed at that instant and bury himself in her body, in her soul, in her life. The demands of his body were strong, nearly overwhelming. He'd waited so long, and wanted her so much, he couldn't stand it another moment.

But he forced himself, straining against time and instinct. Tripp waited.

"Are you sure you know what you're getting into?" he asked.

Kaitlin came to him, snuggling against him, splaying her palms across his chest. "I know…"

She pushed his vest off him and opened the buttons of his shirt and long johns. Dark crisp hair covered his hard chest. She touched him, and he backed away.

Fighting for control, Tripp caught her shoulders and guided her to the big oval mirror on the other side of the room. Standing behind her, he turned her to face the mirror.

"You'll have to look at yourself in this thing tomorrow morning," he said, resting his hands on her shoulders. "Are you sure?"

Passion burned in both their eyes as they gazed at each other in the reflection of the mirror. For Kaitlin, there was no going back, no doubting going forward.

"I'm sure," she whispered. "If I get any more

sure, Tripp Callihan, and you don't hurry up and do something, I'm going to hurt you."

He smiled with her, their joy and love connecting in their reflections.

Tripp eased her wrapper off her shoulders; it pooled on the floor at their feet. Slowly he caressed her neck, until he saw her eyelids sink and she swayed against his chest.

His hands moved down her shoulders, her arms, then parted the fabric of her opened nightgown and laid claim to her breasts. Desire pumped through his veins at the sight of his big rugged hands caressing her milky-white mounds of flesh.

His thumbs circled the tips, then touched them, bringing the tiny buds to life. Her head leaned sideways in surrender, and Tripp sank his lips into the sweet flesh of her neck.

Kaitlin moaned as these new feelings claimed her. His hands were magic, bringing her pleasure she'd never imagined before.

She turned in the circle of his arms and rubbed her breasts against his chest, pressing herself against him, lifting her lips to receive his kiss. He took her mouth hungrily.

Struggling, he pulled off his shirt, then broke away long enough to yank off his boots and socks, and free his arms from his long johns. Then he captured her again and kissed a hot line down her face, into the hollow of her neck.

He eased her nightgown off her shoulders, pushing it back until it fell away. In the mirror Tripp saw their reflection. Kaitlin naked, her long hair curling down her back. He moved it aside, feasting on the

sight of her shapely body. Slowly, he slid his hands along the curve of her hips and captured her soft bottom.

Kaitlin moaned against his neck and dug her hands into the hard muscles of his chest. The coarse hair tickled her palms. Her fingertips roamed him freely, and settled on the tiny disks buried in the swirl of his chest hair.

He sucked in a quick breath and squeezed her tighter. Kaitlin shifted, bringing him against her intimately, and rocked her hips. Tripp swept her into his arms and laid her on the bed.

Quickly, frantically, Tripp stripped off his trousers and long johns and stretched out on the bed beside her. Their bodies matched perfectly, her curves molding against his taut, straight lines.

He explored her with his hands, his mouth, his fingertips, learning every inch, every secret her body held. He took his time. He was as methodical in his lovemaking as with everything else in his life.

Kaitlin gave herself willingly, with no want or desire to stop him. She was powerless to do so.

Tripp rose above her, easing himself between her thighs and into her body. Kaitlin grasped his powerful shoulders, holding him with all her strength. He kissed her until she relaxed, and her tight, untried body accepted him.

Thoughts whirled through her head as he moved within her, thoughts too quick, too wondrous to be named. She could only feel. The swelling of her heart, the rhythm of her hips, the building deep within her.

Faster he moved, pushing her higher, driving her

upward. She was one with him, reaching, climbing. The aching throb within her grew, rising faster and harder until it broke in great pulsing waves, consuming her. She called out his name and arched against him.

Tripp held himself back until the last possible second. His whole body screamed for release, for the exquisite relief only Kaitlin could provide. And, finally, when he'd seen to her complete pleasure, Tripp lost himself in her depths. He poured himself into her, shuddering, emptying his body, but filling his heart.

Morning sunlight peeping around the corner of the window shade woke Kaitlin. Immediately, thoughts of last night, and Tripp, eased into her mind. She opened her eyes and there he was, lying on his side, propped up on his elbow, watching her.

"Good morning," he whispered, and kissed the tip of her nose.

Wrapped in the tangled covers with him, how could the morning be anything but good?

"Sleep well?" she asked.

He grinned. "I hardly slept at all—as you certainly know."

Kaitlin's cheeks flushed and he smiled as if it were the cutest thing he'd ever seen. Everything she did, it seemed, pleased him to no end.

During the night, they'd made love twice more, neither of them able to get enough of the other. She'd tried out some of the things on him that he had done to her. Results had been spectacular, even to her unpracticed mind.

"I admit," Kaitlin said, "I didn't fully appreciate the benefits of how slow and deliberate you are until…very recently."

Tripp snuggled closer. "So I don't drive you crazy anymore?"

"Oh, you still drive me crazy," she said. "But in a good way now."

He looped his arm around her, rolled her on her side, and pulled her against his chest.

"I'm not sure what you mean," he said. "Maybe we'd better try this again and you can show me."

Kaitlin warmed to the idea at once. "I think we should."

Tripp kissed her. "In fact, I say we—"

"Miss Kaitlin?" A soft knock sounded on the door. "Miss Kaitlin?"

She pulled away from Tripp and gasped. "It's Charlie." She suddenly felt guilty, which, of course, she was.

Tripp groaned and fell back on the pillow.

"Miss Kaitlin?"

She sat up, clutching the sheet to her breasts. "What should we do?"

He pointed at her. "*You* won't do anything. I want you right where you are."

The knock sounded again. "Miss Kaitlin?"

"Just a minute, Charlie," Tripp called.

He rolled out of bed and searched the room for the clothing he'd tossed off so frantically the night before. Kaitlin raised on her elbow, watching him. She'd never seen him in the light before. Long legs. Powerful arms. Bulging muscles.

And hair. He had hair everywhere. She gasped as

he turned toward her. Well, it was almost everywhere.

"I'll get Charlie off to school in nothing flat." He pulled on his long johns and shoved into his trousers.

"Are you sure, Tripp? He was up late last night. He might want to stay home today."

He shook his head vehemently. "No. The boy's going to school today."

Kaitlin blushed but couldn't hold back a smile. "We have to open the store soon. Remember?"

"The store can wait."

"But, Tripp—"

He silenced her with a kiss and eased her onto the pillow again.

"Nothing is more important than you and I having this time together," he said. "I waited damn near too long, Kaitlin. We need today. Just the two of us."

Her heart swelled with love and contentment. "All right."

He raised an eyebrow. "Besides, I've got something to tell you."

"Something good?"

"You bet."

She grinned. "I've got something good to tell you, too."

"Stay right here. I'll be back."

Tripp kissed her on the forehead, grabbed his boots and the rest of his clothes, and left the bedroom, closing the door firmly behind him.

Kaitlin languished beneath the covers, listening to the muffled sound of Tripp and Charlie in the kitchen going about their morning routine. Voices, footsteps,

and finally the back door closed. It felt familiar. It felt right.

But being in bed, didn't. Without Tripp, it seemed lonely and cold. Kaitlin pushed back the covers and sat up.

She'd never slept naked before. During the night with Tripp at her side, nothing had seemed so wonderful. Now, it made her uncomfortable.

Kaitlin grabbed her wrapper from the floor and slid her arms into it. She caught a glimpse of herself in the mirror.

Her skin warmed as she recalled the sight of her and Tripp reflected in the glass, and she tingled recalling the feel of him pressed against her.

In the mirror, she saw herself smile. Tripp had said that she'd have to look at herself this morning, have to face what she'd done. Kaitlin had no trouble doing that.

She slid her hand to her belly where the consequences of her actions might be growing at this very minute. The thought broadened her smile.

She bathed at the wash basin and pulled on a fresh nightgown. Tripp would be gone for a while, taking Charlie to school.

In the kitchen, Kaitlin paused by the cookstove and considered putting on a fresh pot of coffee. She had so much she wanted to tell Tripp. That she loved him. That she'd given up her dream of the New York stage for him.

Kaitlin gazed out the window at the back alley and the bright morning sunlight. At this moment, she could have been packing to go to New York. The

stage coach, with Alister Dorsey on it, would leave soon. And now, it would leave without her.

She smiled, knowing that it didn't matter. She could truly be happy here. With Tripp.

An emptiness claimed her at that moment and suddenly she missed him very much. The bond between them was fragile yet, and she wanted him to hurry back from school so she could see him again.

Her need to be near him drew Kaitlin up the stairs to his room. Charlie's little bed was rumpled, and the satchel she'd seen Tripp carry into the store last night sat in the middle of the floor. Clothing hung out of it, scattered across the floor, as if Charlie had gone through it this morning.

"Men…" Kaitlin smiled as she gathered the clothing, folded it, and searched the bureau drawers to put it with Charlie's other things.

So this is what she'd be doing, instead of singing and acting. Simple tasks that bound her to Tripp and Charlie, made a home, made—

Kaitlin's hand stilled as she moved aside a stack of Tripp's long johns. Money. Cash. Stacks of it. Hidden in the bureau.

Her heart fluttered as she dumped the clothing onto the floor. A small fortune in cash. Where had it come from?

She couldn't imagine. Tripp had no money. Neither did she. Every cent each of them possessed went into repairing the store, buying the merchandise. And since their grand opening he'd cautioned her time and time again about spending too freely. They simply didn't have the capital, he'd told her.

What they earned in the store went into their ac-

count at the bank. Tripp took their receipts over every day, like clockwork. He never failed to go. She'd seen him leave every time.

But she'd never seen him put the money in the account.

A chill swept Kaitlin, and she shivered violently. Tripp had gone to the bank—alone. He kept the books. He'd insisted on doing it himself. And that had been all right with her. She trusted him.

Kaitlin pressed her lips together, staring at the money. She wanted to trust him now. At this moment. She wanted to think of some logical explanation of where the money had come from. But couldn't.

Anger surged through Kaitlin. Tripp had been holding out on her. Secreting the money away. Hiding it from her. Deliberately withholding it.

Where else could the money have come from?

Tripp had stolen it from her, and by extension, had stolen her dream. Just as Harvey Stutz had done.

It was one thing to give up her dream willingly. Quite another to have it taken from her. Again.

Kaitlin flew down the stairs and into her room, and pulled her green dress from the armoire. She would not wait around for Tripp to get back. She would find him. If he had some reasonable explanation, she'd listen to it. She would gladly listen.

And if he told her what she feared?

A lump of emotion rose in her throat. She wouldn't lose both of her dreams in one day.

Kaitlin yanked her carpetbag from beneath the bed and pulled it open. One dream was still within her grasp.

She would go to the stage depot. To Alister Dorsey, her gateway to New York.

She'd listen to Tripp explain this situation to her there. If he could...

Chapter Twenty-One

The morning sun had never looked so bright, Tripp decided as he walked away from the schoolhouse. The sky had never looked so blue, either. In fact, nothing in his whole life had seemed this good before.

And it could only get better, he realized. As soon as he got back to Kaitlin.

He walked a little faster and caught himself whistling as he stepped up onto the boardwalk at the edge of town. Visions of Kaitlin still snuggled in bed, waiting for him, filled his mind.

He had so much to tell her. In fact, he couldn't wait to share his news with her. He'd hardly believed it himself when his brother-in-law had told him. Kaitlin would be tickled pink when she heard.

Whistling a little louder now, Tripp rounded the corner and ran straight into Rafe.

"Sorry, Rafe. Didn't see you," he said.

"Don't matter..." Rafe shrugged and nodded toward the stage depot across the street. "I was just killing time."

The stage hadn't pulled in yet, but a crowd had gathered outside.

"What's going on?" Tripp asked.

"Heard that Dorsey fellow was leaving town this morning. He's supposed to make some sort of announcement."

Tripp grinned. He didn't have to be in the crowd to hear what Dorsey intended to spring on the good folks of Porter. He already knew.

And that lifted his spirits higher still, made him that much more anxious to get back to Kaitlin.

But for all of Tripp's good mood, Rafe presented a sad picture. Shoulders haunched, hands jammed into his trouser pockets, he stared at the boardwalk.

Tripp almost felt guilty that his own life was going so well.

"How's business?" he asked.

Rafe sighed heavily. "Doesn't make much difference now, one way or the other. Not without…Julia…."

"Are things any better between you two?"

"The same." Rafe didn't look up, just shook his head. "I don't know why I thought I could ever make her happy. Just stupid, I guess."

"You weren't stupid, Rafe," Tripp said. "You just loved her."

He lifted his head slowly and gazed off down the street. "I guess that doesn't mean much, either."

Tripp just looked at him. Misery, pure and simple, lengthened the lines of his face. Tripp didn't like butting into anybody else's business, but he couldn't stand here and see his friend hurting and not do something about it.

"Yeah, you're right," Tripp said. "Love by itself isn't enough."

"I gave her everything I had," Rafe said. "I worked hard as I could to give her nice things, but—"

"That's the hard part about being married," Tripp said. "Trying to figure out what they want isn't easy. And you, my friend, missed it by a mile."

Rafe shook his head. "I don't know what you mean."

"What she wants is *you*," Tripp said. "Not a man with a good business, who works from dawn to dusk. She wants a man who'll spend time with her."

"But it's my responsibility to take care of her."

"What you need to take care of, Rafe, is *business*. Husband and wife kind of business."

Rafe frowned. "You mean…?"

"Exactly," Tripp said. "Now, get on home and talk to that wife of yours."

Rafe shook his head. "You know how hard it was for me to hold myself back all those times Julia… Well, you know. How's it going to look if I show up at her place just for…that?"

"It might turn out better than you think."

Rafe dug the toe of his boot into the rough grain of the boardwalk. "I don't rightly see how that is going to help anything."

"That's my advice. Take it or leave it," Tripp said. "I've got to get back to the store. I've got a little business of my own to take care of."

Rafe nodded slowly. "Well, thanks anyway."

Tripp hurried along the boardwalk, anxious to reach the store. Across the street, Mrs. Douglas and

the mayor made their way toward the stage depot,
along with most everyone else in Porter.

A little grin tugged at Tripp's lips, knowing he
and Kaitlin would be occupied in other, far more
pleasurable ways when Alister Dorsey broke the
news. In fact, as soon as he got back to the store, he
intended to—

Kaitlin.

Tripp jerked to a stop. He saw Kaitlin trudging
down the street with other townsfolk headed for the
stage depot. What was she doing? He'd told her he'd
be right back, for her to wait and they would—

Tripp's brow creased into a deep frown. Kaitlin
had on her green dress. The one she wore the first
day the two of them arrived in Porter. And just like
that day, she carried a carpetbag.

"Kaitlin!"

She spotted him across the street and stopped short
on the boardwalk. Anger, suspicion and hurt knotted
deep in the pit of her stomach. Kaitlin steeled herself
against the other emotions that tried to present themselves at the sight of him.

Tripp jogged across the street, dodging a freight
wagon and two riders, and cut in front of her on the
boardwalk.

"Kaitlin? What's going on?"

Having him so close, she nearly gave in on the
spot and begged him to forgive her for her terrible
suspicions. She loved him so. How could she have
thought he'd do such a thing?

Still, she had to know.

"I'm—I'm looking for you," Kaitlin said.

He frowned and gestured to the carpetbag clutched in her hand. "With that?"

"Yes." Her chin went up a notch. "*And* I'm on my way to meet Alister Dorsey."

His frown deepened. "Kaitlin, what the hell are you talking about?"

She straightened her shoulders. "Just tell me the truth, Tripp. That's all I ask."

"The truth about what?"

Kaitlin gulped, fighting to contain her emotions. How could she bear it if he admitted that he'd done as she suspected?

"I found it…in your bureau," she said. "The…money."

Tripp pulled on his neck. "Yeah?"

"I deserve an explanation." Kaitlin pulled herself up, fortifying herself for whatever might come next. "Did you, or did you not withhold profits from the store to keep me from going to New York?"

He just stared at her for a moment, thinking, as if trying to make sense of what she'd said.

"Well?" she asked, holding her breath.

Tripp rubbed his chin. "Let me get this straight. You found money in my bureau drawer and thought I was hiding store profits so you couldn't go to New York. Is that what you think?"

She couldn't stand another second of this. "Just answer my question!"

"You think I would actually do that to you?"

"If you won't tell me the truth, then I'm going to New York with Alister Dorsey." She darted around him, and headed for the depot.

"Kaitlin!"

His heavy footsteps thundered on the boardwalk behind her and he jumped in front of her.

"Wait, Kaitlin. You don't mean this," Tripp said. "You'll never be happy in New York."

"Of course I will. It's my life's dream." She cut around him.

He blocked her path again. "Kaitlin, listen. You think that being on the stage like your mama is what you want, but it isn't."

"Move!"

He settled his hands on her shoulders. She jerked away, her heart racing.

"You're just remembering the love for your mama that you felt when she told you those stories," Tripp said. "I think what you're really looking for, Kaitlin, is a family. Somebody to share your love with, like when you were a little girl with your mama and papa, and thinking about the New York stage just reminds you of that."

Kaitlin stopped still on the boardwalk. She'd never considered the thought before.

"Just like I thought living on my pa's farm would make it a home." Tripp glanced away, then at her again. "And like the way I was holding on to my memories of Emily."

She touched her fingers to her lips. Maybe he was right. Maybe a family was what she'd been looking for all along.

"Look, Kaitlin, I've made a lot of mistakes in my life," Tripp said. "I know now that Emily leaving me was…well, it was as much my fault as hers."

"What do you mean?"

"I should have paid more attention to the things

that made her happy. I should have tried harder to give her what she wanted.'' Tripp gazed intensely into her eyes. ''I'm not making that mistake again, Kaitlin.''

She wanted to fold herself into his arms. Lose herself in his touch. Cling to him. Forever.

Kaitlin forced herself to go on. ''What has any of that got to do with the money I found?''

''I sold my farm.''

Breath went out of her in a quick huff. ''You what?''

He nodded. ''I sold my farm while I was seeing Emily. The rancher who owns the spread right next to it has been wanting that piece of land for years. So, I sold it to him. That was the money you saw, Kaitlin.''

Her stomach rolled into a sick knot. ''Oh, Tripp, no. That was your dream. How could you have sold it?''

''Because I found a better dream.'' Tripp took her hand. ''With you, Kaitlin. If you'll have me.''

Tears pressed against her eyes. ''But...''

''A life without you would be like a gift never opened.'' He pulled her against his chest. ''I love you, Kaitlin.''

Tears spilled onto her cheeks. ''I love you, too.''

He kissed her, long and warm, and loving. Then he broke away, but didn't release her.

''I sold my farm, Kaitlin, because I needed the money,'' he said. ''I'm going to build you an opera house right here in Porter.''

''Tripp! You can't be serious.''

''Yep.'' He nodded and smiled. ''It'll be all yours.

You can put on plays, or sing, or dance, or whatever you want.''

''But Porter is such a small town. There's not enough people—''

''I've got that covered too,'' Tripp said. ''You remember I told you that my brother-in-law works for the railroad?''

''Yes, but—''

''He shared a little piece of news with me while I was there. It seems that—''

A cheer went up from the gathering down the block in front of the stage depot. Amid whoops, shouts and back slapping, the crowd broke away, revealing Mrs. Douglas and the mayor shaking hands with Alister Dorsey.

''What's going on?'' Kaitlin waved her hand. ''Mrs. Douglas?''

The mayor's wife maneuvered through the townspeople, smiling broadly.

''The most wonderful news,'' she declared, looking back and forth between Kaitlin and Tripp. ''A banner day for Porter. Just what we need!''

''What is it?'' Kaitlin asked.

Mrs. Douglas drew in a deep breath. ''Our dear Mr. Dorsey has just announced that the railroad is coming through Porter.''

Kaitlin gasped. ''How does he know?''

''He's quite wealthy, Miss Jeffers, and knows all the right people,'' Mrs. Douglas said. ''And, as if that weren't news enough, he also announced plans to build a tannery and shoe factory right here in Porter.''

"My goodness..." Kaitlin's eyes widened. "That means Porter—"

"Porter will grow by leaps and bounds. People will come from all over to work and live. We'll all prosper." Mrs. Douglas moved along. "I must get to the mayor's office. So many plans to be made."

Kaitlin watched her disappear down the boardwalk, stunned. She turned to Tripp. "Can it be true? Really true?"

He grinned. "It's true."

"You knew this all along, didn't you."

"I've been trying to tell you since last night," Tripp said. "Russ, my brother-in-law, works for the railroad laying track. He's bringing his crew to Porter, and told me all about it."

Tripp smiled and eased his arms around her again, drawing her close. "That's when I knew you could have your opera house. There will be hundreds of folks moving to Porter, and they'll need to be entertained."

Her heart tumbled. "You thought of that? Just for me?"

"I love you, Kaitlin." He traced his finger along the line of her jaw. "Say you'll stay here in Porter. Here with me. Please?"

Emotion swelled her throat, choking her words. "Tripp..."

"I want you to marry me."

Tears splashed onto her cheeks and Kaitlin threw her arms around him. "Oh, yes, I want to marry you."

She looked up at him. "But how?"

* * *

An air of celebration still hung over Porter since Alister Dorsey's announcement the day before. Everyone was thrilled by the news, including Kaitlin, of course, since it brought so many people into the store.

The little sitting area at the front door stayed occupied constantly, as the ladies of Porter talked, gossiped, and speculated about the changes that were on the horizon.

Late afternoon sunlight slanted through the store windows as June Hutchinson came inside and squeezed onto the settee between Clara Hadley and Matilda Shaw.

"Seems mighty suspicious, if you ask me," Mrs. Hutchinson declared.

"In what way?" Kaitlin asked, not surprised by the woman's assessment of the situation.

"Why, everyone else in Porter is delighted," Clara Hadley said.

"Humph." Mrs. Hutchinson jerked her chin. "I knew something was up. That Mr. Dorsey in town, wanting to buy up properties, and spending all that time talking with the ranchers. I knew it meant something."

"You were right," Kaitlin said.

"Of course I was right."

"But it worked out for the best," Mrs. Shaw said.

Mrs. Hutchinson lifted her nose a little higher in the air. "It just goes to show you, you can't be too careful about strangers."

"We'll certainly be getting plenty of those," Clara said.

"You can't be sure of anyone's real motives," Mrs. Hutchinson said. "Why, even if—"

The bell clanged over the door and Everette Finch walked into the store. Kaitlin tensed at the sight of him. She wished he would stop coming into the store.

Mrs. Hutchinson got to her feet and looked down her long nose at him. "You have got some kind of nerve showing yourself in here, Everette Finch."

He frowned at her. "I've got a legal claim on this place."

Mrs. Hutchinson gave an unladylike snort. "Seems like a mighty big coincidence that you showed up in Porter with your *legal claim* just after that Alister Dorsey arrived. Seems to me like you suspected something was happening here, and wanted to get a piece of it."

"The law is the law," Finch said.

"I wonder what the judge will have to say about that," Mrs. Hutchinson told him. "Seems mighty suspicious to me."

Matilda Shaw rose from the settee and smiled demurely at Everette. "Good day, Mr. Finch."

He pulled his hat from his head and fumbled with it for a moment. "Why, good day to you too, Mrs. Shaw. I didn't see you sitting there."

She moved closer to him. "I think it's a shame that these two young people might lose their store, after they've put so much hard work into it."

Everette stared at his hat. "Well, business is business."

"Yes, I suppose," Mrs. Shaw said. "But you have

so many other businesses in Porter. Isn't there enough good fortune to go around for everyone?''

"Well…" Everette Finch turned his hat over in his hand. "It's up to the judge to decide…I reckon.''

"Whatever you say, Mr. Finch." She turned to Kaitlin. "I'll be going now, dear. Good evening.''

"Goodbye, Mrs. Shaw," Kaitlin said as she left the store.

Everette stood watching her after the door closed, still fumbling with his hat.

"Mrs. Shaw is going over to the Red Rose for supper," Kaitlin said softly. "Isn't it a shame that she has to eat alone?''

Everette frowned, then crammed his hat on and headed out the door.

"Humph." Mrs. Hutchinson drew in a quick breath. "And with all this celebration going on in Porter, don't you think it's strange that both the blacksmith shop and the millinery are closed? For two days now? Is that any way to run a business?''

Kaitlin pressed her lips together to keep from smiling. "It certainly isn't.''

"And not a sign of Julia or Rafe these past two days," Mrs. Hutchinson said. "It makes you *wonder*, doesn't it?''

"I'm sure everything is fine," Kaitlin said.

"I'd better discuss this with the sheriff." Mrs. Hutchinson headed out the door.

Clara Hadley left on the heels of the sheriff's wife, and Kaitlin spent the rest of the afternoon waiting on customers. She didn't know where all these people were coming from. But they kept coming.

Across the store, Tripp stayed busy, and it was all

Kaitlin could do to hold herself back. Drawn to him so strongly, she struggled to keep a respectable distance. Still, she caught herself stealing glances at him, and most times, found him already looking at her.

When she finally shepherded the last customer out of the store and turned the key in the lock, Kaitlin felt a rush of anticipation. Charlie was playing with Frances Morgan's son down the street and would eat supper there. She and Tripp were alone in the store.

She heard the clink of coins behind her and turned to see him counting the day's receipts, noting them in the ledger. So handsome. So strong. So desirable. Kaitlin felt her cheeks flush.

"Another good day," Tripp said. "Only one way it could have been better."

She crossed the store and stood on the other side of the counter. "How's that?"

"To have gotten rid of all the customers and have had the place to ourselves."

Kaitlin smiled and felt her cheeks grow warmer. "Tripp, we couldn't have done that."

"Why not?" He closed the ledger and circled the counter. "Julia and Rafe did it, and with good results."

Kaitlin looked up at him. "They've been alone over there since yesterday morning. Do you think they've worked out their differences by now?"

Tripp layed his hands on her shoulders and drew her closer. "Might take a few more days. You can never tell."

She snuggled against him. "I'm glad they worked things out."

"There aren't too many problems that rolling around under the covers together won't take care of," Tripp said.

Kaitlin drew back a bit and pursed her lips. "You men. You think that fixes everything."

He grinned. "Well, yeah...pretty much."

"Tripp Callihan, you—"

He smothered her words with his lips until she kissed him back and came fully against him.

"Is that how you intend to fix all of our problems?" she whispered against his mouth.

"Of course."

"Good."

He kissed her again, then locked his arms around her and buried his mouth against her neck. Kaitlin closed her eyes for a moment, reveling in the feel of him.

"Do you think Alister Dorsey asked me to go to New York just so he could buy our store?" Kaitlin asked. "Or do you think his offer was genuine?"

Tripp shrugged. "Probably a little of both."

"He knew all along the railroad was coming through Porter," Kaitlin said. "That's why he tried to buy up those other businesses."

"He didn't get them, though," Tripp said. "But he'll make plenty off his tannery and shoe factory."

Kaitlin grinned up at him. "And so will all the other merchants in Porter."

They were quiet for a moment, content to hold each other. Finally, Tripp spoke.

"I sent that letter today," he said.

Kaitlin looked up and saw him gazing intently at her. "The one to—"

"The lawyer." Tripp nodded. "I don't know how long these things take, but as soon as it's done I want you to marry me."

Her heart thumped a little harder hearing those words. "I can wait, as long as we wait together. And as long as you're sure this is what you want."

"I'm sure, all right," he said. "Don't you doubt that for a minute."

"We have lots to do in the meantime," Kaitlin said. She moved away from him and looked around the store. "Oh, Tripp. What if the judge gives our store to Everette Finch?"

"I've been thinking about that," he said. "It might not be a bad thing, if it happens."

She turned back to him. "You don't mean that. After all our work? All our planning?"

"You're going to be pretty busy with your opera house," Tripp said. "And with all the people and new businesses coming to Porter, I figure there'll be plenty of building going on. I could make us a fair amount of money doing that."

"I hadn't thought of it that way," Kaitlin said.

"Plus, without the store we could set our own hours. Get up when we want." He grinned. "Go to bed when we want."

Kaitlin smiled, then grew serious. "I owe you an apology for yesterday. It must have hurt you to see me on the way to the stage depot, leaving…like Emily."

"No more than it hurt you thinking I'd stolen your money and your dream like Harvey Stutz."

"I'm sorry."

"I'm sorry, too," Tripp said.

"We shouldn't do those sorts of things to each other," Kaitlin said. "Not if we love each other."

"And I do love you, Kaitlin."

She drew herself up. "From now on I promise to talk to you about things and not think about leaving when there's a problem."

Tripp nodded thoughtfully. "And I promise I won't keep anything from you ever again."

"I can live with that."

"Me, too."

Kaitlin extended her hand. "So, it's a deal?"

He folded his fingers around hers. "It's the deal of a lifetime."

* * * * *

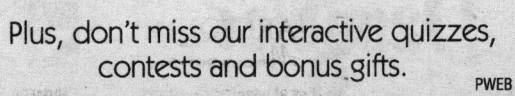

This season,

Harlequin® Historical

is proud to introduce four very different Western romances that will warm your heart....

In October 1999, look for

COOPER'S WIFE #485
by Jillian Hart

and

THE DREAMMAKER #486
by Judith Stacy

In November 1999, look for

JAKE WALKER'S WIFE #489
by Loree Lough

and

HEART AND HOME #490
by Cassandra Austin

Harlequin Historicals
The way the past *should* have been.

Available at your favorite retail outlet.

HARLEQUIN®
Makes any time special ™

Visit us at www.romance.net

HHWEST4

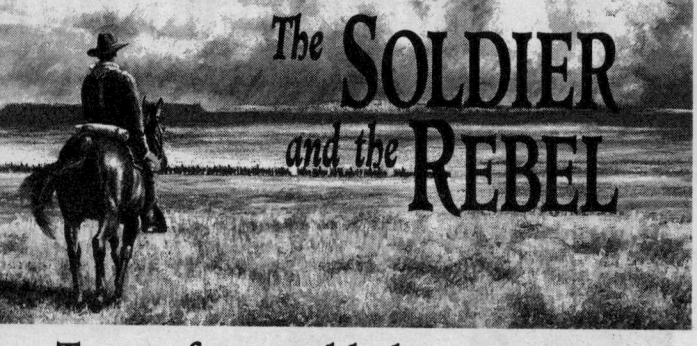

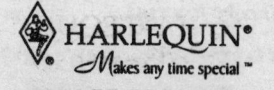